# The Rosenberg Principle

# The Rosenberg Principle

Colin D. Peel

ROBERT HALE · LONDON

© Colin D. Peel 2005
First published in Great Britain 2005

ISBN 0 7090 7814 5

Robert Hale Limited
Clerkenwell House
Clerkenwell Green
London EC1R 0HT

The right of Colin D. Peel to be
identified as the author of this work has been
asserted by him in accordance with the
Copyright, Designs and Patents Act 1988

2 4 6 8 10 9 7 5 3 1

Typeset in 11/14pt Baskerville
by Derek Doyle & Associates, Shaw Heath.
Printed in Great Britain by
St Edmundsbury Press, Bury St Edmunds, Suffolk.
Bound by Woolnough Bookbinding Ltd.

'We are the chosen, we are the only true men . . . . Does it not follow that nature herself has predestined us to dominate the whole world?

'We shall not submit the greatness of our ultimate plan, the context of its particular parts, the consequences of each separate part, the secret meaning of which remains hidden, to the judgement of the many, even of those who share our thoughts.

'We shall paint the misdeeds of foreign Governments in the most garish colours and create such an ill-feeling towards them that the peoples would a thousand times rather bear a slavery which guarantees them peace and order than enjoy their much-touted freedom . . . . Our principles and methods will take on their full force when we present them in sharp contrast to the putrid old social order.'

Alfred Rosenberg
Reichsleiter of the Nazi Party

# Chapter 1

The signs were unmistakable. McKendrick had expected to be impressed, but the satellite photos had failed to convey the real extent of the fire.

By the look of things, this one had stayed underground for the whole of its damn life, not once coming to the surface in a five or six kilometre-long burn through a coal seam that was running deeper than any he'd encountered in Java or Sumatra.

A hungry bastard, McKendrick thought; another Indonesian monster that had already travelled too far under the forest floor for him to consider doing much about it, even if he had the time or could get hold of the right people to fight it.

Beside him, Kalyem had either reached the same conclusion or she was worn out from trying to keep the Land-Rover on a track that was steadily becoming more rutted and less well defined. She was a slightly built Indonesian, a 19-year-old student from the university in Palangkaraya who, for reasons of her own, had volunteered to drive him here – a decision that he thought she might be beginning to regret.

A moment ago she'd allowed the Land-Rover to coast to a halt at the top of a shallow rise so she could stretch her arms and wipe the sweat out of her eyes.

'Why not let me take over for a while?' He could see how tired she was. 'As long as I stay on the track, I'm not going to get us lost, am I?'

'No, no. I am OK, but I think our passenger is not travelling so well.'

She was right. In the back seat, looking distinctly queasy, was their minder for the day, a grizzled old man called Jusaf, a rifle-carrying Dayak from the Kalimantan Ministry of Mines and Energy who had spent most of the journey either asleep or pretending to be. Now that they'd stopped, he was fumbling to light a cigarette, embarrassed to have become the centre of attention.

McKendrick smiled at him. 'That isn't going to make you feel any better.'

'You would like one?' Jusaf offered the packet.

'No thanks. I've had enough smoke to last me for a while.'

'From the fires you chase before you come here?'

'Six on Java,' McKendrick said. 'Eight on Sumatra.'

'That is much bad air for a man to breathe.' Jusaf kicked open his door. 'If we are to remain here for a while, have I your permission to take a piss?'

'Sure. We're not in any hurry.' McKendrick was half-inclined to go as well, hoping that a short walk might help him decide whether it was worthwhile carrying on with the trip.

The girl had already made up her mind. She was using their GPS unit to find out where they were, checking the co-ordinates on her map and comparing their position with the smudge on the satellite photo which showed where the fire-front was burning.

'We are here.' She handed him the map and pointed to a cross she'd drawn on it. 'If the infrared data is correct, we have little more than two kilometres to go.'

'It's not going to make any difference,' McKendrick said. 'We're already too far away from anywhere. You need heavy equipment to fight a fire like this, and even if we could lay our hands on some diggers or bulldozers in Muaratunan, it'd take us days to get them here.'

'We are not so far from Muaratunan; less than thirty kilometres.'

'Yeah, but I'm not going to be around to organize things. My contract finishes tomorrow and I'm due to fly out of Balikpapan first thing on Sunday morning.'

'Oh.' She was disappointed. 'Can you not instruct me what it is that must be done?'

'There aren't any rules in this business,' McKendrick said. 'You make them up as you go along.'

'But you wish to proceed to where the front is burning, do you not?'

He wasn't sure. Intrigued though he was by the size of the fire and the depth at which it was travelling, that hardly seemed a good reason to spend the rest of the day in the middle of nowhere when he had other things to attend to.

Jusaf, too, seemed reluctant to continue. After wandering back to the Land-Rover, he was still looking uncomfortable and appeared to be ill at ease about something.

'What's the problem?' McKendrick asked.

'We are not the first to come here.' The Dayak pointed with his rifle. 'Over there I find tyre marks from what I believe are trucks.'

McKendrick wasn't surprised. If underground fires had a saving grace, it came in the form of the vehicle access they created for hunters and trappers – long clear trails into forests like this one where the vegetation had been poisoned by fumes rising from the burned-out tunnel below.

Jusaf spoke to the girl before he climbed back into his seat. 'We should not stay,' he said. 'You will please drive us back to Muaratunan.'

Evidently annoyed by the suggestion, she swivelled round and began arguing with him in Malay, her voice rising whenever he attempted to interrupt her.

McKendrick was able to understand a few of the words, but soon the conversation became too heated for him to follow much of it at all, forcing him to intervene before things got out of hand. 'OK, OK,' he said. 'That'll do. What's going on?' He held up his hand to stop Jusaf from answering. 'Kalyem first.'

'The old man sees danger where there is none,' she said. 'He is worried that we might run into bad people.'

'What kind of bad people?'

'He is uneducated and too ignorant to know. Terrorists perhaps, men who supply guns to the militia, or those who grow or smuggle drugs. He says that is why he cannot permit us to go further.'

'What do you think?'

'It is not my place to say.' She lowered her head. 'But because I have read how you advise the governments of other countries about these fires, I have paid my own fare to come here from the university.'

'And so far you haven't seen anything interesting or learned anything useful. Is that what all this is about?'

She said nothing, refusing to look at him until he reached across to take the satellite photo from her.

'I can get us to the fire-front in thirty minutes,' she said.

'That's not the point.' McKendrick turned round to find out what their minder had to say. 'How do you know there are gun-runners or drug traffickers operating around here?' he asked.

Jusaf shrugged. 'They are everywhere in Kalimantan, and also in Sarawak. And you are a foreigner in my country.'

'Does being a foreigner make things more dangerous?'

'For you maybe.'

'How fresh are the tyre tracks?'

'They are less than two or three days old, I think. On ground like this, it is hard for me to be certain.'

'So what's the real chance of us running into the wrong people over the next couple of hours?' He knew it was a stupid question.

'At this time of year the chance is not so high, but who can say?'

No closer to making a decision than he had been five minutes ago, he was still weighing up the risk when the girl suddenly thrust a hand-ful of rupiah notes at him. 'It is all I have,' she said quietly. 'If it is not sufficient, for one night I will sleep with you.'

Now it was McKendrick's turn to be embarrassed. Although she'd made it clear how important this field trip was to her, he had no idea she was quite this serious. 'You can keep your money,' he said.

'We shall continue?' Her expression had changed and she was trying not to appear too pleased.

'Yeah, but we're not going to be doing any big analysis when we get there. We'll shoot a few pictures and collect some soil samples to get an idea of what we're dealing with, then we'll be leaving right away. Is that OK with you?'

She nodded. 'Yes. Thank you, but if you would also tell me the special things you know about these fires, later when I have returned to the university I will prepare a report asking the authorities for the money and equipment to put it out.'

McKendrick grinned at her. 'And guarantee yourself an extra good pass mark for your degree.'

'My marks are always good.' She restarted the engine, glancing disdainfully at Jusaf in her mirror before she engaged first gear and put her foot down, not bothering to avoid a ridge of rocks as they set off on the last leg of their journey.

Partly as a result of her enthusiastic driving, but also because the track became progressively wider the further they went, they made good time, approaching the log-strewn entrance to the fire-front shortly before midday.

The sight of what lay beyond was dramatic enough to make Kalyem jam on the brakes.

'It's OK,' McKendrick said. 'There's nothing dangerous about it.'

She hesitated for a second, searching for the best route before weaving her way out on to a large clearing through a minefield of craters left by the roots of poisoned trees that had toppled over.

All around them now, the forest had been replaced by a truly alien landscape that was as familiar to him as it was surreal, but on a larger scale than anything he'd come across before.

For as far as he could see, the ground was the colour and the consistency of brick dust, a desolate expanse of pockmarked soil from which the pure-white skeletons of trees protruded. These were the ones that had remained standing, overwhelmed by heat and the rising tide of toxins to create a dead and twisted forest whose end would come with the next rain or the first good summer wind.

The fire had fanned out, he realized, maybe because it was at last coming closer to the surface where it could consume more of the oxygen it needed to expand or, more likely, because the coal seam had been squashed out sideways at some time in the geological past.

Whatever the reason, locating the front was going to be simple, which meant they wouldn't have to hang around here long. He told Kalyem to stop the Land-Rover and got out, rather wishing he hadn't listened to the bureaucrats in Jakarta who had assured him that the Java and Sumatra fires were fiercer than any on the east coast of Kalimantan.

The bureaucrats had been wrong, he thought, just as they'd been wrong about their commitment to putting the damn things out. After making a lot of noise announcing his appointment as an adviser and trumpeting about their supposed adherence to the Kyoto Protocol, so far they'd failed to allocate anything like the funds or resources that were going to be needed to combat the pollution from fires as big as this one.

His thoughts were interrupted by the girl who had come to stand beside him. She was anxious to start work, holding a flow-pen and the GPS unit in one hand while she tried to stuff a wad of plastic bags under her belt.

'Well,' McKendrick said, 'what do you think?'

'It is not how I imagined it would be.' She coughed on the fumes. 'In a funny way I can see beauty here, but I am also conscious of the heat beneath us. Are you able to guess the temperature of the fire?'

'Hard to tell, but if it's more than thirty metres down, some of the pockets will be over a thousand degrees. If it's an old bastard and it's running as deep as I think it is, it'll be pretty bloody hot. You can tell by the smell: the deeper the burn, the dirtier the smell.' He looked at her. 'You remember what we're trying to do, don't you?'

'Of course.' She was affronted. 'By taking back samples for labora-tory analysis, we will learn of the particles and gases trapped inside the soil at different places, and that is what will tell us where the coal must be excavated in order the starve the fire of fuel.'

'A sample every five metres ought to be plenty.' He wondered if she understood the difficulties of digging out enough of the seam to do the job. 'The front's moving in an arc,' he said. 'The forward edge is prob-ably around twenty metres this side of those trees that haven't been affected yet.'

'Then I had better begin.' She started to smile again, but was over-taken by another fit of coughing.

'Get Jusaf to give you a hand. It'll save you some time.'

'He is asleep again. He is lazy like all Dayaks. Anyway, I do not need his help. I wish to do this by myself.'

McKendrick knew better than to argue. 'OK,' he said. 'Don't forget to write the GPS co-ordinates on each of the bags. I'll take photos while you're getting hot and dirty.' He watched her walk off towards the line of living trees, hoping that half an hour on her knees would slow her down a bit and maybe help reduce her resentment of Jusaf before they had to embark on the long return journey through the forest.

Because of her high cheekbones and her big eyes, she was quite attractive in a skinny sort of way, he thought, and if her offer to sleep with him was still open when they got back to town, she'd be pleasant

12

enough company for the evening.

Rather wishing that the idea hadn't crossed his mind, he returned to the Land-Rover to collect his camera and wake up Jusaf.

The old man was lying on the rear seat with his eyes closed and with his rifle balanced on his chest, but instead of being asleep he was puffing on another cigarette, allowing the smoke to drift out of the open door beside him.

'Hey,' McKendrick said. 'You're not getting paid to spend the day on your back. How about doing something useful?'

'You have a job for me?'

'I will have in a minute. I need you to pace out some distances and measure the ground temperature in a couple of places.'

'I am ready.'

'It's OK. You can finish your cigarette.' Retrieving his camera from the floor of the Land-Rover, McKendrick climbed up on to the bonnet to get a better view and to look for telltale signs of rising smoke.

If there was smoke, he couldn't see it, nor was there the slightest sound. The clearing was eerily silent, completely windless, devoid of bird song and empty of insect life. But he could taste the sulphur, and now he was up higher he was aware of how dry the air was. During the six weeks he'd been in Indonesia, he'd gradually become conditioned to the sweltering daytime temperatures of the tropics, but out here in the middle of the clearing, in place of the normal sweat-inducing humidity, there was nothing except a raw and acrid heat.

Nearer to the edge of the front where the girl was working, the air would be hotter still, McKendrick thought, although she'd be more accustomed to it than he was and, with any luck, she'd be too busy to be bothered by it much.

He used the zoom lens of his camera to find out how she was getting on, focusing on her figure until he could see her clearly through the heat-haze. She was about seventy metres away, standing with her back to him, checking her position with the GPS unit before she bent down to collect another scoop of soil.

Without really knowing why, he took a couple of shots of her, following her progress through his viewfinder before using up more of his film on photos of the clearing – guessing that the prints might be useful to her, even if they were unlikely to be of interest to anyone else.

He was replacing the lens cap when the silence was broken by a scream.

Three men had emerged from the forest. Two had assault rifles levelled at the Land-Rover while the third had seized Kalyem by her wrists. She was struggling to escape, crying out again and fighting to free herself, but falling over when the man pulled her towards him and twisted roughly on her arms.

'Jesus bloody Christ.' McKendrick jumped to the ground, dropping his camera in the process and banging his hip against the mudguard. He was uncertain of what to do and not yet sure of how much trouble they were in, but hoping that Jusaf was going to get them out of it.

He was mistaken. Instead of reacting to the situation, the Dayak was keeping out of sight, peering cautiously through the gap between the two front seats.

'Give me the gun,' McKendrick said. 'Now.'

Jusaf shook his head. 'The danger is too great.'

'If you don't give me the fucking gun, I'll take it off you and shoot you with it.'

'You do not understand. Against so many, what can we do? Look.'

The three men had been joined by at least half a dozen more, all of them armed, standing in a straggly line along the western perimeter of the clearing as though waiting for instructions from someone.

McKendrick's mouth had gone dry. 'Who the hell are they?' he said.

'It is not possible to know.' Jusaf squinted in the sunlight. 'You must go and explain why it is we are here and tell them that the girl is not a threat to them. They will release her then, I think.'

'What if they don't?'

'First give them your watch and your camera, then if it is still necessary you should offer them much money.'

'I didn't bring any money.' He was trying to see if Kalyem was all right. She'd stopped fighting, but remained on the ground, being held down by one of the men who had his boot planted on her stomach.

Keeping his hands out in the open where they could be seen, McKendrick carefully picked up his camera. 'Is it worth offering them the Land-Rover?' he said.

Jusaf nodded. 'Of course, but if they accept it we will have a long walk back.'

'What are you going to do?'

'I think they have not seen me, so it is best I remain here until we learn more of their intentions.'

Knowing that the old man was going to be useless as a back up, McKendrick tried unsuccessfully to think, staring at the still unmoving line of men, unwilling to start out on his walk, but too concerned about Kalyem not to.

He was telling himself that everything might yet turn out to be OK when Jusaf reached out to grip his arm.

'What?' McKendrick kept his eyes on the forest.

'Please listen to me. Because the girl is very young, if you permit her to be taken away, she will be raped by many men and then she will be killed. So it is important you do not let such a thing happen.'

'Yeah, I know.' He didn't want to be reminded about what the penalty for failure might be.

Trying not to gag on the fumes, he took a deep breath and set off across the clearing, walking slowly, no longer conscious of the fire-front, and insensitive to the heat soaking through the soles of his boots.

He headed for the tree line where Kalyem was being held, but before he could reach her a thickset man stepped forwards to intercept him.

The man was an Indonesian, roughly dressed in army fatigues and, like his companions, dirty and unshaven. Although he was carrying no weapon of any kind, his attitude was hostile and aggressive.

McKendrick stopped walking, hoping that whoever he was, and whatever he wanted, he would at least speak English and wondering what to do if he didn't.

The man studied McKendrick for several seconds before he spoke. 'The girl tells me you are not American,' he said, 'but I do not believe her.' He held out a hand that bore a scar and a small tattoo. 'You have documents?'

'Yeah.' McKendrick gave him his passport and waited while the man flicked through it.

'So you are an Englishman who has visited many countries but, like Americans, I think you are not one who follows the teachings of Muhammad.'

'I don't follow the teachings of anyone,' McKendrick said. 'I'm just

15

here doing a job for your government. I work out of Brussels on an environmental programme for the United Nations.'

The man displayed no interest. 'You may leave.' He gave back the passport.

Too relieved to reply, McKendrick called to Kalyem.

'No.' The man shook his head. 'You do not understand. Each month for our business we use this track. It is ours. That is why we keep the girl. When you tell people how she is taken for the pleasure of my men, there will be few who will wish to come this way as you have. She is our payment for allowing you to return unharmed to wherever you wish to go.'

'Like hell she is.' By now, McKendrick had no illusions about what he was up against. His refusal to heed Jusaf's warning had turned an innocent field trip into a full-blown nightmare, and unless he could talk his way out of this in the next few minutes, Kalyem was going to pay an unthinkable price for the worst mistake he could have ever made.

Bargaining for her freedom wasn't going to work, he realized. His camera and his watch would be of no more value to these men than cash he didn't have. They were professionals operating in a part of the world that was already awash with illicit money, and it made no difference whether they were guerrillas, gun-runners or members of a local rogue militia. Here in the east coast forests of Kalimantan, they were the law, and they made the rules.

'The girl's a student,' McKendrick said. 'She's from the university in Palangkaraya. Hurt her and you'll wind up with more trouble than you can handle. In two days there'll be army trucks parked all over this clearing, and you'll have a hundred soldiers hunting you down. I'll go with you instead. The UN will pay you good ransom money for me.'

The man's face was impassive. 'You leave now,' he said.

A knot had formed in McKendrick's stomach. Drenched in sweat and helpless, he felt nauseous and he could feel his heart pounding.

Five metres away a group of men had already started gathering around Kalyem. She'd been yanked to her feet and was being held from behind by a man who had both his arms clamped around her waist.

Leering in anticipation, he let her struggle for a minute before lifting her off the ground to allow his companions to remove her jeans and rip open her blouse.

She was terrified, screaming for someone to help her and kicking out frantically as soon as men began to touch her breasts and grope her between her thighs.

McKendrick couldn't stand it, unable to watch, sickened by a scene that was being made worse now she'd been stripped and he could see how slender she really was.

She had a nice enough figure, but her breasts were smaller than the hands that were fondling them, and overall there was hardly anything of her – a slim young woman not yet twenty, being forced to submit to men who were behaving no better than a pack of rabid animals.

Even if events had been unfolding less swiftly, there would still have been no time for him to consider options because he had none, and because he was already committed to the only course of action he could take – not that anyone would choose a place like this to die, he thought, although in the circumstances it was probably as good a place as any.

The decision had been easy to make. Just as he knew that saving Kalyem was almost certainly going to be impossible, so he knew that he was sure as hell going to try, because if he didn't, as well as betraying her, he'd be betraying everything he'd ever believed himself to be.

Blanking out her whimpering and her cries, he concentrated his attention on a small man who had not yet gone to join the others. He was close, his rifle held loosely across his shoulders, standing less than a couple of metres away, too busy watching to be aware of any danger.

Gritting his teeth, McKendrick was as ready as he was ever going to be. But before he could move, from somewhere behind him came the crack of a rifle and he saw blood spurt bright and red from Kalyem's throat.

She was dead before she hit the ground, released from an ordeal that could have only had one end, her spine shattered by the same bullet that had penetrated the chest of the man behind her.

He was taking longer to die, but McKendrick was already looking elsewhere.

It had been Jusaf who had fired the shot. Repelled by a spectacle that had been getting more dreadful by the minute, he'd taken the responsibility of doing what he'd known McKendrick could never have done – an act not of a coward, but of a courageous man who had

17

neither doubted himself nor given any thought to his own survival.

He fired twice more, wounding the small man in front of McKendrick and killing another outright before he changed position, ducking out of sight behind the Land-Rover.

McKendrick had frozen, isolated and exposed with nowhere to go, expecting to be cut down by gunfire that had erupted from what seemed like every corner of the forest.

Men who a moment ago had been otherwise engaged were seeking shelter in the trees or lying prone using automatic weapons to direct a hail of bullets at the hidden gunman, calling for fresh magazines and continuing to fire until a rocket-propelled grenade reduced the Land-Rover to a heap of smoking scrap.

But somehow Jusaf had remained alive. Out in the open, bleeding terribly from a wound that had all but severed his left arm, he carried on working the bolt of his rifle with his one good hand, supporting himself against a chunk of burning tyre.

His bravery was short-lived. He died on his knees, his body almost cut in half, but still gripping his gun in a final gesture of defiance against odds that he had always known would be too great.

For McKendrick, too numb to comprehend why he alone had been allowed to live, the horror was not yet over. He stood where he was as the man with the tattooed hand came over to speak to him.

'For the long walk you have ahead, you will need this.' The man held out a plastic bottle. 'It is best you do not waste this water I give you by staying here where it is so hot.' He turned to leave. 'After what has taken place, please be certain to tell your friends that it is unwise for anyone to use this route.'

McKendrick couldn't answer. He couldn't do anything, realizing that, because of his stupidity, not only had Kalyem and Jusaf lost their lives, but that he had no one to blame but himself for the events to which he had just borne witness.

He continued standing in the clearing until the men had dispersed and he heard the distant growl of engines starting, overwhelmed by his guilt and wondering how in God's name he was ever going to forget what had happened here today.

It took him several minutes to come to his senses, and only then, perhaps to guarantee that he never would forget, or in response to some unconscious need, did he use his camera to photograph what was left of Jusaf and the smouldering Land-Rover.

Dealing with Kalyem was much harder. Her eyes had stayed open, and her skin was still moist and she was still very warm.

He retrieved her shoes and managed to put her clothes back on, then carried her in his arms to the base of the tallest and the whitest ghost tree where, with the aid of the jack-handle from the Land-Rover, he excavated a shallow grave, laying her gently to rest and closing her eyes before he covered her with soil that was as red as the river of blood that had run down between her breasts.

# Chapter 2

**M**cKendrick always enjoyed his visits to Hawaii, often stopping-over here between flights back to Europe in order to wind down and reacquaint himself with the real world.

Today, though, Waikiki seemed tacky and artificial, and no more real than the world he'd left behind.

For most of his flight from Balikpapan he'd been able to keep his mind off what had happened in the forest, but after making the mistake of falling asleep four hours out of Manila on the second leg of his journey to Honolulu, he'd experienced the first of the flash-backs.

The second had occurred earlier today when he'd been standing on the balcony outside his hotel room, and a car had backfired in the street below. Since then, by making a determined effort to keep his thoughts on the present, there hadn't been another one, although McKendrick knew better than to believe he'd got on top of his problem.

He'd left his hotel after lunch, heading for nowhere in particular and spending some time in Kapiolani Park before wandering back along the beach until he'd found himself here outside the Royal Hawaiian where, as usual, a group of Waikiki's beautiful people were at play. They were all in their late teens or early twenties, young men and women with tanned and buffed bodies, none of them wearing much even though, by Indonesian standards, the October sun had little heat in it, and McKendrick was finding the day quite cool.

He watched some girls who were throwing a frisbee around, wondering how he was going to handle the next few days with

20

Andrew and hoping that he hadn't forgotten how to talk to a 10-year-old.

How well they'd get on together would depend on him behaving like any other father, he decided, a job that, in the circumstances, might not be as easy as he would wish it to be.

He spent the remainder of the afternoon at the beach, returning to his hotel shortly before six, relying on the traffic noise, the crowds and the smell of suntan oil to remind him of where he was and why he'd come here.

The lobby was full of people, including a Japanese tour group and a number of elderly women who were lined up at the check-in. McKendrick avoided them all, going to the far end of the desk where a youth was busy at his computer.

'Hi.' McKendrick placed his swipe card on the counter. 'Could you see if there are any messages for me, please?'

'Yes, sir.' The young man made a point of finishing what he was doing before he cleared his screen and punched another button. 'Your wife phoned from California,' he said.

'I don't have a wife,' McKendrick said. 'I have an ex-wife. What did she want?'

'Just to confirm that your son Andrew is arriving on flight UA14 tomorrow morning at 8.45 A.M. And there's a guy from the navy who's been waiting to see you – a Lieutenant Goddard. He's over there by the fountain.'

'Thanks.' McKendrick was fairly certain he didn't know anyone in the US Navy, and the name didn't ring a bell either.

He pushed through the people, making his way over to the fountain where an officer in full naval uniform was standing by himself at the window. The man was about thirty with closely cropped hair and already transferring his briefcase to this other hand now he'd seen McKendrick coming.

'Adam McKendrick?' he asked.

'That's me.'

'I'm Dean Goddard.' He shook hands. 'I'm really sorry to be interrupting your lay-over, but I figured this was probably the only chance I'd have to say hello.'

'What can I do for you?'

21

'That's kinda hard to answer.' Goddard smiled. 'I wish I knew, but if you can spare me half an hour, maybe we can both find out. If you have the time I'd be glad to buy you a beer.'

McKendrick had the time, but he wasn't sure if he wanted to spend it drinking with a stranger. But nor was he much inclined to spend the evening alone either: in which case, sitting in a bar might be a better idea than sitting in his room looking at the wall. 'How did you find me?' he asked.

'I sent a couple of faxes to your office in Brussels and tried to e-mail you. When that didn't work, I phoned the UN and spoke to a woman there who gave me your contact address in Indonesia.'

'And she said I'd be calling in here on my way back?'

'Right.' Goddard hesitated. 'How about that drink?'

'OK.' McKendrick followed him across the lobby to a small half-empty bar that had piped Hawaiian music playing in the background.

Choosing a booth at the rear of the room, Goddard waited for McKendrick to sit down before opening his case and taking out a thin manila folder. 'I've got a desk job that drives me crazy,' he said. 'Three years ago up in the Gulf I took a chunk of shrapnel in my leg. Instead of the navy invaliding me out, they gave me a nice office here in Honolulu.'

McKendrick had noticed his limp. 'Were you part of the Iraqi occupation?' he said.

'I'd go back tomorrow if they'd let me. I've had enough of rattling around with a lot of paper pushers. That's why I got started on this goddamn witch-hunt.' Goddard opened his folder. 'If you're wondering how I got your name, it's because I spent half a weekend sifting through stuff on the Internet, and yours just kept on turning up – mostly on the website the UN are running for their Environmental Programme. As far as I can tell, of all the people who know about underground fires, you know more about them than anyone else.'

McKendrick grinned. 'You don't want to believe what you read on the Internet. If someone says they understand underground fires, they're either stupid or they've never seen one. Why's the US Navy interested in them?'

'They're not. The navy wouldn't recognize an underground fire if they fell into one headfirst. It's me who's interested. It's a kinda personal project – because of something that happened to my sister Bridget. She was killed by a hit and run driver six weeks ago in Germany.' Goddard paused. 'She was only twenty.'

One year older than Kalyem, McKendrick thought, a reminder he could have done without.

'It's a bad luck, good luck story with a lousy ending,' Goddard said. 'If it's going to make any sense I'll have to bore you with some family history if that's OK.'

'Fine. Go ahead.' McKendrick wasn't bored yet, but unable for the moment to imagine where all this might be leading.

'My sister and I were born and raised in Logan County: that's a region in West Virginia. It's a tough place for kids to grow up in. It used to be coal country, but it isn't anymore. Most of the mines have closed, the economy packed up years ago and just about all the miners there are unemployed. You can find whole families on welfare or others that have sold everything they own just to buy food.' Goddard stopped talking while a waiter placed beers on the table.

'Is that the bad luck bit?' McKendrick asked.

'If you don't count mining accidents and occupational sickness. Our father and both our grandfathers died from black lung disease. That's what you get if you spend your life working underground breathing in coal dust from mines that have badly filtered air.' Goddard leaned back in his seat. 'But ten years ago, things got a bit better – after the US Mine Safety and Health Administration filed a successful seven million dollar civil action against mining companies who'd been falsifying their test results of air quality. A few families got compensation: about four per cent of them, I think it was. That's the good luck part.'

'Because your family was one of the lucky four per cent?' McKendrick said.

'We never did find out why, but there was enough money coming in for our parents to put me through naval college and send Bridget to university.'

While Goddard had been speaking, people had been drifting into the bar to occupy the other booths. Some were obviously hotel guests, but there were also three or four native Hawaiians and an attractive, olive-skinned woman in an evening dress who had chosen to sit on a stool near the door. She was about Goddard's age, with a good figure and shoulder-length dark hair, smiling at McKendrick now she'd realized he was staring at her.

'Forget it,' Goddard said. 'You haven't been away from home that long. If she's not waiting for someone, you're looking at a thousand dollars a night.'

'If I had a thousand dollars to throw away, I wouldn't be going home at all,' McKendrick said. 'I've got business that needs finishing in Indonesia.'

'Putting out more fires?'

'Not exactly. It's a sort of personal project like yours. What was your sister doing in Germany?'

'She got herself mixed up with the wrong people – well, maybe not that wrong – just a bunch of environmentalists who were out to solve the world's problems. Because of her family background and where she came from, Bridget really cared about things like air pollution, ground pollution, water quality and car emissions. You name it, Bridget was out to fix it. She even had a thing about the contamination of city storm water by people who wash their cars in the street. She went to Europe on a working holiday – after she'd heard about a company call Linder International who are supposed to be building a new kind of power station at the foot of the Rocky Mountains in Wyoming. To someone like Bridget, Linder International were the enemy. She sent them letters, she wrote articles about them for Wyoming newspapers and she had thousands of bumper stickers printed saying that Linder were environmental terrorists.'

McKendrick wasn't sure what to say. 'Was this new power station a nuclear job?'

Goddard shook his head. 'Coal-fired, but without mining the coal first. It's not rocket science. Apparently the concept's been around for a while.' He took some sheets of paper from his folder. 'The technology's called UCG: Underground Coal Gasification. Have you heard of it?'

'I think I might have read an abstract or seen something about it in a journal.' McKendrick was finding it hard to get his mind on track. 'As far as I can remember, the idea is to drill a couple of holes into a deep seam somewhere and burn the coal where it is for years on end.

You pump air or steam down one hole to provide oxygen for the fire and use the other hole to siphon off the combustion gases so you can drive a whole lot of gas turbines to generate power on the surface. Is that what you're talking about?'

'Yep.' Goddard began to read from one of the sheets. 'UCG is the in situ combustion of an underground coal seam to produce gas for use as an energy source in power stations located near or above the seam itself. The technique is conceptually very simple, but the development of working systems is proving to be difficult in practice.' He looked up. 'Do you want me to go on?'

McKendrick drained his glass. 'Not if you're going to be reading that stuff to me for half an hour.'

Goddard smiled slightly. 'Bear with me. This is the good bit.' He read out a statement from another page. 'Although the deliberate ignition of underground coal seams promises the prospect of clean, cheap and greenhouse-friendly energy, environmentalists claim that large-scale blazes that may last for decades or even centuries will not only kill thousands of acres of vegetation and create forest fires, but will poison aquifers and other water sources with cancer-causing toxic chemicals.'

'Which is why your sister got involved,' McKendrick said.

'And the reason she went overseas. She phoned me before she left to borrow some money and tell me what she was doing. Apparently she'd found out that there are pilot plants operating in at least four countries: small ones in China and Russia, a Spanish one that's about to be closed down and another that's just started up in England.'

'But none in Germany.'

'No. She'd spent weeks trying to get information about the environmental impact of these foreign installations, but none of them has been up and running long enough for anyone to know whether they're dirty or not.' Goddard paused. 'But then Bridget tripped over a report describing a real old plant that the Nazis had operated for a couple of years at the end of World War Two. The document she got hold of was all in German, so she had to get it translated.'

'And because the plant had been closed down for over half a century, your sister figured she ought to go and have a look at it,' McKendrick said, 'so she could see if there had been any long-term problems.'

'Right. Can you handle another beer?'

McKendrick shook his head. 'I'm fine for the minute.'

'Look, I know this must sound pretty much off the wall to you. If you don't want to hear the rest, you only have to say.'

'It's OK. Carry on. What did she find out?'

'I'm not sure.' Goddard closed his folder. 'All I know is that she visited a lake on a private estate near Weiskirchen in western Germany. I looked the place up on a map. Weiskirchen's a village in the Saar district between Saarbrücken and Trier – more or less in the middle of what the Germans call the little Ruhr because of the industry there. I guess that's why the Allies bombed the shit out of it in 1945.'

'It's probably why the Germans built the power station there to start with,' McKendrick said. 'They'd have been running short of power for their factories at the end of the war, so it would've looked like a pretty good solution at the time – quick and easy, and without them having to dig new mines or transport coal from somewhere else halfway across the country.'

Goddard nodded. 'That's what I figured, too.' He took out a small box and an envelope from his briefcase. 'Two days before Bridget got run down she sent me this video tape and this letter. By the time her package arrived here I already knew what had happened to her, so I didn't play the tape or open her letter right away. I should have, though. If you read between the lines, it sounds as though she thought she was on to something.'

'Like what?' McKendrick was becoming more curious.

'She said the lake and everywhere around it is completely dead and that the tape shows how milky the water is. And she said the water smells like antiseptic.'

'A video tape doesn't prove anything,' McKendrick said. 'She ought to have taken samples.'

'She knew that. In her letter she said she was going back the next day to get some, but I don't know if she ever made it.'

Their discussion was interrupted by the waiter coming to ask if they'd care to reorder. McKendrick declined, hoping that by doing so he might hurry things along, or at least find out what advice or assistance Goddard was expecting him to offer.

The naval officer took his time to refill his glass from a freshly opened bottle before he spoke again. 'Can I ask you a couple of questions?' he said.

'Ask away.'

'Do you really think a lake in Germany could still be polluted by an underground coal fire that stopped burning sixty years ago?'

'Maybe.' He tried to remember how old some of the fires in China had been. 'If there's ground water leaching into the empty tunnel, it might rise up again under the bottom of the lake at certain times of the year.'

'Why would a lake be milky and have an antiseptic smell?'

'Hard to know.' McKendrick thought for a moment. 'There's a fair chance the water could be contaminated with phenol – that's carbolic acid. You can get a whole lot of nasty chemicals left behind in burned-out seams – particularly if the coal hasn't had enough air or oxygen to keep it going properly over a long period.'

'What about gases?'

McKendrick shook his head. 'Not after sixty years. I don't think it'll have anything to do with the methane or the carbon dioxide or hydrogen, but there might be some bad oxides still hanging around, or even just plain old tar.' He hesitated. 'Why do you want to know?'

'Because of Bridget – because something's not right about the way she died. You see, she was supposed to have been riding a bicycle when she got slammed into, but I know damn well she hadn't been near a bike since she was seven years old. There was no reason for her to have been on one when she had a perfectly good rental car sitting back in the car park of the hotel where she'd been staying.'

'What did the German police have to say?' McKendrick thought he was beginning to understand.

'All I can tell you is what I got out of them over the phone. There was a mangled-up bike lying beside her in the ditch where she was found, and they had a witness – a local farm labourer who claimed he saw her that night riding along the road in the dark with no lights.'

'Do you think he was lying?' McKendrick kept his voice level.

Goddard avoided the questions, clearly recognizing the need to tread more carefully now he'd blown his cover. 'My sister was a fit and healthy young woman,' he said. 'Even if she'd been on a bike, she wouldn't have fallen off it in front of a car or a truck. The Germans did an autopsy and found nothing. She wasn't drunk, she didn't have needle marks on her arms and, except for some residual novocaine in her system from where she'd had a couple of her teeth filled, there wasn't a trace of anything unusual in her blood.'

McKendrick looked at him. 'So you've decided it wasn't an accident at all. You've come up with your own explanation. You think that because your sister was making waves for Linder International about their Wyoming power station, they'd been keeping an eye on her – which meant she was in trouble the minute she stumbled on this German lake.'

Goddard seemed to be relieved to have his theory out in the open. 'It's not as crazy as it sounds,' he said. 'Why let a twenty-year-old girl screw up a billion dollar construction contract? Once Linder realized what Bridget had seen and how big a threat she was going to be to their project, they arranged to fix the problem permanently.'

'How much do you know about Linder International?'

'A fair bit.' Goddard reopened his folder. 'Do you want to see a copy of their last year's annual report?'

'Just tell me who they are.'

'Their headquarters are in Zurich in Switzerland. The company's run by its founder: a guy called Ron Linder. He made his name ten years ago designing and manufacturing turbines for wind farms, but since then he's diversified into other energy fields. The company has contracts for solar generators and desalinization plants in the Middle East and they've got wave and tidal projects running all over the world. Coal gasification is just one arm of their business.'

'Look,' McKendrick said, 'I know you don't want to hear this, but I've worked for some hard-nosed international companies, but I can't remember a single one of them even thinking of doing what you believe Linder's done. Big-name outfits don't behave like that. They can't afford to, and they don't need to.'

Goddard's expression remained the same. 'I know I've got squat for evidence,' he said. 'And I know a guy like you must get sick and tired of hearing dumb-ass conspiracy theories, but I'm not here to try and convince you of anything.'

Interesting though Goddard's story was, McKendrick had heard enough. In spite of not wishing to appear rude, with problems of his own, and with Andrew arriving tomorrow, he was too preoccupied to pick his words with any care. 'So why are you here?' he said.

'To ask for a favour: to see if you'd give me an opinion.'

'On what?'

'I want to know if it's worthwhile me going to have a look at that lake in Germany. I've got leave due to me, and I could be there and back in a few days.'

'Unless you happen to call in on Linder as well,' McKendrick said.

'Which is why I need your opinion. If you think the lake won't tell me anything, I'll have to figure out another way to prove Linder had my sister killed.' Goddard slid the folder across the table and placed the videotape on top of it. 'Those are her notes and the footage she shot in Weiskirchen.'

McKendrick decided to be blunt. 'I'm sorry,' he said, 'but even if I had the time, right now I have trouble remembering what day it is. I've had six tough weeks in Indonesia, and first thing in the morning my son's arriving here from San Diego. We haven't seen each other since Christmas, and I've only got two days with him before I'm due to fly out again to Brussels. You'll be better off talking to someone else.'

'Can I leave the notes and the tape with you anyway,' – Goddard stood up from the table – 'in case you have half an hour to have a look? I'll call by for them on my way home tomorrow, if that's OK with you.'

'No promises.' McKendrick waited for the lieutenant to settle the tab, then accompanied him out of the bar.

'Do you think I'm crazy?' Goddard stopped walking while he searched for his car keys.

'I know how you feel, if that makes any difference. I've got more or less the same problem.'

'That unfinished Indonesian business of yours?'

McKendrick smiled. 'My problem might be easier to fix than yours, though. Thanks for the beer.'

'My pleasure. Thank you for listening to me. I'll see you tomorrow.' Goddard limped away, pausing briefly to wave goodbye from the hotel entrance before he disappeared out into the street.

For McKendrick, the evening had been a muddled end to a muddled day. Too unsettled to consider eating in the hotel restaurant, he went to his room where he phoned the front desk to ask if someone could bring up a VCR for him to use.

He shouldn't have bothered. By the time it arrived an hour later, McKendrick's mind was back in Kalimantan and he was as reluctant to view the tape as he was to read the notes of a young woman he'd never met and never would meet.

Telling himself that instead of thinking about her, he'd be better off thinking about tomorrow, he ordered coffee and sandwiches from room service, then wandered out on to the balcony, ready for another backfire, uneasy at the prospect of another night of flashbacks and wondering if being reunited with his son might somehow push away his recollections of the past.

McKendrick had forgotten how to keep up with a 10-year-old. After a day that had been variously described by Andrew as awesome and full-on, it was easy to see which of them was the more tired and who was more in need of rest.

For the moment, McKendrick had secured some breathing space. Under the pretext of watching the evening news before they went out again, he was slumped in a chair in front of the television while Andrew was continuing to explore the hotel suite, experimenting with the bathroom shower before he began going through the drawers and the cupboards in the lounge.

McKendrick had enjoyed the day, as willing to play tour guide as he had been to assume the less familiar role of being a father: something that had come more easily to him than he'd expected. The exercise had been good therapy as well, he thought, preventing him from dwelling on the events in Indonesia, because there had been no more time to do that than there had been time to consider what, if anything, he was going to do with the material Goddard had given him.

'Hey, Dad.' Andrew had discovered McKendrick's sketches. 'Did you draw these?'

'They're nothing. Put them back where you found them.'

Instead of doing what he was told, Andrew brought them over.

'What are they?' he asked.

'Drawings of a tattoo I don't want to forget.'

'Are you getting one like it?'

McKendrick smiled. 'I don't think so.'

'Why's it important?'

'It's sort of complicated.' He changed the subject. 'Might be an idea for you to start figuring out what we're going to do tomorrow,' he said. 'If we're planning on driving to Diamond Head and having a look at the Blowhole, I'll need to organize a rental car for the morning.'

'You said we could go to Waimea Falls.' Andrew returned the sketches to the drawer. 'And Mom said you'd take me to the Sea Life Park. I know how to find it. I looked it up on the map.'

'We can go where we like.' McKendrick switched off the TV. 'If you're ready for that ice cream, how about we see if the snack bar behind the fountain is still open? Will that be OK?'

'I suppose.'

'Don't you want to go?'

Andrew came and perched himself on the arm of the chair. 'The kids in my class all know my father has a really neat job,' he said, 'but when they ask me about it, I don't know what to tell them. All I've got are the photos and postcards you send me. I'm nearly eleven, Dad. You don't have to keep taking me places as an excuse not to talk to me about things.'

McKendrick was surprised. 'I'd better do something about it, then, hadn't I? We'll go and have an ice-cream each, but I guarantee that before you've finished yours, you'll have enough stories to keep your friends happy for the rest of the year.'

Judging by the smile on Andrew's face, McKendrick thought he might have recovered the situation, even though by the time they'd taken the elevator down to the lobby he still wasn't sure how suitable some of his stories might turn out to be.

He made a quick detour to leave a note for Goddard at the front desk in case the lieutenant were to call by early, then went over to the snack bar where Andrew was in the process of ordering two large multi-coloured sundaes.

'You'll be sick,' McKendrick said.

31

'No, I won't.' Andrew pointed. 'We can sit over there.' He was expectant, looking forward to learning about the more lurid aspects of his father's job.

To avoid disappointing him, McKendrick began by describing one of his more notable experiences – an accident that had occurred when the ground had collapsed beneath two mechanical diggers that had been excavating on the wrong side of a burning seam in the jungles of Brazil. Because one of the operators had died, McKendrick had been arrested and thrown into a filthy village jail where he'd stayed for nearly two weeks, unable to prove that the men had acted against his advice until a translator had arrived from a neighbouring town, and the surviving operator had recovered sufficiently to help McKendrick clear his name.

It was hardly a ripping yarn, but it seemed to have the right effect on Andrew.

'Is that really true?' he said.

'Sure it is.' He was preparing to add some authenticity by describing the jail in more detail when he saw Goddard at the door.

The lieutenant came over and smiled pleasantly at Andrew. 'Hi there,' he said. 'My name's Dean.'

Andrew shook hands with him, evidently impressed by the naval uniform.

'Do you want to join us?' McKendrick asked. 'We're only talking about this and that.'

'Just for a minute.' Goddard put his car keys on the table and sat down. 'I know how it is when people haven't seen each other for a while, and you're short on time. Have you had a good day?'

'Busy,' McKendrick said. 'And another busy one coming up tomorrow.' He hesitated. 'I didn't get a chance to check out that stuff of your sister's yet, but if you don't mind me hanging on to it, I'll be happy to take it back to Brussels and go through it there. That's not a brush-off. If you let me have your e-mail address, I'll get back to you with my opinion sometime next week.'

'I'd sure appreciate it.' Goddard was pleased. 'The address is in Bridget's folder along with my phone and fax numbers.'

Now Andrew had finished his ice-cream his eyes were fixed on a small enamel badge attached to Goddard's key ring. 'Have you got a Porsche?' he asked.

'Sure have.' Goddard showed him the emblem. 'Do you know about Porsches?'

'The father of one of the kids in my class races a GT3. I haven't seen it, though. He only drives it on the track.'

'I'm afraid mine's only a plain old 911,' Goddard said. 'I bought it from a friend who was posted back to the mainland about a year ago. It's right outside if you want to take a look.' He stood up. 'I'd better get going. I'm supposed to be over at the National Memorial at seven.'

Letting Andrew go on ahead, McKendrick accompanied the lieutenant to the front door of the hotel where a porter was arranging taxis for a number of people – among them the woman who'd been drinking in the bar last night. She was standing by herself, speaking into her cell phone, too preoccupied or too busy soliciting business to notice him as he walked past her and went out into the street.

'Dad, over here.' Andrew was admiring a black Porsche that was parked at the kerb behind an SUV.

'Have a sit in it.' Goddard opened the passenger door to allow Andrew to climb in, then turned to shake McKendrick's hand. 'I don't need much of an excuse to have a run at Linder,' he said. 'If you think my sister was close to finding something I can use to screw the bastards, I'll get some attorneys on the job.'

'Hey, Dad, look.' Andrew had discovered the Tiptronic gearshift. 'Isn't this cool?'

'Real cool, but you'd better get out now. The lieutenant has another appointment.'

Goddard checked his watch. 'It's OK. I'm fine. I'd be glad to give Andrew a ride round the block if he'd like that.'

The offer was a kind one and perfectly genuine, but McKendrick was uneasy with the idea, not prepared to take risks while the consequences of his mistake in Indonesia were still so fresh and vivid in his mind. 'I'd rather he didn't,' he said. 'You know how it is.'

'Sure.' Goddard wasn't in the least offended. 'I guess if I had a son I wouldn't want him being driven around by someone I didn't know.'

Andrew had overheard. 'Oh Dad,' he said. 'Come on. Please.'

'Out,' McKendrick instructed. 'Now.'

Once Andrew had vacated the seat, Goddard made a point of shaking hands with him as well. 'It's been a pleasure meeting someone who likes fast cars,' he said. 'I hope you have a great day with your Dad tomorrow.'

Andrew said nothing, standing beside McKendrick on the sidewalk and remaining tight-lipped even after Goddard had waved a farewell and driven off into the traffic.

'You can have a ride another time,' McKendrick said.

'When? You're the same as Mom. She never lets me do neat things either.'

An accusation for which there was no obvious answer, he thought, and certainly not one that would satisfy an impatient 10-year-old boy.

He was about to suggest they had a walk along the beach when, in the distance, the sky was illuminated by a sudden flash of light and he heard the roar of an explosion.

The blast had come from somewhere along Kalakaua Avenue, close to an intersection where Goddard's Porsche would have been at the time – a possibility that McKendrick found unnerving, but nothing like as unnerving as the possibility of the blast having come from the Porsche itself.

Wondering if his imagination was getting the better of him, he looked for rising smoke, refusing to believe the worst because, if he did, it meant that, but for his earlier misgivings, Andrew would have been a passenger in the remains of the black car he could just see through the queues of traffic.

The car was on fire, and the outline of it was familiar.

Andrew's expression showed that he had recognized it too. 'Wow,' he said. 'Do you think Lieutenant Goddard's OK?'

'I don't know.' McKendrick started propelling him back to the hotel. 'We'll switch on the TV. That's the quickest way for us to find out.'

'I want to watch from here. It's like the movies.'

'No, it's not.' Skirting round the gathering crowd of people, McKendrick marched him inside, took the first available elevator and had him back in the room before the first of the sirens began to wail.

Eager to see what was going on in the street, Andrew went straight out on to the balcony, leaving McKendrick to wonder if the boy understood how incredibly lucky he'd been. Worryingly, since seeing the flames, he'd said little, and even allowing for the natural resilience of someone his age, he seemed to be taking things too easily.

McKendrick, though, was not, aware now that it had been his guilt over the deaths of Kalyem and Jusaf that had saved his son, but unable to accept the idea of Andrew being alive because they were not – a trade-off too disturbing for him to contemplate.

And then there was Goddard himself, a victim not of a simple traffic accident, but almost certainly of something more sinister. Even if the Porsche had been travelling at a stupid speed, and its fuel tank had been ruptured in a collision, McKendrick knew very well that the blast would never have been so severe.

Andrew came back into the room and went to switch on the TV, sitting down in front of it cross-legged on the floor.

'Could you see anything outside?' McKendrick asked.

'Just some flashing lights. The balcony doesn't face the right way. If Lieutenant Goddard crashed into something he could have got out in time, couldn't he?'

'Maybe.' McKendrick was wary of sounding optimistic, but his caution was unnecessary. Crawling along the bottom of the TV screen were the latest local newsflashes.

Andrew read them out loud. 'More Maui fish killed by pesticide run-off: Kalakaua rush-hour car explosion injures bystanders: details on the hour.' He glanced up. 'Shall I switch it off now?'

'Whatever you want. Find a music channel, but keep the volume down.' He needed to think, guessing that people would remember seeing him with Goddard, and already worried that the police might find the note he'd left for the lieutenant at reception.

Either way, it didn't matter, he decided, not while he had Andrew to think of and when, suspicious though the explosion had been, offering the Honolulu police a half-baked, unsubstantiated reason for it would be as pointless as attempting to implicate Linder International in a conspiracy for which there was not the slightest evidence.

In case he was wrong, and because events had taken such a sudden and alarming turn, he went to get the information that Goddard had given him, searching everywhere for it until he came to realize that, whoever had been so carefully through the room while he'd been out, had also taken the video and the folder with them.

# Chapter 3

The morning traffic in Brussels had been fairly dense, but here in downtown Zurich it was a good deal worse. Even the taxi driver was becoming frustrated. He'd stuck his head out the window in an attempt to see how far the congestion extended along the Bahnhofstrasse, but seemed unwilling to suggest that his passenger might as well walk the last few hundred metres.

McKendrick made the decision for him. 'This is fine,' he said. 'Thanks for the ride.' He handed over some francs and got out, annoyed with himself for not catching an earlier flight and no longer prepared to waste time when he had such a tight schedule ahead of him.

Not that his irritation was altogether a bad thing, he thought. In recent days, his animosity towards Linder had been tending to dissipate, and starting off his meeting with them in a lousy mood might just be what was needed.

Now he was here in Zurich he felt less confident, and the plan that had been festering in his mind for the last three weeks seemed this morning to be less well-defined or even a little stupid.

He was also starting to wonder if he was trying to accomplish too much in one day, rather wishing he hadn't agreed to present his paper at this afternoon's conference. It had been a spur of the moment decision, a convenient excuse to combine official UN business with his own so he could confront Linder and show them that they weren't as fucking invulnerable as they thought they were – even if he was beginning to question the wisdom of such a direct approach.

Despite the sunshine, people were hurrying along the sidewalk with their collars turned up against the same kind of chill wind that had swept through Brussels earlier in the week, a harbinger of a coming winter that McKendrick was hoping to avoid by spending it somewhere else.

Growing colder by the minute, he crossed the road at the Bleicherweg intersection and searched for the right building, eventually finding a pair of glass doors bearing a gold-coloured logo above the name Linder International.

Inside it was much warmer, and after the noise and bustle of the street, the silence came as something of a relief.

The foyer was understated but large, a carpeted area that was either intended to intimidate visitors or designed to show off some of Linder's grander and more scenic projects. Each wall was hung with panoramic photographs of wave generators, wind farms or aerial pictures of solar panels sitting out in the middle of a desert somewhere.

The receptionist had guessed who he was. 'Mr McKendrick to see Mr Linder,' she said. 'Is that correct?'

He nodded. 'Sorry I'm late.'

'I'm sure it's all right.' She smiled and pushed a button on her intercom. 'Lucy Mitchell will be right out.'

McKendrick didn't have to wait to discover who Lucy Mitchell might be. From a door behind him a young woman was already coming over to say hello. She was smartly-dressed in a sleeveless white blouse, knee-length black skirt and high-heeled shoes, but instead of the standard issue corporate secretary he'd been expecting to meet, he found himself being introduced to a pretty redhead who was so smothered in freckles that the effect was startling.

'I'm Mr Linder's PA,' she said. 'If you'd like to follow me we can go through to his office.'

Linder's office was almost as big a surprise as his personal assistant. In contrast to the foyer, the room was small, cluttered up with books and papers, and the only picture on the wall was an abstract painting of some unrecognizable fruit in a bowl.

Linder himself was equally low-key, a fine-featured, small man in his thirties who was wearing jeans and a chequered open-necked shirt.

He left his desk and came to shake hands. 'You'll have to excuse the mess,' he said. 'I've been trying to catch up on work I should have finished a week ago.' He removed some books from one of the chairs. 'Do please make yourself comfortable. Has Lucy offered you coffee?'

'I'm fine thanks. I'm kind of short on time.'

'Because of the conference you mentioned over the phone when we spoke yesterday?'

'I have to be there before two o'clock.' McKendrick sat down, not yet sure if Linder was as relaxed as he appeared to be. The man's English was faultless except for a slight accent that could mean he was French or German, or even Swiss; although these days it didn't matter where people came from, McKendrick thought: the bad bastards were still bad wherever they came from and whatever language they spoke.

The girl had remained in the room, seated on a chair beside Linder's desk with a notepad on her knee. 'We're not entirely clear why you've come to see us,' she said. 'The references you gave us were helpful, but apart from the websites telling us you're an expert in the field of underground fires and that you're presently under contract to the UN, we don't really have much information about who you are.'

'Do you need to know who I am?' McKendrick asked. 'Don't you speak to people you don't know?'

She flushed slightly. 'I didn't mean that.'

Linder was amused. 'I think Lucy was trying to say we're not certain how we can help you.' He sat on the edge of his desk. 'You said you'd prefer not to discuss your business over the phone, so we're rather in the dark.'

'It might be more a question of how I can help you.' McKendrick had rehearsed the line, conscious of the need to open the subject cautiously in case he got cut off at the knees before he'd even started. 'The reason I'm here is because of someone called Dean Goddard who called to see me three weeks ago while I was in Hawaii. He wanted to have a chat about his sister Bridget.' McKendrick paused. 'Do their names mean anything to you?'

Linder started to shake his head, but his assistant corrected him.

'Bridget Goddard,' she said. 'The bumper-sticker girl – you know, the one in America who kept writing to us about the Wyoming project.'

'Oh God, her.' Linder grimaced. 'The girl who thinks we're eco-terrorists. She's been trying to stir up trouble for months.'

'She won't be doing that any more,' McKendrick said. 'Nor will her brother. They're both dead.' He looked for telltale signs of uneasiness, aware that Linder had been smart enough to refer to Bridget in the present tense, but otherwise failing to detect any alarm either in the man's manner or in his expression.

'I'm sorry to hear that,' Linder said. 'I can't pretend Bridget Goddard was anything but a nuisance to us, but it's always unfortunate when family members lose their lives together – a car accident, I presume.'

'Not exactly. Bridget Goddard's supposed to have been killed by a hit and run driver while she was on a working holiday in Germany, and as soon as her brother started investigating what had really happened to her, someone planted a bomb in his car. According to the Honolulu newspapers, the police found bits of detonator that are used by Middle East terrorists, so unless you have a suspicious mind, there's nothing to connect the two deaths together.'

Linder raised his eyebrows. 'I see, or rather I don't see. Can I take it you're suggesting there is a connection?'

'What do you think?'

'I don't understand why you expect me to have an opinion.'

'Bridget Goddard only went to Germany for one reason,' McKendrick said. 'She wanted to have a look at a lake that's been polluted by a disused underground coal gasification plant the Nazis built during the last World War. And, if you don't already know, she was going to use that lake as evidence to shoot down your Wyoming power station project.'

'How interesting.' Linder had become more attentive, but he was displaying no signs of concern.

'Bridget did something else as well,' McKendrick said. 'She sent a video tape of the lake to her brother – along with a letter describing what it was like. Now do you understand why I expect you to have an opinion?'

'I hope you're not suggesting that we were in some way responsible for the deaths of these people.'

'I'm not suggesting anything,' McKendrick said. 'I'm telling you. The way I see it, you've got a loose cannon operating in your company – someone who made sure Bridget and Dean Goddard wouldn't interfere with your nice UCG project in the States – one of your senior managers maybe.'

By now, Linder's attitude had changed. He slid down off his desk. 'Are you representing the interests of the Goddard family?'

'I'm representing my own interests. Five minutes before Goddard's car blew up, I stopped my son from having a ride in it. If I'd let him go, I wouldn't have a son any more. He'd be as dead as Goddard and his sister are. I'm fairly pissed off about that – which is why I expect you to find out who the fuck in your company has gone off the rails.'

'And if I don't find out, you will – by taking over where you think the Goddards left off?'

'If I have to. It's up to you.'

'Where precisely is this lake supposed to be?'

'North of Saarbrücken, on a private estate near Weiskirchen.' McKendrick was careful not to mention the absence of any lake on the maps he'd bought this morning at the airport.

'Well, thank you for your frankness, even though I find your accusations preposterous and offensive. I can't imagine what proof you have of my company's involvement, but if you intend taking this further, I can assure you there are no courts that would even begin to listen to such nonsense. What did the Hawaiian police say to you?'

McKendrick kept his mouth shut.

'You have spoken to them?'

'No.'

'Mr McKendrick, I've had the courtesy to meet you this morning and I've listened with interest to what you've had to say, but I'm afraid you're wasting your time, and you're certainly wasting mine. I have no need whatever to justify myself to you. However, to prevent any further misunderstanding, I'd like you to go away knowing how false your allegations are.' Linder turned to his PA. 'Lucy, perhaps you could fetch the Wyoming file and order a taxi for our visitor. Mr McKendrick will only be staying a few more minutes.'

McKendrick knew his plan was falling round his ears. Instead of Linder being defensive or evasive, he was as self-assured as he had been ten minutes ago. Or was he, McKendrick wondered? Was he being so damn smooth and so uncompromising because he was lying?

Now the girl had left the room, Linder had gone to sit in the chair behind his desk. 'Some of our overseas projects attract threats from pressure groups or greens,' he said, 'but no one's accused us of killing people before. I find the experience distasteful.'

Before McKendrick could think of a suitable reply, the girl re-entered the room carrying a blue folder from which she extracted a number of documents and letters.

'I think you'd better see these.' She gave them to him. 'Your taxi will be here shortly.'

The first of the letters was a communication from the office of the Governor of The State of Wyoming, typed on official notepaper and informing Linder of the State's intention to withdraw all funding for the proposed UCG power station project. The tone was formal, but the last paragraph expressed regret, and whoever had drafted it had evidently realized that they were slamming the door on the project once and for all.

The second letter was Linder's written response, dated a week later and signed by Linder himself. It was equally formal, stating that in the light of the Wyoming State's decision, Linder International would not be proceeding with further geological or environmental impact studies, and that, accordingly, all consultancy contracts had been terminated, and the project cancelled.

McKendrick did no more than thumb through the rest of the correspondence, trying to convince himself that it was part of an elaborate cover-up, but knowing it wasn't because there were simply too many documents confirming that the project had been killed off before it had even started.

Altogether there were at least half-a-dozen letters, among them claims from third parties invoking penalty clauses in survey contracts that had already been let, and statements from the US Environmental Protection Agency hinting at their support should Linder International wish to consider similar UCG projects in the future – evidence that was as impossible to refute as it was to disbelieve.

McKendrick felt defeated, embarrassed by a search for information that had backfired in his face and made him look like an idiot.

'Mr McKendrick.' Linder put his fingertips together. 'When was it that Bridget Goddard had her accident?'

'September.'

'And what are the dates on those letters you've just read?'

The question was unnecessary. He'd already checked. 'May and June,' he said quietly.

'Which means, does it not, that our Wyoming project had been abandoned three full months before the Goddard girl went to Germany?'

'I guess.'

'Good. Then I imagine you'll also agree that my company had made the decision to cut its losses five months before her brother was killed by the bomb you mentioned.'

'You don't have to spell it out,' McKendrick said.

'I think I do – for your sake as much as mine. Can you honestly believe now that my company, or anyone in it, could have had anything to do with the deaths of these people? And, perhaps more to the point, can you see any possible reason to blame Linder International for what could perhaps have happened to your son in Hawaii?'

'No.' McKendrick stood up. 'I'm sorry. I should've done my home-work better.'

'Indeed you should.' Linder remained at his desk. 'I would have thought you could have managed a rather more gracious apology given the seriousness of your accusations, but I suppose that would be expecting too much. I can't say it's been a pleasure meeting you, Mr McKendrick. Lucy will show you out. Goodbye.'

Avoiding eye contact, the girl escorted him to the foyer, turning her back on him at the door before McKendrick left the building and stepped out into a wind that seemed to have become suddenly much keener and altogether colder than it had been earlier.

The post-conference banquet had turned out to be a dreary affair, more boring than the conference itself had been, and the kind of dinner that McKendrick had guessed he wouldn't enjoy long before he'd sat down here at the table to endure what seemed like several hours of mind-numbing small-talk.

He'd agreed to attend the dinner principally because it would have been bad manners not to – particularly after his lecture had been well received – but also because he'd been hoping that the company of other people might help keep his mind off this morning's fiasco at the offices of Linder International. Rarely had he felt so foolish: a case not just of jumping to the wrong conclusion, he thought, but a knee-jerk reaction to something that could've happened to Andrew but which, in reality, had not happened at all. Or was it his guilt over the events in Kalimantan, he wondered? Was that the reason he'd gone off half-cocked and, if so, how long was he going to wait before he did something about it?

The heavily perfumed woman to his left was speaking to him again, asking if his wife minded him being away from home so often.

'She used to,' McKendrick said. 'But she doesn't mind any more.'

The woman nodded understandingly. 'I expect she's got used to it,' she said. 'Most wives do in the end.'

'Mine didn't.' He smiled pleasantly at her. 'She ran off with a guy who owns an art gallery in the States. He's home all the time.'

'I see.' The woman cleared her throat. 'I'm sorry.'

Before McKendrick could find out why she should be sorry, one of the English-speaking waiters came over with a note for him.

'A young lady outside asks me to give you this,' he explained. 'I am to wait for your reply.'

The note was brief, handwritten on a folded sheet of paper:

*Dear Mr McKendrick,*
*I apologize for interrupting your dinner, but Mr Linder has asked me to contact you before you leave Zurich. I would be grateful, therefore, if you could let me have the address of your hotel so I may telephone you first thing in the morning, or perhaps call to see you if that would not be inconvenient.*
*Lucy Mitchell*

The waiter produced a ballpoint pen and a fresh sheet of paper.

'It's OK.' In his present circumstances, McKendrick would have welcomed any reason to leave the table. 'Where is she?'

'Please to follow me.' The waiter removed McKendrick's chair for him. 'You would like to take your wine with you?'

He didn't bother, nor did he bother to make his excuses to the woman beside him who'd been eavesdropping and endeavouring to read the note he'd been given.

Lucy Mitchell was standing outside the banquet room reading a copy of the conference brochure. She was wearing an expensive cream-coloured coat and holding what appeared to be an ultra-thin laptop computer.

'Oh.' She smiled at him awkwardly. 'I didn't mean you to come out. I just wanted to make sure you didn't leave town before I had a chance to speak with you. You're not catching a late flight back tonight, are you?'

McKendrick shook his head. 'Complimentary overnight accommodation if you present a paper, and you get to have a free dinner with a whole bunch of people you've never met before. Is there something I can do for you?'

'It's a bit complicated to explain tonight.'

'I've got the time if you have.' He studied her face, aware of a slight thaw in her attitude towards him, but unable to identify what it was that made her so attractive.

'Is there somewhere here we can talk?'

'Let's see.' He walked over to one of the lecture rooms, discovering that the doors were still unlocked and that the lights were still switched on. 'How about this?'

She nodded, following him down an aisle to a row of seats at the front. 'Is this the room where you gave your paper?'

'It might be. I'm not sure. Auditoriums all look the same to me.'

Leaving her computer on one of the seats, she stepped up on to the stage and read out loud from a page in the brochure. '*Extinguishing Underground Fires with Water or by High-Explosives: an overview by Adam McKendrick*.' She glanced at him. 'I thought those kinds of fires couldn't be put out with water.'

'They can't. It's the first thing everyone tries, but it never works.'

'But explosives do?'

He shook his head. 'You can excavate ahead of a front with Semtex or dynamite, but unless the seam's near the surface, mostly the ground just cracks open and that lets the fire grab more oxygen. The title of the paper was supposed to be a come-on.' He waited for her to return, wondering how much longer she intended skirting around whatever it was she'd come to ask him.

'You made a lot of work for me today,' she said.

'Tough being a PA.'

'Mm.' She came to sit beside him. 'Mr Linder wants me to go and see that lake in Germany tomorrow and he thinks you might like to have a look at it as well.'

'Why's he so interested all of a sudden?'

'In case there really is some evidence of long-term pollution there. The information would help us on other UCG projects.'

'Do you have any other UCG projects?'

'No. That doesn't mean we won't have, though.'

'Why would I want to go to Weiskirchen?'

She was surprised. 'Isn't that obvious?'

'Not unless you think I might be going anyway. Does your Mr Linder want you to make sure I don't make more trouble for him?'

'No.' She frowned. 'You do believe we had nothing to do with the deaths of Dean and Bridget Goddard, don't you?'

He knew he was missing something, but for the moment, the point she was making remained obscure. 'Look,' he said, 'I haven't had much of a chance to figure out anything since this morning. What are you talking about?'

'The lake, of course. Don't you see? If you're right about what happened to Bridget Goddard, and you're certain we weren't involved in any way, she was still killed by someone because of something she saw when she went there.'

McKendrick might have been slow to understand, but he was making up for it now, angry with himself for not taking the trouble to think things through properly.

'We were sure you'd want to see the lake for yourself,' she said.

'Because whoever killed Dean and Bridget is the same person who could have killed my son? Is that what you've decided?'

'Yes – well, it's more of a guess, I suppose.' She took off her coat and removed a cell phone from one of the pockets. 'Can I tell Mr Linder we'll be going together?'

'I'm riding shotgun for you, am I? Or isn't he worried about you going there alone?'

'He didn't say he was worried.'

'Maybe he ought to be.' McKendrick was growing suspicious. She was endeavouring to be professionally detached and cool, but trying too hard. 'You might have a problem finding the lake,' he said. 'It does-n't show up on any of the maps I've seen.'

'I know exactly where it is, and I know what it looks like, more or less. You see, Bridget Goddard didn't just mail a copy of her tape to her brother in Hawaii; she sent one to us as well. I know we should have told you this morning, but Mr Linder didn't think it was any of your business then.' She paused. 'Until you turned up, we weren't even sure what country the lake is in. All we had was the tape and a rude letter from Bridget Goddard asking us to explain how surface water could still be contaminated from a UCG installation that was closed down sixty years ago.'

'Then I came along and told you it's near Weiskirchen, so your boss thought he'd do some checking – just in case you could learn some-thing useful from the place?'

'Mm.'

'How long's the tape?' McKendrick was careful not to sound inter-ested.

'Didn't you see Dean Goddard's copy?'

'He gave it to me, but I never had the chance to play it. Someone stole it out of my hotel room in Hawaii.'

'Oh.' Her expression changed. 'I wish you'd told us that before.'

'Why?'

'It explains the break-in we had about six weeks ago at the office. We lost two computers, a new flat-screen plasma television, our VCR and a drawerful of video tapes.'

'Including the tape from Bridget Goddard?' McKendrick said.

'Yes. We didn't think much about it at the time, but it makes more sense now.'

'That's not the worst of it.' McKendrick had remembered some-thing. 'Bridget must have told someone who'd she sent the tapes to.'

'It wasn't a secret, was it? It wouldn't have been that big a deal to her.'

'It was to someone else – whoever caught her out at the lake the next day when she went back to collect water samples – someone who'd have wanted to know what the hell she was doing there.'

'She'd have explained right away.'

'Sure.' McKendrick nodded, 'but if they didn't believe her, they'd have tried pretty damn hard to get what they thought was the truth out of her.'

'If you're saying what it sounds as though you're saying, I don't believe you.'

'Think about it,' McKendrick said. 'According to the report her brother got from the coroner, Bridget had novocaine in her system and two new fillings in her teeth. Who the hell visits a dentist when they're slap bang in the middle of a project that's really important to them? If I got someone to hold you down while I drilled a couple of holes in your teeth, you'd tell me everything I wanted to know in fifteen seconds.'

'You said her teeth had been filled and that she'd had a novocaine injection.'

'Afterwards,' McKendrick said, 'to eliminate the evidence before she was got rid of on the road.'

He'd been intending to issue Lucy Mitchell with a warning, but instead he seemed to have succeeded only in frightening her. She was looking apprehensive and fiddling with her watchstrap.

'I still don't believe you. You're making this up as you go along.' She picked up her phone. 'I'd better tell Mr Linder about your stolen tape; he'll want to know.'

The remark confirmed McKendrick's suspicions. She hadn't been lying, but she was almost certainly withholding information – either on Linder's instructions or for some reason of her own.

He reached out to stop her making the call. 'How about you and I sort out a few things first?' he said.

'What things?'

'This isn't about you collecting data on the lake for future projects, is it?'

'I've already told you it is.'

'Look,' McKendrick said, 'you've taken the trouble to come here; why not tell me what's going on?'

'I can't. It's none of your business: it has nothing to do with you.'

'If it's nothing to do with me, why are we talking to each other?'

She was hesitant, apparently unwilling to trust him, but aware that he was giving her little choice. 'It's about the Weiskirchen estate,' she said. 'After you'd left this morning, and after Mr Linder had made

47

some private phone calls, he asked me to find out what I could about the place.'

'And.'

'It belongs to an old German family who've owned it for generations. It used to be a sort of country retreat as far as I can make out, but about ten years ago it became a centre for an international institute.'

'What kind of institute?'

'One that fosters closer relations between Christian and Muslim countries. It's called ICIS; Institute for Christian and Islamic Studies.' She opened the lid of her laptop. 'I'll show you. ICIS has websites in Europe, the US and another one in the Middle East.' She pressed a button on her keyboard. 'This is a summary of what they do.'

In order to see more easily, McKendrick climbed over into the seat behind and leaned over her shoulder, trying not to be distracted by the profusion of freckles on her neck and arms while he read what was on the screen:

### INSTITUTE OF CHRISTIAN AND ISLAMIC STUDIES

- Privately owned, international organization established in 1996 by founder Günter Zitelmann to promote religious tolerance between countries and societies which are either predominantly Christian or predominantly Islamic.

- Committed to harmonizing these religions by concentrating on common teachings of the Bible and the Koran. Publicity highlights the following unreferenced quotation: 'The sum of man is the sum of all men united by faith in their own beliefs.'

- Dedicated to healing rifts caused by Islamic fundamentalist violence directed at the West, and by Christian imperialism imposed upon Muslim countries by recently elected North American and European leaders.

- Regards itself as the modern face of religious unification, and believes this can be best accomplished by:

Offering theological courses in numerous countries.
Publishing high-quality, multi-language pamphlets expressing ICIS views and philosophy.
Funding low-technology, self-help projects in underdeveloped Middle East countries.
Facilitating trade deals which benefit Christians and Muslims on an equal financial and cultural basis.

- Provides cultural advisory service to companies involved in:

    Textiles and phosphates from Syria.
    Salt from Jordan.
    Oil from Saudi Arabia and Iraq.
    Cement and aluminium from United Arab Emirates.
    Cotton and carpets from Pakistan.

- ICIS is headquartered in Weiskirchen, Germany: offices in New York, San Francisco, London, Paris and Riyadh.

'A do-good outfit,' McKendrick said.

'If you want to be that cynical. It's the man running ICIS who interests Mr Linder.' She cleared the screen and turned round in her seat.

'This guy Zitelmann?'

'Yes. You see, Zitelmann is the son of a Nazi war criminal who was found guilty of crimes against humanity at the big Nuremberg trials in 1946. Günter Zitelmann's father was one of the commandants at the Nazi concentration camp in Dachau. He was responsible for the gassing of God knows how many Jews. After Mr Linder saw the name Zitelmann on that document I've just showed you, he asked me to access anything I could find about ICIS.'

'Why?'

'His family comes from a long line of German Jews. Three of Mr Linder's grandparents died in Dachau.' She paused. 'With that kind of family history I don't think he'd ever trust anyone called Zitelmann.'

By now, McKendrick was able to assemble more pieces of the jigsaw. 'Does your boss think ICIS is a cover for something?'

'He doesn't know. But now you've told him your story about Dean and Bridget Goddard, he thinks he ought to find out. People like him have awfully long memories. Now do you understand why he's interested in the lake?'

McKendrick nodded. 'Except that if there is something going on there, he shouldn't be asking you to go there alone.'

'He isn't: he's expecting you to go with me – so you can find out why your son was nearly killed when that car blew up.' She looked at him. 'Or isn't that a good enough reason any more?'

It wasn't. No matter how intrigued McKendrick happened to be, he had no intention of getting mixed up in something as complex and as convoluted as this. If Linder wanted to learn more about ICIS, he was welcome to do so, and if Lucy Mitchell wanted to visit the lake, she could damn well go there by herself.

'I'm sorry,' he said. 'I've got a problem of my own, thanks.'

'Can I ask you what it is?'

'Something I have to fix in Indonesia.'

'Suppose Linder International could fix it for you.' She placed her hands together on her lap. 'Maybe we ought to see if Mr Linder would pay you for your expertise and for your time.'

'Why would he do that? He doesn't know me from a can of fish.'

'He likes you. I don't know why, but he does. He told me. Anyway, you don't know how he operates.'

'But you do?'

'Yes. It's what I get paid for.'

McKendrick smiled at her. 'If your boss wants information on this ICIS organization, he ought to be digging it up himself.'

'He can't. He's flying out to Chicago in the morning. He'll be away for three weeks. Are you going to tell me about your problem, or not?'

McKendrick was unsure, doubting that it would do any good and reluctant to compromise himself in case he was to receive an offer that might be hard to refuse. She was being direct on purpose, he realized, hoping to discover how he would use the money so she could decide how badly he needed it.

He stepped over the seat back and sat down again. 'Do you really want to hear why I could use some cash?'

'Only if you want to tell me.'

'It's a pretty nasty story.'

She said nothing, sitting beside him quietly in the lecture-room, waiting for McKendrick to explain something he didn't know how to explain.

Conscious of talking to someone he'd met for the first time today, he started in the wrong place, attempting to justify the decision that had led him to the fire-front in the clearing before he gave her a brief description of the man with the tattooed hand. From there on, because it became progressively harder for him to find the words to explain what had happened to Kalyem and Jusaf, he cut his account short, keeping his voice free of sentiment and barely mentioning his two-day trek back out through the forest to Muaratunan.

When he'd finished, he couldn't understand why he'd begun. There was no sense of having shed a burden, and no discernible easing of his guilt. Instead, the events seemed to have been brought back into sharper focus – something he'd wanted to avoid.

'I can't imagine how awful it must have been,' she said. 'But you shouldn't go on blaming yourself. It wasn't your fault.'

'Yes it was. That's why I need the money. It won't help Kalyem or Jusaf, but I can sure as hell guarantee no one else runs into the same kind of trouble.'

'How?'

'You don't want to know, and I'm not going to tell you. Are you going to phone your boss?'

'Yes, I am.' She stood up and pressed a speed-dial button on her phone. 'I think I'd rather not have heard what you've just told me.' Turning her back on him, she walked away, speaking quietly into her phone in fluent German.

McKendrick wasn't interested in overhearing, preferring to sift through what he'd learned this evening while he tried not to look at Lucy Mitchell for too long. He'd found himself doing it before, aware that he was, but unwilling to stop until he'd determined what was so different about her.

It was her hair, or the shape of her mouth, he decided; or her voice, or simply the way her breasts occasionally brushed against the fabric of her blouse. Except that it wasn't just one thing: it was all of her – or at least all of her he could see now she'd finished talking on the phone and was facing him again.

'Ephelides,' she said.

'What?'

'Ephelides – freckles. They're not contagious.'

He swore under his breath. 'Look, I'm really sorry,' he said. 'I don't usually stare at people.'

'I'm used to it.' Ignoring his discomfort, she walked over to the foot of the stage. 'All expenses plus two thousand francs a day – or in US dollars if you'd prefer that.'

The offer was fairly generous, McKendrick thought, a useful contribution towards a return trip to Kalimantan – if and when he received information on the whereabouts of the men he intended to find there.

'How many days' work?' he asked.

'Is it important?'

'I suppose I can phone my office and invent some extra business to do while I'm here.'

'Does that mean you're accepting?'

'I guess so.' He knew it was the wrong decision, but there seemed little point in worrying about it now. 'What else did Linder have to say?'

'Only that he hasn't any useful contacts in Indonesia. And he wanted to know if I'd showed you Bridget Goddard's tape yet.'

'You said it was stolen from your office.'

She smiled slightly. 'We're a very efficient company, McKendrick. We store everything on disk – I mean everything.'

'So you can run it for me on your laptop?'

'Only if you and I come to an arrangement first.' She came to collect her coat. 'You've had dinner, but all I've eaten since eleven-thirty this morning is some chocolate. If you'd like to start using your nice expense account by buying me a sandwich, we can have a look at Bridget Goddard's home movie in the coffee shop round the corner.'

A bar would have been better, but he decided against the idea in case there wasn't one handy where he could view the disk in peace and revise his opinion of Lucy Mitchell.

She followed him out of the lecture-room, going on to wait for him at the front door while he handed in his name tag and shaking her head when he asked if she wanted him to call a taxi.

Outside the conference centre the wind had eased, but the temperature had dropped significantly. As a result, and because the coffee shop round the corner turned out to be several blocks away, it wasn't until they were inside and seated at a table that McKendrick began to thaw out again.

'Too many weeks in a hot climate,' he explained. 'I've forgotten how cold Europe can be at this time of year.'

'That sounds as though you'd rather be somewhere else.' She took a mouthful of her sandwich. 'You're not going back to Indonesia just to put up warning signs, are you?'

He didn't want to think about it, nor was he prepared to discuss it with her. 'Let me see the video,' he said.

Repositioning her laptop on the table, she flipped up the screen. 'Don't blink or you'll miss it,' she said. 'It's not very long.'

McKendrick was ready to be disappointed, but more interested than he cared to admit, particularly now he knew it was the tapes that formed a link between the deaths of Dean and Bridget Goddard and connected two separate burglaries that had occurred in two different countries.

The opening scene was a shaky, long-distance shot of three brick buildings. They were grouped together, the one in the middle being substantially larger than the other two. The impression was that of an elegant, ivy-covered seventeenth or eighteenth-century mansion house flanked by a stable-block and perhaps what had once been a lodge or a worker's cottage. Although the view showed the rear of the buildings only, in between them there were glimpses of a courtyard and an expanse of well-kept lawn.

The shot had evidently been intended as an introduction to the Zitelmann estate, the camera lingering for no more than a second or two before moving to the right and panning downwards to pick up on the foreshore of a small lake.

Determining its shape was as difficult as getting a fix on its size, but however big the lake was, it lay some distance from the buildings – anything up to half a kilometre, McKendrick estimated, more than far enough away for Bridget Goddard to have felt safe while she'd zoomed-in on the wide border of sterile soil that ran around the water's edge.

The soil was yellow, a sickly colour he'd seen before in dried-up rain puddles above freshly extinguished underground fires. But this was no puddle, and the poisons in this water were coming from a fire that had stopped burning more than half a century ago.

Lucy pointed to the left of the screen. 'Any second now,' she said. 'There. Do you think that used to be the power station?'

If it had been, there was little left of it now. One end of the building was still standing, but the rest of it was in a state of extreme disrepair, making McKendrick wonder if it had been targeted by Allied bombs during the War. The prefabricated concrete panels from which it had been constructed had either fallen over or cracked in half to let the roof collapse, and several large trees had taken root among the rubble.

Before he could decide what purpose the structure could have served, there was a single close-up shot of the lake surface and then the screen went blank.

'Is that it?' he asked.

'I told you it was short. What do you think?'

'Forget the buildings,' McKendrick said. 'It's the lake that'll give us answers. Bridget shouldn't have gone on such a sunny day. There's too much reflection off the surface to see how milky it is. About all we can be sure of is that the water's full of dissolved chemicals.'

'Because nothing's growing around it?'

'We'll know more when we've had a look.'

'Yes we will, won't we?' She packed up her computer and got to her feet. 'I'll be at your hotel at nine o'clock sharp tomorrow.'

'No you won't − not unless I tell you where it is.'

'That won't be necessary.' She smiled. 'We've had the information since this morning. Thank you for my sandwich. It was very nice. Goodnight Mr McKendrick.'

# Chapter 4

Instead of taking one of the Karlsruhe exits, Lucy was keeping the Mercedes in the outside lane of the autobahn, increasing her speed to such an extent that, not for the first time this morning, McKendrick was beginning to wonder when she was going to back off.

The car belonged to Linder, an expensive SL600 – a great means of getting anywhere in a hurry, McKendrick thought, particularly if it was being driven by a young woman who was prepared to use its performance whenever she had the opportunity to do so, and frequently even when she didn't.

'Are you trying to hit warp speed or something?' he asked.

'Do you want me to try?' She spoke without taking her eyes off the road, braking slightly now they were bearing down on a BMW that was being slow to get out of the way.

'If this was my car, I don't think I'd let you anywhere near it,' McKendrick said.

'I always look after it when Mr Linder's away. He likes to have it exercised.'

Exercising was not the word McKendrick would have chosen to describe their high-speed journey north to Germany, but she was safe and confident enough behind the wheel, and if she was hoping to impress him or frighten him, she hadn't quite succeeded yet.

It was largely because of her driving that they'd made such good time, losing only a few minutes in merging traffic near Strasbourg and reaching Baden Baden in a little over two hours on an autobahn that had been remarkably free of heavy trucks on this cold, clear morning.

So far, apart from outlining her proposal for the day, and complaining about the extra work she'd had to do last night, she hadn't said much, happy to answer the odd question, but otherwise content apparently to concentrate on her driving.

For McKendrick, the journey had been a further opportunity to consider what he was doing and why the hell he was doing it. Yesterday evening, his motives for accepting Linder's offer had seemed reasonably straightforward, even if his decision had been made without much thought. By this morning, though, he'd started to believe he'd been too hasty and perhaps too willing to spend more time in the company of someone he hardly knew while he embarked on an exercise that was likely to prove exactly nothing.

It was his own fault, he decided, a matter of one thing leading to another without him bothering to consider how easily he'd fallen into a trap of his own making. Had events in Indonesia turned out differently, or if Andrew hadn't been so fascinated by Goddard's Porsche, neither Linder nor Lucy Mitchell would have had more than a passing interest in the lake.

To try and forget the past, he consulted the map, searching for a cross-country route to Saarbrücken before they reached what appeared to be a maze of intersections between Heidelberg and Mannheim.

'Are you looking for the N10?' Lucy asked.

'Is that the road to Landau and Pirmasens?'

'Yes, but it'll be quicker if we carry on and take the E12 autobahn. I know the N10 looks good on the map, but it's always jammed up with traffic.'

'We're not in that much of a hurry, are we?'

'I just thought that the sooner we check into our hotel in Saarbrücken, the longer we'll have to explore Weiskirchen this afternoon. I know the lake can't be much more than half an hour's drive from Saarbrücken, but we don't want to run ourselves short of time, do we?'

She'd suggested this preliminary visit to the lake before they'd left Zurich earlier this morning, an idea that McKendrick was no happier with now than he had been then.

'Have you been to Saarbrücken before?' he asked.

She nodded. 'The company which makes the propellers for our wind turbines has its factory there. Don't you think we should go to the estate this afternoon?'

'If we do, it'll only be for a quick drive-by – just to see where it is, so I can figure out how we're going to play this.'

'Why should it be you who decides? You might be able to find your way around countries where there are lots of fires burning underground, but I know more about how things work in Germany than you do.'

He'd been half-expecting this, aware of her reluctance to accept advice from him, but also conscious of the need to establish some ground rules early on.

'Look,' he said, 'you and I aren't going to get far unless you stop trying to score points. If you want to do this by yourself, that's fine by me. You can drop me off at the airport in Saarbrücken and I'll have a nice flight back to Brussels.'

'I'm not trying to do anything.' She was careful not to look at him. 'I just don't see why you think you have all the answers when you're as much in the dark about why the Goddards died as I am.'

'The Goddards aren't my problem,' McKendrick said. 'I've already told you; I've got other things on my mind.'

'If you mean what you're planning to do in Indonesia – or what I think you're planning to do, it won't stop you believing you made a mistake when you were last there, will it?'

He didn't need any reminders from her, and he wasn't going to let her lecture him about things that were so far outside of her experience that she couldn't even begin to understand them.

'OK,' he said. 'How about this? You're out in a desert thirty clicks from anywhere. You know there are drug-runners and guerrillas operating in the area, but you've still decided you can use some help from a 19-year-old girl who wants to learn about the solar energy panels you're setting up for her local village. But before you can finish the job, a whole bunch of terrorists comes out of the sand-hills and makes you watch while they rip off her clothes and rape and kill her. How are you going to feel about that? You'd just walk away and forget all about it, would you?'

She started to reply, but thought better of it, sitting tight-lipped behind the wheel and allowing the Mercedes to slow to a more reasonable speed.

'Your Mr Linder won't be too pleased if you wind up in a ditch like Bridget Goddard,' McKendrick said. 'And I figure that might be a bit of a waste as well, so I'm going to make sure it doesn't happen.'

'Well, how reassuring.' She gave him an artificial smile. 'I don't think that's the most flattering compliment I've had from anyone, but I don't believe I've met anyone like you before, Mr McKendrick.'

'Adam,' he said. 'Call me Adam.'

'I'm not comfortable with first names of people I don't know.'

'You know more about me that I know about you.'

She glanced across at him. 'What would you like to know?'

'Anything. You're not Swiss, are you?'

'My parents are Irish, but they went to live in Preston before I was born, so I'm English, I suppose.'

'Do you have a husband?'

'I don't seem to have had time to find one.' She paused for a moment. 'That's not the whole truth. You'd be surprised how limited the market is for someone who's covered from head to foot in freckles. I think that's one of the reasons I buried myself in an arts degree. But it didn't work out, so I took a job where I could practise my languages and learn about commerce. I was in London about eighteen months before the company was taken over by Linder International.'

'And you landed the job of being Linder's PA.'

'Mm. As long as you can speak three or four languages, you can get work almost anywhere in the EU nowadays.' She manoeuvred the Mercedes into the centre lane and reached out to adjust one of the heater controls. 'Are you warm enough?'

'I'm fine. It still looks pretty damn cold outside, though.'

She nodded. 'There was ice on the windscreen first thing this morning, and the weather forecast isn't good either. Do you really think we ought to be careful at Weiskirchen?'

'It won't do us any harm. But that doesn't mean we have to waste time there. If the estate's as deserted as it looked in Bridget's video, we can collect our water samples after dark and have a look around then.'

'I wasn't expecting us to go at night.'

'Did you happen to bring dark clothes and sensible shoes?'

'I think I can find some, and before you ask, I happened to bring binoculars and my camera, too.'

'How about film canisters?'

She shook her head. 'It's a digital camera. Why?'

'They're good for storing soil and water samples. We'll buy some in Weiskirchen.'

'It'll be easier if we get them in Saarbrücken. I'm not sure how big Weiskirchen is. Do you know what Weiskirchen means in English?'

'No.'

'Churches, or a point of churches. There could hardly be anywhere better for a religious institute, could there?'

'Depends if you have a polluted lake sitting in the middle of your grounds,' McKendrick said. 'Nobody's going to want to walk on water that's full of nasty chemicals. Did you find out any more about who's running the place?'

'Mr Linder has. After I'd left you last night, I called round to see him at his home. Günter Zitelmann's on record as having a science degree in biochemistry, but he seems to have always been more involved in theology. When he was younger he churned out religious articles for German and Austrian magazines – mostly about how faith can save the world, but that was before he used his family's money to found ICIS and went global with his ideas. He doesn't sound a very sinister sort of person to me.'

'Is that a polite way of saying you think your boss is chasing shadows?'

'I'm not sure what to think.' She kept her eyes on the rear-view mirror. 'Did you call your wife to tell her what you're doing?'

'If I still had a wife, I would've done, but I haven't so I didn't. You'd be surprised how limited the market is for husbands who spend all their time overseas.'

She was amused. 'I'd trade my freckles for your job. I never go anywhere exciting – well, except for today, or when I'm installing solar panels in imaginary deserts full of imaginary terrorists.'

McKendrick pointed across to her window. 'There's some excitement for you.'

'I know. He's been on our tail for the last ten minutes.'

In the outside lane, a lime-green Nissan Skyline had drawn level with them, the young male driver staring at Lucy now he could see her at close range, and evidently more interested in her than he was in the

Mercedes. He blew her a kiss and put his foot down hard.

The gesture had been inoffensive, but not to Lucy. Either to see if she could match the blistering acceleration of the Skyline, or because she was pleased about something, she responded by pulling out into the fast lane and letting the big V12 have its head.

Whatever her excuse, or the reason for her change of mood, it was another example of her unpredictability, McKendrick thought, unless she was simply taking the opportunity to show him that exercising the Mercedes was a lot more entertaining than listening to anything he had to say about himself, or about the possibility of danger at the lake.

His impression of the Saar district had been wrong. Earlier today, during their drive into Saarbrücken, the region had seemed to be nothing more than a densely populated and heavily industrialized part of Germany nestled up against borders with France and Luxembourg. But this afternoon, once they'd left the outskirts of the city and headed north towards Weiskirchen, there was less evidence of what was supposed to be the second largest coalfield in the whole of Europe and, gradually, the smoke-stacks, steel-mills and factories had been replaced by a pastoral landscape that differed little from the open countryside further to the south and east.

From what McKendrick had seen of Saarbrücken itself, the city had seemed a pleasant if somewhat characterless place, although they'd stopped there only long enough to check into their hotel and grab a sandwich and some coffee.

Out here, though, on the road from Schmelz to Zerf, the villages, the fields and the hedgerows were as non-industrial and as full of character as they would be anywhere else in Germany on such a cold, grey afternoon.

The sun had long since disappeared, obscured by a blanket of low cloud which was making him wonder about the prospect of the moonlit or partially moonlit night that he was hoping for.

If Lucy shared his thoughts, she was keeping them to herself. She was also driving in an altogether different manner. After leaving the Skyline driver in her dust on the autobahn this morning, she no longer appeared to be interested in testing the performance limits of the Mercedes, preferring instead to enjoy the scenery, and rarely exceeding 80 or 90 k.p.h. except when she was forced to overtake the odd tractor or one of the slower-moving trucks they were encountering from time to time.

Over the last half-hour, she'd made an obvious attempt to be more co-operative, asking McKendrick questions about Andrew, and on one occasion coming close to saying that she had no wish to question his suggestions for tonight.

How genuine or how long-lasting her change of attitude might be, he wasn't sure, but he remained wary, sitting back in his seat with his eyes half closed while he waited for her to spring the next surprise.

It came shortly after they'd passed through the village of Losheim when she began to slow the car to not much more than walking pace.

'Are we lost?' McKendrick asked.

'That farm labourer lives along here somewhere – you know, the one who said he saw Bridget Goddard on a bicycle the night she was run over. I thought we'd call in on him to say hello.'

This time McKendrick was really annoyed. Interrogating the labourer was not on the agenda, and she'd clearly avoided mentioning the idea before because she'd known how opposed to it he'd be.

'You just happen to know his address, do you?' he said.

'Mr Linder had the transcript of Bridget's inquest e-mailed to him. The address was in one of the appendices. You don't mind, do you?'

They weren't going to learn anything new about ICIS, McKendrick thought, and a visit could be positively unwise. He was about to explain why when she jammed on the brakes and brought the Mercedes to a halt on the verge outside a broken wooden gate.

'This is it,' she said. 'You're coming, aren't you? I don't want to go in there by myself.'

'Pull another stunt like this, and you'll be going everywhere by yourself,' McKendrick said. 'What do you expect to find out here?'

'I don't know.' Endeavouring to avoid the worst of the mud, she accompanied him up a driveway that led to a dirty, brick-surfaced yard where a woman was in the process of gutting a small pig.

The carcass was equally dirty, hanging from a beam in front of a derelict hay-barn – a scene that, to McKendrick, seemed more reminiscent of a third-world country.

The woman had seen them coming. Leaving her knife in the belly

61

of the pig, she wiped her hands on her apron and walked over to ask what they wanted.

Lucy introduced herself, giving the woman a business card and speaking quickly to her in German while McKendrick took the opportunity to look around.

Except for a very new Ducati motorcycle that was partly covered with a tarpaulin inside the barn, there was little to see.

The farm was badly run down, and the house was in no better shape. Tiles were missing from the roof, several windows had cracks in the glass and the guttering had become detached in so many places that rain had spattered up lines of mud along the bottom of each wall.

Lucy's charm had failed her. The woman was becoming angry, raising her voice and pointing back towards the driveway to show that they were to leave the property at once.

Lucy retreated and came to take McKendrick's arm. 'Be nice,' she whispered. 'Try to smile.'

He didn't bother, pleased that her enquiries had blown up in her face and amused by the haste with which she returned with him to the car.

'Did you get a mouthful?' he asked.

'Arrogant, interfering city bitch who ought to be minding her own business – or words to that effect. I should've worn different clothes.' She climbed back into the Mercedes, resting her hands on the top of the steering wheel for several seconds to regain her composure before she started the engine and pulled out on to the road. 'What a waste of time that was,' she said.

'Maybe not.' He resisted the temptation to tell her it was her own fault. 'Did you see the motorcycle?'

She nodded. 'It must belong to her son. He was the witness. But she wouldn't say where he's working today.'

'He could have been paid enough so he doesn't have to work for six months.'

'Paid to lie at the inquest?'

'You have to sell a lot of pigs or do a lot of labouring to buy a top of the line Italian motorcycle.'

'You're guessing.'

'It fits,' McKendrick said. 'It's one thing to prop up Bridget

Goddard in the middle of the road while you get someone to knock her over, but if you pay a local farmhand to say he saw her cycling without lights on the same night, it's going to sound a whole lot more like an accident.'

'That doesn't help us, though, does it? And it doesn't prove Zitelmann's guilty of anything.'

McKendrick smiled at her. 'Stop trying to run before you can walk. We've only been in Germany for half a day. How much further to the estate?'

'I don't know. We can ask directions when we get to Weiskirchen.'

Directions were unnecessary. They were travelling on the Zerf to Primstal road, less than five minutes away from Weiskirchen when Lucy saw the first of the ICIS signs. It was attached to a post in a small field, discreetly sign-written in several languages and giving the distance as one kilometre.

'Drive right past,' McKendrick said.

'Don't you want to use my camera? It's in the glove box with the binoculars.'

'No point. Pictures aren't going to do us any good.' He was trying to make out where the estate began, guessing that the moss-covered stone wall he could see was the northern boundary of it, but not being certain until they'd passed two further signs and approached what appeared to be the entrance to the institute itself.

The gates were suitably imposing, made of wrought iron and supported by large stone pillars on which were mounted brass plates giving the name of the institute in German and in English.

At the end of the driveway, the main house, the courtyard and the two other buildings were clearly visible, but the lake was not.

In the few seconds it had taken them to drive past, he had seen nothing of interest. Nor had he been able to determine whether or not there were any people around. No smoke was curling from the chimneys of the house, not a single car was parked outside and, if a theological course was being held at the institute today, there was little sign of it.

If anything, the place seemed to be unoccupied, he decided, in which case they'd have the choice of dispensing with the precautions he had in mind for tonight as well as the option of extending their investigation beyond the confines of the lake as long as they could find the damn thing.

Lucy was awaiting instructions, driving at normal speed to avoid attracting attention from anyone who happened to be watching at an upstairs window, but impatient to hear what McKendrick had to say.

'See if you can find a side road that'll take us round the edge of the estate.' He checked for one on the map. 'Bridget shot her video from the south end of the lake so, unless she climbed over the wall in broad daylight, she could have found an easy way in where she'd have had the cover of some trees or something.'

'And a safe place to hide her car.' Lucy glanced at him. 'I read about her rental car in the inquest transcript.'

McKendrick's hunch had been right. A tree-lined, pot-holed lane did indeed follow the wall around to the south – although there was no indication of it being a dead end, and he wasn't sure whether Lucy would be willing to reverse the Mercedes all the way back out of it if there was nowhere for her to turn round.

She had no such reservations, driving through several deep puddles as she swung the nose of the car into the lane and engaged low gear.

'How far shall we go?' she asked.

'Half a kilometre ought to get us to where I think the lake might be.'

'I can already see it. Look.' She pointed between the trees.

If the video had failed to convey the true colour of the water in bright sunlight, there was no such problem in late afternoon on an overcast November day.

The lake wasn't particularly milky, but it certainly wasn't clear, and the combination of an unnaturally yellow foreshore with the lack of vegetation was imparting a distinctly otherworldly appearance to the whole surrounding area.

On the left side of the lane, Lucy had found a patch of mud on which to park. Leaving the engine running, she took her binoculars from the glove box. 'We can park here when we come back tonight,' she said.

He shook his head. 'We'll need headlights,' he said. 'We don't want anyone wondering who's driving down here in the dark. It'll be safer if we leave the car somewhere on the main road and walk back.'

To avoid arguing with him she used the binoculars. 'There's a wire fence all the way round the lake,' she said.

McKendrick had seen it already. He'd seen something else as well – a narrow, gravelled path leading from the house to a rusty steel gate in the fence. The gate had strands of razor wire strung across the top of it and appeared to provide access to the remains of the power station, if that's what it once had been.

The fence was a good two metres tall, sagging between old steel posts and made from woven wire that was even rustier than the gate – except for one section that looked as though it had been replaced in recent months.

The place where Bridget had cut her way in, he wondered? Or had she simply hopped over the wall and stuck her camera through the first hole in the wire she'd come to?

Lucy handed him the binoculars. 'It's not a very big lake, is it?' she said.

'Are you disappointed?'

'No – well, not yet. Have you seen those signs on the wire?'

'Do they say no trespassing?'

'*Achtung, verschmutztes wasser*. That means keep out, contaminated water. So someone probably knows what kind of chemicals are leaching out of the seam.'

He doubted it. So faded and so old were the signs that whoever had put them up was likely to have passed away many years ago.

Viewed through Lucy's binoculars, the lake was unremarkable apart from its unpleasant colour and the sterile shoreline. It was more like a large pond, a hundred metres long at the most, not dissimilar to a figure of eight in shape, but with the far end heading off at an angle.

How deep it might be was difficult to tell. He couldn't tell if there was any odour to it, either, although a slight easterly breeze could be carrying the smell away, he thought.

Lucy had put away her camera without taking any photos and seemed anxious to depart. 'Well,' she said, 'what have you decided?'

'A couple of flashlights, a good pair of wire-cutters or bolt-cutters and the film canisters.' He gave the binoculars back to her. 'We'll buy what we need in Saarbrücken before the shops close, then grab a few hours' sleep at the hotel before we come back.'

'Don't we have to find someone who'll be able to test our samples for us in the morning?'

'We can try a medical laboratory or the university.' McKendrick paused. 'I've got a feeling we'll be wasting our time with the lake. That's not what your boss is interested in. He just wants to know if Zitelmann's Institute for Christian and Islamic Studies isn't an institute at all.'

'If it isn't a cover for something, why would Bridget Goddard have been murdered, and why did someone put a bomb in her brother's car?'

'Who knows?' McKendrick had been hoping that the lake would provide at least some clues. But so far it had provided them with nothing. 'We need to figure out what that gravel path and the gate are used for,' he said. 'And maybe try the house.'

'Oh.' She engaged reverse and started backing the Mercedes expertly out of the lane. 'I didn't expect you to take this so seriously. I thought you were doing it mostly for the money.'

'You don't have a 10-year-old son who had to watch Goddard's car blow up.'

'And I didn't have to watch a teenage girl being raped and shot either, did I? You really don't have to keep on justifying yourself to me. As long as we're helping Mr Linder, I don't care what we look at.'

By now, McKendrick was able to recognize the signs. Apparently, in spite of her earlier comments, she still resented being told what they were going to do. But that was her problem, he decided, and if she wanted to be consulted about everything, she was shit out of luck.

He made a point of not replying, content to let her smoulder while he attempted to understand why he'd allowed himself to be talked into someone else's business, not yet willing to admit that Lucy Mitchell could have more to do with it than the money he was being paid and, for the second time in two days, wondering if he could be on the verge of making another fairly large mistake.

# Chapter 5

The moonlight was unreliable, breaking through the clouds every minute or so to illuminate the lane, but usually not for long enough. As a result, Lucy was stumbling in and out of puddles she couldn't see and twice had nearly fallen over.

McKendrick was faring better. His night vision was continuing to improve, although he was beginning to feel the cold, and where he was gripping the bolt-cutters and his flashlight he was losing the feeling in his fingers.

'How much further?' Lucy asked. She steadied herself on his arm while she scraped the mud off her shoes. 'We must be just about there.'

'We are.' He risked switching on his flashlight, shielding the beam with his hand until he'd established where they were. 'We'll be going over the wall between those two trees. With any luck that new section of fencing won't have too much grass growing up through it, so we might have a chance of crawling underneath. I'll check it out. You stay here.'

'I don't want to stay here.'

Instead of insisting, he bent down and scraped up a handful of mud. 'You need to let me put some of this on your face,' he said. 'You stand out a bit in the moonlight.'

'What about you?'

'I don't have fair skin and I've still got a tan from being overseas.'

She was hesitant. 'You said you didn't think anyone's home at the house.'

'Better safe than sorry.' Hoping that the precaution was unnecessary, he used a finger to smear some mud across her forehead and her cheeks, stepping back to inspect his handiwork when he'd finished.

In place of the suede jacket and designer jeans she'd worn during the day, tonight she was dressed in a thick, dark-blue sweater and matching tracksuit pants – a combination that, together with the mud, made her quite difficult to see except for the moonlight shining on her hair.

She wiped a spot of mud off her lips. 'Are you happy now?'

'You'll do. Let's go and see what we can see.' After helping her over the wall, he left the cover of the trees, heading directly for the fence and searching out shadows on the odd occasions when the clouds parted or became thinner for a moment or two.

He'd been right about the wire. The repair had been poorly executed, and the whole panel was slack, allowing them to slither underneath without the need to sever any of the strands.

'Leave the cutters here,' Lucy whispered.

They were cold but, because they were reassuringly heavy, McKendrick decided to take them with him anyway.

He could smell the chemicals now – not the mild antiseptic smell he'd anticipated, but something a good deal more powerful.

'Do you want me to get the water samples?' Lucy was eyeing the lake with some apprehension.

'I'll do it. You can fill these with mud.' He gave her four of the canisters. 'Scoop up some of the soil where it's softest and the most yellow. Clip the lids on tight and don't lick your fingers afterwards.'

McKendrick let her go on ahead, then walked carefully down to the water's edge.

Instead of the foreshore being soft and slimy as he'd expected it to be, the ground was firm underfoot, and there was evidence of what he thought could be small crystals embedded in the soil. More of them were clustered along the waterline, in places so many that they formed a crust.

Or had his imagination got the better of him, he wondered? On a night as cold as this, could he simply be looking at a film of ice? The water was freezing when he filled the canisters, adding to the numbness in his fingers and making him fumble as he tried to wipe off the residue on his sleeve.

He was jumpy, he realized, too conscious of having another young woman as an assistant, and far from certain that coming here at night had been such a great idea.

In daytime the appearance of the lake had been dominated by the unnatural colour of the water and the shoreline. But at night, illuminated only by moonlight filtering through the clouds, the entire area was almost colourless and filled with so many shadows that the impression he had of it was slightly sinister.

To his left, nearer the north-west shore of the lake where Lucy had started work, the deepest of the shadows was being cast by the derelict power station, the building that McKendrick thought might hold more information – if in reality there was any information to be found here at all.

Wondering if they were on a fool's errand and endeavouring to decide whether or not he should risk breaking into the house, he went to see how she was getting on.

She'd finished, but was still trying to clean the muck off her hands. 'Do you know where the smell's coming from?' she asked.

'Not yet. We'll have a look inside the building. That ought to tell us. If it's worse in there, we can be pretty sure that toxins are still being washed up out of the seam. Are you OK?'

'Yes.' She shivered. 'I don't like it here, though.'

McKendrick didn't like it either, but he said nothing, checking the sky for clouds before he set off for the concrete ruins, skirting the lake and keeping well clear of the crystal impregnated soil in case the poisons turned out to be more unpleasant than he thought they were.

If gases from the burning seam had been used to generate power inside the building sixty years ago, there was little hardware left to confirm it. From the outside, there were no signs of old chimneys or rusted-out steelwork, and if the lake had originally been a feed source for boilers or for a cooling system, the pipes that had carried the water here had long since corroded and vanished.

What hadn't yet collapsed or disappeared was the part of the structure that McKendrick remembered seeing in the video, an ugly, rectangular box that looked as though it had been repaired at some point in the distant past.

There were no windows in it he could see but, in the centre of the west-facing wall, Lucy had found a door or a pair of doors.

They were substantial and made of thick wood, but secured only by a padlock that proved to be no match for the bolt-cutters.

Pleased that he'd decided to bring them with him, he eased open one of the doors, then moved Lucy out of the moonlight so he could check the interior before he allowed her to accompany him inside.

'I can't see anything,' she whispered.

'Pull the door to, then we can use our flashlights.'

The effort was hardly worthwhile. The building was nothing more than an implement shed for the estate. An orchard tractor and a ride-on lawnmower were parked against the far wall on which a variety of garden tools were hanging from hooks, while alongside a worn-out wheelbarrow, half-a-dozen bags of grass seed were standing on wooden pallets in the corner.

Adding to McKendrick's disappointment was a marked lack of smell. If anything, the atmosphere was fresher in here than it had been outside, although it was hard for him to be certain because the air was so damn cold. It was like being in a refrigerator, he thought, or maybe even in a deep freeze.

Lucy had gone to explore by herself, bending down to direct the beam of her flashlight on to a number of cans or drums.

'What are these?' she asked.

They weren't cans of paint. Nor were they drums of liquid fertilizer. They were twenty-litre screw-top containers, each bearing the international poison symbol and the word PHENOL printed in large black letters.

'Jesus.' He sniffed one of them.

'What's phenol?'

'Carbolic acid. The toxins aren't coming up from the seam at all. Someone's pouring this stuff into the bloody lake.'

'What for?' She frowned. 'Why would they?'

'God only knows.' He shone his light around, unable for the moment to think of any explanation and slow to appreciate why the tyre of the wheelbarrow seemed to be glittering until he realized that the reflections were coming from crystals that had been carried up in a layer of lakeside mud.

He showed Lucy. 'Super-low-tech delivery system,' he said. 'Whenever the water in the lake gets too clean, someone trundles down one of these drums and tips in a slug of nice raw phenol to top it up.'

'Why would anyone want to do that? It doesn't make any sense.'

'Nor does this.' Behind a moth-eaten burlap sack hanging from a nail on the wall, McKendrick had discovered a small white sign above what appeared to be some kind of electrical switch. The wiring to it was insulated in modern PVC, the switch was of a type that could have never existed in the 1940s and the sign was printed on finest twenty first century plastic.

He read out the words on it. '*Warnung. Notfall Flutung*. What does that mean?'

'Warning. Emergency flood. Do you think it's to flood the lake with fresh water – you know, to clean it out?'

McKendrick had no chance to answer her question.

From the ceiling high above them, something had made a whirring noise. The sound had been faint and short-lived, but they'd both heard it.

He used his flashlight, sweeping the beam backwards and forwards over the cobwebs and the rafters until he picked out the gleam of a glass lens.

'Shit.' He cursed his stupidity.

'What is it?' Lucy was trying to see.

'Motion-sensitive, CCTV surveillance camera. We're being taped on closed-circuit television.' He extinguished his light. 'We need to move right now.'

'What about going to the house? You don't know the tape's being watched by anyone.'

'We're not going to wait to find out.' He spun her round and shoved her out the door. 'Straight for the fence,' he instructed. 'Don't run and look where you're going.' He considered taking the bolt-cutters, but changed his mind and left them where they were. 'Go on. Now.'

For a moment he hung back, waiting for the lights in the house to come on suddenly, and half-expecting to hear alarms or sirens.

But there was nothing – nothing to see and, apart from a slight creak from the door when he closed it behind him, nothing to hear either.

Now there were fewer clouds about, or perhaps because, after the darkness of the building, the moonlight seemed brighter than before, he could pick out Lucy almost as clearly as he could have done in daylight. She was making good progress, not wasting time by seeking out shadows and already nearing the fence.

McKendrick caught her up. He'd stopped glancing over his shoulder, still furious with himself for making such a fundamental mistake, but relieved that their break-in had gone undetected.

He could not have been more wrong.

Lucy was halfway under the wire when there was the hiss of a high-velocity bullet, and a patch of mud exploded in her face.

'Jesus Christ.' Throwing himself down beside her, he used one arm to lift the wire and his other to push her on through. 'Run,' he shouted. 'Run like hell. Get to the wall.'

Too scared to watch in case she'd be cut down before she could reach safety, he struggled to get a hold on his nerves, waiting for another bullet, knowing what an easy target he was and hardly able to believe what was happening to them.

Lucy had made it, but only just. No sooner had he slithered under the fence and started out on his own run than a round screamed off the wall where she'd been a second ago, and bullets began thudding into the ground all round him.

Gritting his teeth, he began to weave, doing his best not to slip on the wet grass and praying that the shadows from the trees would confuse whoever it was that had them in their sights.

How many men or guns there were, he couldn't tell. He'd heard no stuttering of automatics and no crack of rifles – not because the shots were coming from silenced weapons, he told himself, but because the gunmen were firing at long range from the upstairs floors of the house – too far away even in bright moonlight for them to be able to guarantee a kill.

It was a vain hope.

He reached the wall in one piece and was vaulting over it when bullets ricocheted off the stonework, driving a shower of fragments into his eyes and mouth.

Lucy was scared witless, too terrified to speak and trembling so badly that he had to shake her to make her pay attention.

'Listen to me,' McKendrick said. 'There's a chance we can get to the car. From here on we've got trees on both sides of us, and if we can reach the main road ahead of them, they won't know which way we've gone.'

'I've lost a shoe.' She couldn't look at him. 'It came off on the wire.'

'You'll be fine.' He pointed towards the darker shadows along the east side of the lane. 'We'll start over there. Are you ready?'

She nodded.

'OK.' He pulled her to her feet. 'Let's do it then. Fast as you can.'

He should have known his strategy would be unworkable. They were nowhere near the main road when the potholes and the cold began to take their toll on Lucy's foot. She was in obvious pain, wincing whenever she trod on a jagged stone and slowing down with every step she took.

Adding to his sense of helplessness now was the odd glimpse he had of the house. The whole place was ablaze with light, and twice he'd imagined he'd heard the sound of barking dogs.

Lucy made him stop so she could catch her breath. 'How much further to the road?' she said quietly.

'Fifty metres; maybe a bit more. Can you keep going?'

'I'm too frightened not to.' She started walking again, attempting to take longer steps. 'If we don't reach the car, we're going to be shot, aren't we?'

'We'll get there.' He was endeavouring not to think about it, worrying instead about the apparent lack of pursuit. There had been plenty of time for men to have taken a short cut from the house, but no one had come to intercept them in the lane, and no more shots had zipped towards them out of the darkness.

So what the hell was he overlooking? Where was the surprise going to be, and what form would it take?

He had his answer almost at once. They were approaching the T-junction when, through the trees, he saw the headlights of two cars. They were leaving the house, accelerating rapidly up the driveway to the front gates.

Urging Lucy to hurry, he guided her on to the grass at the side of the main road, supporting her as well as he could, but beginning to think they'd be better off abandoning their run for the car and seeing if they could lose themselves somewhere in adjoining farmland.

But could they outrun a pack of dogs? Was there a chance of passing traffic? At this time of night, would any driver be prepared to help?

Straining his eyes, he started counting under his breath, knowing that in a few seconds both cars would have cleared the gates and be on the road.

The first of them had turned left and gone the wrong way. The second one hadn't. But, instead of it sweeping round the corner behind them, the driver was crawling along in low gear, swinging the nose of his car from one side of the road to the other in order to scan the hedgerows and the ditches with his headlights.

So suddenly had their luck changed that it took McKendrick a moment or two to realize they might still have a chance of reaching the Mercedes.

'Get your car keys ready,' he yelled. 'And if you get boxed in, put your foot down and ram the bastards.'

His advice was meaningless, and for the second time tonight he had miscalculated.

The Mercedes was already boxed in. Parked in front of it was a black Peugeot. And in the shadows beside the Peugeot stood a man with a gun. He was wearing night-vision goggles, stepping out from the lay-by to confront them now he'd seen them coming.

Despairingly McKendrick wrenched on Lucy's arm, using all his strength to swing her to one side.

He was too late. Before she could change direction, without warning the man opened fire at point blank range, and all McKendrick could see were muzzle flashes, and all he could hear was the awful hammering of a machine-pistol.

# Chapter 6

Unharmed but blinded by the muzzle flash, McKendrick did the only thing he could do. Certain that Lucy was dead, he let go of her and prepared to launch himself at the vague outline of the gunman.

The man had anticipated the move but, instead of firing again, he backed away and held the gun up high above his head. 'Whoa there,' he said. 'Take it easy.'

McKendrick remained in a crouched position, muscles bunched, still ready and trying desperately to recover more of his sight.

The man removed his goggles. 'How about we give your friends another fright?' he said. 'We don't want them trying to be brave, do we?'

Not sure that he properly understood, McKendrick straightened himself. There was no sign of Lucy, but what he could see was the car from the institute.

The driver had panicked. With both his headlights shot out, he'd attempted to reverse at high speed and had become bogged down in mud on the grass verge.

Engine screaming and wheels spinning, he finally found sufficient traction to continue his retreat – but not before the man beside McKendrick had time to fire another warning burst.

Simultaneously, Lucy appeared from nowhere. In some distress and smothered in mud as a result of being flung to the ground, she limped over to join McKendrick at the roadside. 'I don't know what's happening,' she said.

He didn't know either, so relieved to see her that he was slow to ask if she was all right.

'What do you think?' She leaned against him to take the weight off her foot. 'Of course I'm not all right. I'm frightened to death. I'm cold, it feels as though I only have one leg and you just about pulled my arm off.'

'Better than having a hole in your head.' It was the man who spoke. He smiled at her. 'Hi. My name's Harland. I work for the US Government.'

'Doing what?' McKendrick asked. 'What the hell are you doing here?'

'I've been kind of hoping you could tell me.' He held out the machine pistol. 'Do you know how to use one of these?'

'Why?' McKendrick took it from him.

'Well, seeing as how we seem to have a common interest, I figure the three of us ought to have a bit of a talk somewhere. If you want to follow me in my car, maybe one of you can scare off anyone who gets too close behind. It's an old Uzi. Just stick it out your window and hold the trigger back. It works real well so long as you're not trying to hit anything.' He smiled again at Lucy. 'If you're not too strung out, I think we can fix you up with a hot shower and some brandy. What do you say?'

Too bewildered to say anything, Lucy stared at McKendrick who'd already realized that holding a conversation in the middle of the road was a fairly stupid idea while they were still so close to the institute and while there was still another vehicle around somewhere.

Harland had reached the same conclusion and was on his way over to the Peugeot. 'Are you coming or not?' he called. 'Or are you going to stay and play with the bad guys?'

'We're coming.' McKendrick helped Lucy to the Mercedes. 'How far?'

'I'm staying at a place on the 268 this side of Zerf. It's just up the road.'

'OK.' Intending to take over driving duties, McKendrick reached out for the car keys.

'No.' She clamped her fingers round them. 'If I can walk I can drive. You're the one who thinks you're being paid to ride shotgun for me, so here's your chance.'

Unlocking the door, she slid behind the wheel and started the engine, waiting for the Peugeot to pull out of the lay-by ahead of her before she switched on her lights and set off after it. 'I'm sorry,' she said. 'I didn't mean that about you riding shotgun.'

He didn't care what she'd meant, too concerned about the possibility of a chase car suddenly rounding the bend before they were up to speed, and too busy wondering how a stranger from the US Government could have so conveniently appeared out of nowhere at one o'clock in the morning on an otherwise deserted road in Germany.

That Harland's presence was more than a coincidence hardly seemed worth questioning. But his interest in ICIS was a greater mystery still. Or had he simply followed them? And if not, what other reason could he have for being in the lay-by?

Lucy had more immediate and more practical matters on her mind. 'This is crazy,' she said. 'We haven't the first idea who that man is. We can't just follow him. We have to go to the police.'

'And tell them what?'

'Everything. We're not in Chechnya or the Middle East. This is Germany, and we've just had people firing guns at us. We can't pretend nothing's happened.'

'Think for a second,' McKendrick said. 'You haven't been shot and nor have I, so who's going to believe us if we start claiming ICIS isn't a religious institute when everyone around here knows that's exactly what it is. We can't prove a thing. We can't prove Bridget Goddard was murdered. We can't prove her brother's death has anything to do with her, and if Zitelmann wants to disinfect his lake with phenol and stick security cameras all over his property, why shouldn't he?'

'We could still try.'

'You're wrong,' McKendrick said. 'Once someone discovers our bolt-cutters and sees your name on the business card you gave to that woman this afternoon, we're more likely to have the police coming after us.'

She chose not to reply, struggling to prevent the Mercedes from drifting on to the other side of the road and shivering so badly that he thought she might be going into shock.

'How's the foot and the arm?' he asked.

'Better now the heater's going – well, my foot's coming round and my arm's not hurting so much. Do you really believe Harland works for the American Government?'

'I can't see why he'd say that if it's not true and, if he wanted to trick us into something, he wouldn't have given me his gun, would he?'

'What if he's emptied the magazine?' She glanced at McKendrick.

'He hasn't: I checked. Stop worrying about Harland. My guess is that we'll find out more about ICIS from him than we'd ever find out by ourselves. It depends on what he was doing there.'

She directed more warm air into the foot-well. 'I need to know something else.'

'What?'

'I want to know why you weren't frightened back there at the lake.'

He smiled at her. 'I was. You'd have to be brain-dead not to be frightened when someone's shooting at you like that. I was as scared as you were.'

'Have you been shot at before?'

'Couple of times: once when I was on an assignment in Brazil and another time in China. If you go around following underground fires in out of the way places, sooner or later you end up where you shouldn't be. That's pretty much what happened to me in Indonesia.'

'And now it's happened to you again.' She changed into a lower gear. 'Thank you for helping me to the car.'

He tried to see her face. 'You're not doing too well,' he said. 'Why don't you let me take over? Your boss isn't going to mind me driving his car for a while, is he?'

'No, but I'm all right. I can't imagine what I'm going to tell Mr Linder about tonight, though.'

'How are you going to tell him anything? He's in Chicago, isn't he?'

'He said he'd phone me at the hotel in the morning.'

'I'll speak to him,' McKendrick said. 'With any luck, we'll have a fix on where our American friend fits into all this by then. How do you think we should play things with Harland?'

She made no attempt to answer, closing up the gap between the Mercedes and the black Peugeot as though she was worried about falling behind, but seemingly reluctant to continue with the conversation.

McKendrick was less concerned about them getting lost than he was about Lucy herself. Although she'd stopped shivering, and her driving was not as erratic as it had been five minutes ago, he could see how tense she was – in which case, the sooner they reached wherever it was they were going, the better it would be for everyone, he thought.

Harland had mentioned the town of Zerf and highway 268, but there were no signs of street lights or suburbs when he suddenly turned left into a side road and brought the Peugeot to a halt, waiting for Lucy to draw up alongside before he wound down his window to speak to her.

'Over there,' he said. 'Where that brown gate is. If you go on ahead, you can put your car in the garage where no one who's looking for it is going to see it.'

She drove past him without saying anything, swinging the Mercedes into the open gateway and carrying on until they reached a small, detached garage standing in the grounds of what appeared to be a traditional German hunting lodge.

Like the gate, the garage doors were open, but Lucy was cautious, waiting for McKendrick's nod of approval before she parked the car inside and got out to stand nervously in the shadows.

Harland had left his Peugeot in the driveway and gone to unlock the front door of the house. 'Come on in,' he said. 'I'll wake up Emily while you go on through to the lounge.' He switched on a light in the hall and pointed. 'It's down there. I'll be back in a minute.'

The lounge was wonderfully warm, smelling faintly of wood-smoke and illuminated by wall lights and the dying embers of a log that had been burning in the fireplace.

As well as being warm, the room was comfortably furnished, if a little overcrowded. Competing for space with a leather lounge-suite and a walnut coffee table were a pair of large wicker chairs, while a dresser crammed with porcelain figurines occupied most of one wall and blocked off part of a window.

Lucy went to stand by the fire, keeping her foot off the carpet now she'd caught sight of her torn and bloodstained sock.

'You'd better let me have a look at that.' McKendrick knelt down.

'No.' She pulled her foot away. 'You don't have to fuss over me.'

'If I don't fuss over you, who else is going to?'

'Emily will. She's on her way down.' Harland walked into the room and came over to McKendrick. 'I guess you must be Linder,' he said.

'What makes you think that?'

'Swiss number on your car. I've been watching that estate for four days and three nights, so when you arrived out there this afternoon, I ran a check on your plates. According to my office, your car's registered to someone called Ron Linder of Linder International in Zurich.'

'I'm Adam McKendrick.' He shook hands with Harland. 'I'm working for Linder. This is Lucy Mitchell. She's his PA.'

Harland smiled at her. 'You could've fooled me with all that make-up you're wearing.'

'Oh.' She wiped the mud off her face. 'I don't usually go visiting looking like this.'

'I don't usually get to blow the rust out of my Uzi in the middle of the night.' Harland stopped talking and went to greet an elderly lady who'd come to stand in the doorway. She was tiny and rather frail, wearing a pink dressing-gown and with a number of coloured curlers in her hair.

'Say hello to Emily,' Harland said. 'She owns this place. Emily's the great aunt of one of the translators who works for us in Bonn. I stay here whenever I get the chance, which isn't anything like often enough. Emily enjoys having visitors and she's the best cook in the whole of western Germany.'

Harland was a man who would know, McKendrick thought. The American had the build of someone who liked his food. Not yet out of his thirties, he was fleshy-faced and already running to fat, but with an underlying intelligence and toughness about him that went with his somewhat direct approach to matters.

Emily's manner was equally direct. Ignoring both Harland and McKendrick, she took charge without being asked, escorting Lucy from the room, clearly as pleased to discover that she had a German-speaking guest in her home as she was to meet a young woman who was in need of some attention.

'Plenty of spare rooms upstairs,' Harland said. 'If it's OK with you, I'll have Emily make up beds for you and your girlfriend. I don't think the pair of you ought to be going anywhere else tonight, do you?'

'Lucy isn't my girlfriend. I only met her yesterday.'

'Doesn't take long to get yourself into deep shit if you don't know what you're doing.' Harland went to the dresser. 'How about a Scotch? I've got half a bottle of Johnny Walker here.'

'Scotch is fine. Are you going to tell me why you've been watching ICIS?'

'Maybe.' The American brought over two glasses. 'Do you know you've cut your lip open?'

'It's just from a stone chip. One of the bullets came pretty close. If you hadn't been around, I'd have more than a cut lip to worry about.'

'You don't know that. If some dumb bastard hadn't parked his car in front of yours, you'd have had a free run out of there.' Harland gave McKendrick one of the glasses, then sat down and placed a wallet on the table. 'Inside flap,' he said. 'Check it out.'

The wallet held a card issued by the Drug Enforcement Agency of the United States of America, a thin plastic card embossed with the insignia of the DEA on one side, and with a small photograph and the name and signature of Craig Harland on the other.

'OK,' Harland said. 'The way I see it, that card means I've got more angels on my side than you have on yours, so I figure you owe me an explanation more than I owe you one.'

'So you want me to go first.' McKendrick gave him back the wallet.

'Unless we have a conflict of interest because you're working for an outfit I've never heard of.'

McKendrick had already decided it would be best to volunteer his side of the story while Lucy was out of the room. 'I've already told you,' he said. 'Right now, I'm working for Linder – or I was.' He waited while Harland put a fresh log on the fire, taking the opportunity to collect his thoughts and swallow a mouthful of whisky before he began to speak again.

He started by providing an account of the events that had brought him from Hawaii to Switzerland, and then went on to explain the reason for tonight's abortive visit to Weiskirchen. Although he avoided mentioning the incident in Indonesia and said nothing about his reasons for accepting Linder's offer, he was careful to take the blame for what had happened at the lake, playing down the danger they'd been in before finishing his summary by describing how they'd discovered the drums of phenol and the camera in the shed.

'What kind of camera?' Harland asked.

'I didn't get much of a look at it. Why?'

'If it was an infrared job, those guys at the institute will have a tape of you and Lucy. That'll make you easy to recognize if they want to find you.'

'Why would they bother?' McKendrick was hoping the question might prod Harland into disclosing more information.

'Why bother to get rid of Bridget Goddard and her brother?' The American drank some of his Scotch. 'If you're right about what happened to them, and if Zitelmann's that paranoid about whatever it is he's up to, he isn't going to sleep too well now he knows you're on to him.'

'Lucy and I aren't on to anything. You're the one who knows what he's up to, not us.'

'I wish.' Harland smiled. 'That's where this whole thing turns to shit. I've no more idea what he's doing than you have.'

The statement was implausible, so much so that McKendrick knew it wasn't true. 'Look,' he said, 'you wouldn't have Zitelmann under surveillance unless he's bringing drugs into Europe or trafficking them into the States.'

'If he was, I could have the Germans nail him. But he isn't. As far as I can make out, all he's doing is running his religious institute.'

'So why are you watching him?'

'I'm not. I've been watching someone else – or trying to.'

'Who?'

'Hold on a minute.' Harland stood up from his chair. 'Change of priorities. Here's my brandy customer.'

Fresh from her shower with a neat white bandage on her foot, Lucy had a towel round her head and another one wrapped around her waist to compensate for the shortness of what looked like a spare dressing-gown that Emily had found for her.

How well she was recovering was hard to tell, but McKendrick could see she was less on edge and in better spirits than she had been. He'd also seen the difficulty Harland was having in keeping his eyes off her.

The American's interest came as no surprise. The effect she had on men seemed to be more or less universal, a reaction McKendrick had first noticed during his lunch with her in the Saarbrücken restaurant where the number of stares she'd attracted had been almost embarrassing – the irony being that she genuinely believed it was because of her freckles, when in reality the reason was rather more straightforward.

'How bad's the foot?' he asked.

'Just bruising – well, mostly. The bandage was Emily's idea. I don't need it really.' She sat down in one of the leather chairs. 'What have I missed?'

'Not much. I've just been explaining a few things.'

'Oh.' She looked at Harland. 'What is it you do for the American Government?'

'Drug enforcement. I work for the DEA in Washington, but for the last three years I've been stationed in Europe – in Bonn. Here, get this inside you.' He gave her a glass that was nearly half full of neat brandy.

'Has McKendrick thanked you for what you did?'

'No need. If my car hadn't been in the way, you could've outrun a fighter jet in that nice Mercedes you were driving.'

'Nothing like this has ever happened to me before.' She smoothed the towel down over her legs and sipped at her drink. 'It's funny, until those men started shooting at us, I didn't really believe Zitelmann could've arranged to have the Goddards killed.'

'Do you believe it now?' McKendrick asked.

'Mm.' She nodded. 'I think I do, but we still don't know why.'

'Nor does our friend here. He hasn't been watching Zitelmann. He's been watching someone else.'

'Really.' Unwrapping the towel from her head, she leaned forwards and began to dry her hair in front of the fire. 'Who?'

'Long story,' Harland said. 'One that doesn't tie in with yours – which makes things more interesting for all of us. Your story started in Hawaii: mine begins in Brazil. I'm part of a South American project the agency's running down there.'

'Hard drugs?' McKendrick said.

'It's a US initiative to strangle the American market for heroin and cocaine by putting the suppliers out of business. Washington has this great idea of throwing experts and dollars at South American governments so they'll be able to fix the problem for us. We've got agents in

Colombia, agents in Bolivia and Peru, and a whole fucking department operating out of Brazil.'

'And an office in Bonn,' Lucy said.

'Not much of one. Staff of three for about a dozen projects. I got mixed up in this one last week, after I had a phone call from the States saying that a South American dealer was due here sometime in mid-November. Washington loses a lot of sleep worrying about narcotic routes into the US via Europe, so I was asked to keep an eye on things at this end. That's what I was doing tonight.'

'Who's the dealer?' McKendrick asked.

'Depends which passport she's using. Her real name's Maria Kessel. She's Brazilian, but her family's German. Her grandfather was one of those Nazi war criminals who took off to live in South America at the end of World War Two, so the Allies couldn't get their hands on him.'

The link with Zitelmann's background was peculiar, but McKendrick was more surprised to learn that Harland had been staking out a woman. 'Did you know Zitelmann's father was a Nazi?' he asked.

Harland nodded. 'Doesn't sound as though the family have ever tried to cover up their past, though, and there's no evidence of Zitelmann being involved with drugs of any kind. Until tonight, I figured Kessel was visiting him on legitimate business.'

'Does she have a legitimate business?'

'Yeah, she does. When she's not busy doing something else, she runs a company that exports aquarium fish. It's a good cover for her, and if you think the fish business is a bit tame for someone who sells narcotics, you'd better think again. Last year the world trade in aquarium fish was close on a billion dollars – $90 million out of Singapore, $400 million out of Asia and about the same for Europe and North America.' Harland went to fetch the bottle of Scotch. 'But that's not all our Maria exports, of course. Most of her money comes from heroin and cocaine that she traffics into the Middle East, and from an employment agency she runs that supplies the Arab market with South American prostitutes.'

'Exporting girls, you mean?' Lucy stopped drying her hair.

'Officially they're hired as housekeepers or domestic maids or servants, but they know what they're going there to do.'

'So why has Kessel come to Germany?' Lucy said. 'Why would she be visiting Zitelmann?'

Harland smiled. 'Because he buys his fish from her. If you believe what you read, Zitelmann's a leading fancier and a regular contributor to magazines that specialize in exotic fish. Sounds to me as though he spends as much time thinking about fish as he does thinking about religion.'

'Oh.' She folded up the towel and placed it on the arm of her chair. 'None of that showed up on my Internet search.'

'Why would it?' McKendrick said. 'You weren't researching Zitelmann; you were looking for information on ICIS.'

Harland refilled his glass. 'So now you see the problem,' he said. 'There's no proof of Maria Kessel supplying narcotics to the US through Germany so, unless we can figure out what she has in common with Herr Zitelmann besides fish, the DEA are going to lose interest in her real quick.'

McKendrick couldn't make sense of any of this. 'If she's exporting drugs and prostitutes, why the hell don't the Brazilian police arrest her?' he said. 'Don't they know what she's doing?'

'Sure they know, but as long as she's earning export dollars by getting hookers off the streets, and providing she doesn't start importing drugs into Brazil, why would they care?' Harland settled back in his chair. 'There's something really weird in her file, though. Because she's recruiting more and more girls every month, she has an arrangement with a medical laboratory in São Paulo who get paid to check each of them for disease before she arranges their new jobs in the Middle East.'

'What's so strange about that?' Lucy asked.

'I'll tell you.' Harland looked at her over his glass. 'One of the DEA guys in our Brazil office got hold of the medical test results for every girl who'd applied to Kessel for an overseas job in the last three months. I don't know why he bothered, but it doesn't matter. The thing is, as far as anyone can make out, Kessel's only supplying girls who are proved to be HIV positive. Any of them with a clean bill of health miss out. They don't get a free airline ticket to anywhere and, instead of them making all that nice money lying on their backs in some nice Arab country, they get tossed back into the brothels they came from.'

If McKendrick had been hoping for meaningful information, this was most certainly not it. 'That's crazy,' he said.

'Right, but it gets more interesting. Once the DEA started following Kessel's money-laundering trail, they found it all led back to one guy in the States – someone called Justin Quaid. Have you heard of him?'

'No.' Lucy shook her head.

McKendrick hadn't heard the name before either, nor could he imagine why any of this should be important. 'Who's Quaid?' he said.

'He used to be a neo-Nazi or white-supremacist – one of those smooth-talking, evangelical bastards who believes American society is being undermined by anyone who doesn't look like him or think like he does. But, about a month after September 11, he either had a wet dream, or someone gave him a real good idea for his birthday. That's when he started up the US branch of the Christian Freedom Party.'

Lucy interrupted. 'I've heard of them,' she said. 'There's one here in Germany, and I think there's another one in France, but I don't know anything about them.'

Harland smiled at her. 'You're lucky. They're pseudo-religious, pseudo-political racists who've decided that Christianity is the only true religion. They've been established in Europe for a while, but our Justin saw September 11 as a message from God and figured that an international union of Christian Freedom Parties was the answer to world peace. Trouble is, these guys believe world peace is unattainable as long as there are Muslims around, so poor old Quaid had to turn himself into an anti-Islamicist overnight.'

'Which he did?' McKendrick said.

'Bet your life he did. And he's done it well. He's got a fair-sized following here in Europe, the American public love him and, if he carries on the way he's going, he'll be real trouble for the US Administration. The Democrats have no idea what to do about him, and he scares the shit out of the Republicans. It's the same in other countries – particularly now these bastards are more influential because of the Twin Towers and Madrid, and because Christian free-dom parties have suddenly got more money than they know what to do with.'

'From people like Maria Kessel?' Lucy said.

'Probably.' Harland drained his third glass of Scotch. 'Which leaves us with the problem of Zitelmann and those trigger-happy assholes down the road. Anyone running an institute that preaches religious tolerance would have to be stupid to even think of doing business with people like Kessel or Quaid.'

'What do you know about ICIS?' McKendrick asked.

'Not a lot.' Harland screwed up his face. 'How does it go now? The sum of man is the sum of all men united by their faith.'

Lucy corrected him. 'United by faith in their own beliefs,' she said.

'Yeah, that's it. More like something you'd hear from a football coach. Tell you what, though, if that's the best Zitelmann and his institute can come up with, he's pissing against the wind compared with these Christian freedom party pricks. They're in a league of their own.' Taking a sheet of paper from a file on the coffee table, Harland read out loud. *'Islam is a religion in which Allah requires you to send your son to die for Him. Christianity is a faith in which God sends His son to die for you.'* He looked at McKendrick. 'How does that grab you for a slogan?'

It wasn't a slogan, McKendrick thought. It had the resonance of a proverb – one that had been cleverly worded to have the widest possible appeal.

'Have you got the drift?' Harland asked. 'Or do you want to hear some more?'

'I've got the idea. Is that your file on Maria Kessel?'

'Do you want to see it? There's nothing classified.'

'Not now. I'm too wiped out. I'll go through it in the morning.'

'Just check out the pictures. You're not too tired to look at them, are you?' Harland passed him the file. 'You'll find a couple of Quaid in there, and you might as well see what the lovely Maria looks like before you go to bed.'

Clipped inside the front cover were two A4-sized photographs showing a tall middle-aged man. In the first photo, he was standing on some steps outside a white-painted church, holding a cross and wearing a white cassock while he addressed a gathering of white people.

The message in the second photograph was less subtle. In this one, the cassock had been replaced by a military uniform and, instead of the cross, the man had a Bible clasped to his chest and was brandishing a rifle.

'Is this Quaid?' McKendrick held up the photo.

'That's him. Finest Alabama white-trash stock, not too bright, but well read, great on television, good public-speaker and as dangerous as a cottonmouth snake.'

'What about this guy?' McKendrick had found a print showing someone else.

'That's Jürgen Meyer. He's Maria Kessel's hard man. Meyer does all the dirty work for her. He hires the mules who traffic the heroin and cocaine out of Brazil, and he's the contact for the girls who are recruited for export. He's a real bundle of fun – your regular twenty-first century white slaver. There's a fact sheet on him in there somewhere. It should be underneath the pictures of Kessel. Have you found it?'

McKendrick didn't answer, too stunned by the sheaf of photos he was studying now even to think of answering.

There were more than a dozen of them: close-up shots, long-distance shots, some in black and white and others in colour, but every single one showing the same woman – the olive-skinned woman with dark hair who'd been in the hotel bar at Waikiki, and the same woman who'd been using her phone in the hotel lobby on the night that Goddard's Porsche had exploded in a ball of flame on Kalakaua Avenue.

# Chapter 7

**M**cKendrick knew he'd overslept, but he was reluctant to leave the warmth of his bed, not yet ready to face a new day before he'd cleared his mind of the flashbacks and dreams that had made for an unpleasantly disturbed and restless night.

The worst of the flashbacks had been the familiar one of Kalyem, although he'd managed to wake himself up before the usual end point – a trick that had failed to work for his other dreams which had been longer-lasting if less vivid, most of them jumbled collages of people and places, including two in which Lucy had turned into someone resembling Maria Kessel, presumably because he'd drunk too much Scotch before he'd gone to bed.

At least things had become clearer by the light of day, McKendrick thought. In common with Harland and Lucy, he had no doubt that it had been Maria Kessel who'd planted the bomb in Goddard's car. Whether she'd triggered it herself, or instructed her associate, Meyer, to initiate the blast was unimportant. Nor did it matter whether it had been her or Meyer who had stolen the videotape from his hotel room in Waikiki.

What mattered were the extreme measures that were being taken to snuff out any investigation of the lake – first by eliminating Bridget Goddard, then by making certain that her brother could discover nothing about the way she'd died, or why she had died – proof enough of a connection between the Brazilian-born Kessel and the German owner and founder of ICIS, even if it was harder to imagine what might link the pair of them to a politically motivated racist in Alabama.

Zitelmann, Kessel and Quaid, three names that rolled off the tongue, McKendrick thought; three people from three different continents with a single purpose? Or could Harland be right? Was Maria Kessel visiting Zitelmann for an entirely legitimate reason – surely an invalid explanation once Bridget's fatal survey of the lake was factored into the equation, and after everything else that had occurred.

So what now, he wondered? Was he sufficiently intrigued to carry on taking Linder's money? Would Linder be sufficiently intrigued to keep on paying it without proof of anti-Semitic activity on Zitelmann's part – more questions for which he had no answers, let alone an answer that would allow him to figure out whether he should continue to be influenced by the presence of the young woman who'd accompanied him here to the lodge last night.

In the space of two days and two nights, his preoccupation with her had become intrusive, a development he hadn't expected and one that in his present circumstances was as unwise as it was inappropriate. Not that she'd showed any signs of minding, or none he'd detected – presumably because she was attributing his interest to her freckles.

For the second time since he'd been awake this morning he could hear her voice drifting up from the hall where she was speaking in German on the phone again.

To discover who she was talking to, McKendrick climbed out of bed and put on his clothes, making a quick detour to the bathroom to check for blood on his lip before he went downstairs.

Lucy was sitting cross-legged on the floor by the phone, wearing a shoe on her good foot and one of Emily's slippers on the other. She was scribbling notes on a scrap of paper, but not too busy to smile and whisper a good morning to him.

'Who is it?' he asked.

'I'll tell you in a minute.' She pointed towards the kitchen. 'Toast and coffee.'

There was rather more than toast and coffee on offer in the kitchen. Despite the lateness of the hour, the table was still laid for breakfast, and now Emily had heard his voice she was cracking eggs and throwing strips of bacon into a frying pan on the cooker.

At the far end of the table, Harland was staring at the screen of a battered laptop while he drank from a mug of coffee. 'How did you sleep?' he asked.

'Too much to think about.' McKendrick pulled up a chair. 'Who's Lucy talking to?'

'Linder. She's been worried about him trying to get hold of her at the hotel, so she called someone at her office first thing and asked them to fax him this number so he could phone her here. He sounds like a pretty regular guy.'

'Have you spoken to him?'

'Lucy asked me to.'

'About what?'

'This and that. Mostly this.' Harland angled round his screen to show McKendrick. 'You never know your luck until you try, do you?'

The data on the screen was presented in three columns, each listing a dozen or more heavily abbreviated facts:

| GÜNTER ZITELMANN | MARIA KESSEL | JUSTIN QUAID |
| --- | --- | --- |
| Religious institute | Narcotics/Prostitution | Political aspirations |
| German | Internationally active | American |
| Pro-Christian/Pro-Islam | Brazilian/German | Anti-Muslim |
| Bridget Goddard link | No religious affiliations | Borderline legal |
| Lake poisoning | Dean Goddard link | Former neo-Nazi |
| Cameras/Armed security | No political interests | Knows Kessel |
| Imports fish | Nazi heritage | High public profile |
| Nazi heritage | Knows Quaid | Christian Freedom Party |
| Low public profile | Exports fish | White-supremacist |
| Internationally active | Illegal operations | Launders Kessel's cash |
| Knows Kessel | Knows Zitelmann | Internationally active |
| No political interests | No public profile | No Goddard links |

'I know it's rough as guts,' Harland said. 'But what do you think?'

McKendrick wasn't sure. Nothing seemed to jump out at him, and any items that could possibly be common to all three columns were either ambiguous or tenuous at best.

'I've told Linder it doesn't prove anything,' – Harland put down his mug – 'but he's asked me to e-mail him a copy anyway. I've tried a few tricks, but it always comes back to the same things.'

'What do you mean?'

'If you take out the fish because they're just Zitelmann's hobby and Kessel's cover, this is what you're left with.' Harland pressed a key.

On the screen now, replacing the lists were three short statements:

- Kessel connects Zitelmann to Quaid
- All have international operations
- All have Nazi or neo-Nazi backgrounds

'Too thin,' McKendrick said. 'And it doesn't work – not when Zitelmann teaches religious tolerance and Quaid's a rabid anti-Islamicist. You're looking for a thread that isn't there.'

'Yeah, I know. The Nazi connection's still weird, though, don't you think?'

'No weirder than Zitelmann pouring phenol in his lake, and Maria Kessel hiring HIV-infected girls.'

'That's more or less what Linder said, and why he's asked me to sound you out on something.'

Sensing he'd been outmanoeuvred, McKendrick went to see how Emily was getting on. 'I don't do business through other people,' he said. 'If Linder has something to say to me, I'll hear it from him, not from you, and not from Lucy, thanks.'

'You need to hear it from me because I'm part of the deal.' Harland closed the lid of his computer. 'No one's trying to screw you behind your back.'

'What deal?' McKendrick returned to the table, but remained standing, wondering whether he should interrupt Lucy's phone call so he could speak to Linder before Harland had the opportunity to put his case.

He hadn't made up his mind when Emily came over and placed two plates in front of him.

'For you,' she said. 'Please to stop your talking, otherwise your food will grow cold.'

McKendrick sat down, confronted now by a breakfast that gave new meaning to the word substantial.

On one plate, as well as eggs and bacon, there were four sausages, two slices of ham, some salami and a chunk of fresh pineapple. The other plate was smaller, but piled high with a selection of coarse-textured German bread on top of which was balanced a croissant and two small pots of marmalade.

'Thank you.' He returned her smile. 'I don't think I'll be able to eat all this.'

'You try.' Bobbing her head at him she went back to the bench to continue making what he thought was an apple strudel.

'Now you know why I like staying here.' Harland leaned back in his chair. 'Look, you and I don't have to start banging our heads together. How about we sort out a few other things first?'

'Such as?' McKendrick spoke with his mouth full.

'Such as you and Lucy needing to understand that you're playing hardball with some real nasty bastards. You're in shit up to your armpits, and in case you haven't figured it out for yourselves, you'd better believe Zitelmann knows the colour of your eyes by now.'

'Because he's got us on that surveillance tape from last night?'

'Forget the tape. You were seen talking to Goddard in Hawaii, and you and I both know Zitelmann wouldn't have had to drill holes in poor little Bridget's teeth to find out she'd sent one of her tapes to Linder International. Then there's that local kid in Weiskirchen with his nice new motorcycle. If he's made himself a few more euro by selling Lucy's business card, Zitelmann wouldn't even have had to look up her phone number to make a call he's probably already made.'

'To the States? To Quaid?'

Harland shook his head. 'To Lucy's office in Zurich. All he had to do was pretend to be a businessman who needed to get in touch with her in a hurry.'

McKendrick was slow to appreciate the implications. 'And someone in reception would've given him the number of our hotel in Saarbrücken. Is that what you're saying?'

'Right, which means neither of you want to go back there. So if it's OK with you, I'll arrange to have your stuff picked up. If you haven't got anywhere else to go while you're figuring out your next move, you're welcome to stay here for a couple of days.'

The offer had been made too easily, McKendrick decided: as though the American was assuming they had no options. 'You still haven't told me about this deal of yours,' he said.

'If Lucy's finished on the phone, you can ask her. It's more her idea than mine.'

Lucy had finished. Favouring her injured foot, she limped into the room and went to steal a piece of apple from the bench. 'I'm sorry I've been so long,' she said. 'It's because Mr Linder thinks last night is all his fault. He's feeling really guilty about it.'

'But that hasn't stopped him coming up with some kind of plan with a bit of help from you,' McKendrick said. 'One that he doesn't want to bounce off me.'

'It's only a suggestion. I was going to talk to you about it first, but Emily said not to wake you. Have you seen Harland's list of things we know about Zitelmann and the woman and that Christian Freedom Party man?'

McKendrick nodded. 'Did you tell Linder there's nothing anti-Semitic that makes much sense?'

'Yes, but it's made him more interested in ICIS than he was before – because of the Nazi connection, I suppose. He didn't explain. He just wanted to know if I believed there was anything else you could help him with.'

'And you think there is?'

'Well.' She looked awkward. 'It depends on you.'

She hadn't expressed herself well, McKendrick thought. What she meant was that it depended on how persuasive Harland was going to be, and to what degree Linder might benefit from any new arrangement.

Judging by her expression, she wasn't expecting him to agree to very much at all. She was far less self-assured than she had been yesterday and treading carefully, aware of having bitten off more than she could chew after having had a taste of the big bad world outside of Linder International, and reluctant to talk him into anything in case her idea was to backfire in her face.

'Better tell me the plan then, hadn't you?'

'It's not really a plan.' She smoothed back her hair. 'Mr Linder's asked me to see if you'd be prepared to follow Maria Kessel to wherever she goes next. He said he doesn't care if it's Budapest or Paris or Moscow, and he's happy to pay you whatever you like.'

'Does he think Kessel is the key to what's going on in Weiskirchen?'

'I suppose so. He's speaking to a friend of his as well – about them enrolling in one of Zitelmann's ICIS study courses – you know, so they can have a look round inside the house because we didn't get that far.'

'Where or how does Harland fit in?'

'Well.' She hesitated. 'I guessed you probably wouldn't be interested in carrying on unless someone could help you with your Indonesian problem, so I asked Harland if he could.'

McKendrick was annoyed. 'My problems are none of your damn business,' he said. 'And they sure as hell aren't any of Harland's. With a job like yours, you ought to know when to keep your mouth shut.'

She flushed. 'You're not giving me a chance to explain.'

'You don't have to explain.' He pushed his plate away. 'You're so busy trying to be smart that you're beginning to believe you are. If you want to impress your boss that much, ask him to take you away on a dirty weekend somewhere. Then you won't have to involve other people. I'm glad you're his PA and not mine.'

'That's not fair.' Her cheeks were burning now. 'I haven't been trying to impress anyone. I was trying to help you.'

Harland had been listening with some amusement, waiting for an appropriate moment to interrupt. 'Why don't you go outside and throw rocks at one another,' he said. 'Then, when you've finished, maybe we can do some work and see if we can help each other.'

'I don't need any help, thanks,' McKendrick said.

'Suppose I could sort out things for you in Kalimantan? What if I told you the DEA has people working with the *Kopassus* in Samarinda? You know who they are, don't you?'

McKendrick knew of the *Kopassus* all too well, the vicious special forces unit of the TNI, or the Indonesian military, who were saturating the countryside with blood in their search for members of subversive militias.

'Why would the United States DEA want to help me with anything?' he said. 'What's in it for them?'

'Figure it out. You give us a leg up with Kessel, and we'll see what we can do for you in South-East Asia.'

'Even though you're ninety per cent certain she isn't running drugs into the US?' McKendrick could see that Harland had become more cautious.

'It's like I said: once I tell Washington there's no sign of Maria pumping South American drugs into the States via Europe, they'll choke off their surveillance funding faster than you can zip up your fly. But that doesn't mean we're going to forget about her.'

'In case she gets more ambitious in the future?'

'No. Because of Dean Goddard. He wasn't one of ours, but he was still a lieutenant in the US Navy who got himself killed for nothing. That doesn't sit too well with a lot of people I know, so if you can do us a favour, why shouldn't we do one for you?'

McKendrick didn't know whether to be surprised or not. At face value, taking over the surveillance of Maria Kessel in return for a favour in Kalimantan was not such an outlandish suggestion, but without guarantees and in the absence of hard information about where all this might end up, he was unwilling to entertain the idea.

'I track fires for a living, not people,' he said. 'And I fix my own problems. If you're after justice for Dean Goddard, leave it to Linder: he's got his own agenda.'

Harland showed no signs of disappointment. Lucy, though, was apparently not quite ready to give up.

'Everything's all right, then, is it?' she said. 'You never actually met Bridget Goddard, and you only spoke to her brother twice, so they don't count. Your son didn't actually go for that ride in Goddard's Porsche, so that doesn't matter any more, and those men who shot at us last night didn't actually manage to kill you, so that means you can forget all about what's happened, does it?'

McKendrick knew she'd intended to sound scathing, but the tone of her voice had been more sulky than resentful. 'Do you get a salary increase if you can talk me round?' he said.

'No. And you don't have to be rude. All Mr Linder's said is that he'll pay for me to take a two-week holiday somewhere. He thinks it might be dangerous if I stay on in Germany.' As if wanting to change the subject, she came over and inspected the cut on McKendrick's lip. 'I'll bring you back some salve for that,' she said. 'Is there anything else you want?'

'Are you going somewhere?'

'I need to get some things in Trier.'

'What's wrong with Zerf?'

'There won't be the right kind of shops in Zerf.'

'I'll go for you.' He collected up his plates and carried them over to the sink. 'You stay and talk to Harland. What do you need?'

'A pair of shoes for a start.' She gave him the one she was wearing. 'The same size as that, only with low heels and only in brown.'

'Harland's having our stuff picked up from Saarbrücken,' McKendrick said. 'Haven't you got spare shoes back there?'

'I don't want to wait, anyway I need socks and clean underwear too, so you'd better write down my waist and bra size. Then you'll have to get me Tampax and panty-shields, facial cleanser, non-allergenic lipstick and, unless Emily thinks I can wash and dry this sweater and my track-suit pants overnight, you'll have to find a shop where you can buy a cotton blouse, a pair of jeans and some kind of lady's jacket: one with a lined hood would be nice.'

'OK,' McKendrick said. 'Forget it.'

'What?'

He ignored the question and gave her back the shoe. 'If you're going now, you'll have to ask Harland to move his car.'

'I know. I'm sure he won't mind.'

Harland didn't mind. He accompanied her from the room, smiling briefly at Emily and raising his eyebrows at McKendrick on his way past.

Emily had been keeping herself busy, but now it was safe for her to speak, she had some advice for her guest. 'It is never wise to tell a young woman what it is she may do or what it is she should not do,' she said. 'If you wish to be her friend, it is necessary for you to understand this.'

McKendrick smiled at her. 'I'll try harder. Sorry I couldn't finish my breakfast.'

'You have too much on your mind, I think. My English is poor, but from what I learn this morning, it is best if you listen to Herr Harland. He is a good man who does not often help people he does not know well.'

Unless he has good reason to, McKendrick thought. Harland was simply exploiting an opportunity, suggesting an alternative means of keeping tabs on Maria Kessel at someone else's expense now that the DEA were about to lose official interest in her.

So was the proposal worth considering, he wondered? And if it was, where if anywhere did Lucy Mitchell fit into things?

He was still wondering when the American returned to the kitchen.

'Has she gone?' McKendrick asked.

'Foot down and flat out.' Harland bit the end off one of McKendrick's uneaten sausages. 'What do you expect with red hair and so many goddamn freckles you'd think she'd been got at by some mad bastard with a spray-gun. Spend a dirty weekend with her and you'd go crazy trying to find out if she's like it all over.'

Until now, the possibility was not one that had occurred to McKendrick. 'She's not pissed off with you,' he said. 'It's me. Emily says it's because I keep telling her what to do.'

Harland grinned. 'Serves you right. You might as well save your breath.' He finished the sausage and wiped his hands on a paper towel. 'Have you thought any more about why Zitelmann's pouring that stuff into his lake?'

McKendrick had all but abandoned his search for an explanation. 'Hard to tell,' he said. 'If I had to guess, I'd say it's just to keep people away from the estate. Phenol could've leached up into the lake for anything up to ten or fifteen years after the seam stopped burning, so he could've decided to keep topping up the concentration artificially.'

'Why go to all that trouble to stop a bunch of schoolboys from catching tadpoles or going fishing?'

'Maybe he uses the water to disinfect his fish tanks. How the hell would I know?'

'Walk away now, and you never will know, will you?'

'I haven't said I'm walking away. I just can't see a lot of point in running Linder's witch-hunt for him. If Zitelmann's in bed with Maria Kessel, and if she's being screwed silly by the leader of the US Christian Freedom Party, that's fine by me.'

Harland selected another sausage, but changed his mind and put it down again. 'How about Indonesia? Or is that too hard as well?'

'I haven't decided.' McKendrick looked at him. 'What if I sent your people in Samarinda five thousand US dollars for the *Kopassus*? Then all the *Kopassus* would have to do is keep their eyes open for anti-government terrorists who use the same track through the forest each month. I can fax a sketch of the tattoo on the hand of the guy they need to take out first, and the Ministry of Mines and Energy in Balikpapan have copies of my photos of the girl who was raped and of the old man who was our minder for the day.'

'I thought you were a guy who liked to fix his own problems.'

'I am, but why would I go halfway round the world and back if I can pay someone who's already there for a better and quicker job?'

'Because if you follow Kessel to wherever she's going next, Linder will pay you for your trouble, and I'll see what the DEA can do for you in Indonesia without it costing you anything. That way you'll be making money instead of spending it.'

'I don't need that kind of work – not while I've got a contract to finish for the UN. Will you think about what I've said?'

'I'll think about it, but it's a bit of a stretch to expect us to help you if you're too busy to give us a hand.' Harland packed up his computer. 'I have a couple of jobs to do. If you need anything, ask Emily. We'll have another talk when Lucy comes back. Maybe she'll twist your arm for you.'

McKendrick doubted that she'd bother – particularly now she'd been given an expenses-paid holiday by her employer, and now that Linder was intending to use his own contacts to uncover the truth about Zitelmann's Institute of Christian and Islamic Studies.

To stop himself from thinking about Lucy, he thanked Emily again for his breakfast, then made his way outside to explore the grounds of the lodge, wandering around in the cold for nearly twenty minutes, and only returning to the house after he'd heard the old lady calling to him from a kitchen window.

'What is it?' he asked.

'It is Lucy. She wishes to speak with you on the telephone.' Emily ushered him into the hall. 'Please, you will hurry. She says it is important.'

Wondering what the rush was, he picked up the receiver. 'Hi,' he said. 'Are you in Trier?'

'I haven't got there yet. I'm calling on the car phone.'

'Did you forget something?'

'No.' She sounded uneasy. 'I think I'm being followed. There's been a blue Audi behind me almost since I left. I didn't worry about it to begin with, but when I kept seeing it in my mirror I slowed right down, but the driver won't overtake me.'

'OK. Hang on a second.' Endeavouring to keep calm, he turned to Emily. 'Get Harland,' he said. 'Quickly.'

Lucy had misinterpreted the delay. 'Are you there?' she said. 'McKendrick, tell me you're there.'

'I'm here. Take it easy. Nothing's going to happen on a highway full of traffic in broad daylight. If the Audi draws up alongside, just put your foot down.'

'They won't try. I've already told you they won't. What shall I do?'

He wished he knew. Last night during their frantic sprint along the pot-holed lane he'd been able to support her physically. But this was different. If she was right – if, somehow or other, men had been lying in wait for the Mercedes – who the hell was going to help her now?

Harland had arrived, alerted to the emergency and clearly concerned now he'd seen the expression on McKendrick's face. 'Where is she?' he asked.

'Still this side of Trier. She's calling from the car.'

'And she thinks someone's on her tail?'

McKendrick nodded. 'Sounds like it.'

'OK. This is how we play it.' Harland's manner became more professional. 'First you tell her she has to double back before she gets anywhere near Trier, so we can rendezvous with her somewhere on the 268. That means she has to stay on the 268. Then you tell her she has to keep moving. If she stops at lights or gets stuck in traffic, she could find herself in more trouble than any of us will know what to do with.' He gave McKendrick a pen. 'Write down the number of her car phone on your hand and say we'll be in touch on my mobile the minute we're on our way.'

Lucy had overheard and was already supplying the information, speaking so quickly that McKendrick had to ask her to repeat the numbers.

'Right.' Harland checked his watch. 'Before you hang up, tell her to lock all her doors, and you'd better make sure she understands about not stopping – not anywhere, not for anyone or for anything. Scare the shit out of her. Explain that if she goes off looking for help by herself there's a chance we'll miss her.'

Conscious of how scared she was, McKendrick expected her to

receive the instructions with alarm. What he hadn't expected was silence.

'Hey,' he said. 'Listen to me. You can burn off an Audi without even trying. All you have to do is keep going.'

'I can't.' Her voice was wavering and she'd begun speaking far more slowly. 'The low-fuel light came on in Zerf, but I was too frightened to stop at any of the service stations there. I can't keep going.'

He had no idea what to say, searching for words to reassure her, anxious to tell her she'd be all right – wanting to, needing to – but balking at the prospect of taking the blame for allowing her to go out alone, because he already knew that if they failed to reach her in time, he would have indeed made another awful, unforgivable mistake.

# Chapter 8

**H**arland was a brutal driver with a skill level that was making McKendrick sweat.

The 268 was a good road, consisting largely of fast straights and long sweeping bends that could have been taken at high speed if the Peugeot had been set up correctly for them, and if Harland had got his braking over before he tried to compensate for the heart-stopping slides that were taking them either into the path of oncoming traffic, or dangerously close to roadside trees and ditches.

'For Christ's sake ease up,' McKendrick said. 'We won't be much use to Lucy if you slam us into a truck or roll us over.'

'We're not going to be much use to her if she runs out of gas before we get to her either.' Ramming his gear lever into third, the American overtook a white van that had been impeding progress. 'Find out where the hell she's got to.'

Over the last kilometre or so, the reception on the cell phone had been marginal, the signal occasionally cutting out altogether while McKendrick had been speaking to her and, in the last few minutes, suffering on and off from interference of some kind.

'Lucy, can you hear me?' he said.

'Yes, I can.' She sounded more positive. 'I've turned round like you said. I used a side road, and the Audi went straight past without the driver seeing me. There are two other men in the car with him – one in the front and one in the back.'

'OK. Look for road signs – anything with distances on it, so you can tell us where you are.'

'The last one said four kilometres to Zerf. I'm sure it did. How far away from there are you?'

He braced himself against a door pillar while he checked the map. 'About five minutes, if we carry on at the rate we're going. How's the fuel gauge holding up?'

'I've stopped looking at it. If I run out will there be any warning, or will the car just stop on me?'

'I don't know. Don't worry about it.'

'How can you say that?' Her voice faded for a moment. 'McKendrick, I can't see them behind me any more. They're gone. They think I'm still going north.'

It sounded too good to be true, but he was reluctant to dent her optimism. 'There you go then,' he said. 'Hang on a second while I tell Harland you've lost them.'

The American had already guessed what the good news was, but like McKendrick, he was wary. 'Too easy,' he said. 'She's not dealing with a bunch of fucking amateurs. What did you do with my Uzi?'

'It's still in the Mercedes.'

'See if she can get at it.'

McKendrick had reservations about mentioning the idea to her. 'Harland's gun's lying on the floor somewhere,' he said. 'Put it on the seat beside you.'

'In case of what?'

'Surprises. Have you got it?'

'Yes, but I don't know anything about guns. I've never fired one. I don't think I could.'

'It's just insurance,' McKendrick said. 'Are you still watching for road signs?'

'I don't need to. I'm already in Zerf.' Her voice was suddenly brighter. 'I'll stop for petrol at the first place I see.'

'Don't,' McKendrick said. 'Don't do that. Wait until we meet you. We're nearly there.'

'It's more dangerous for me to keep going. The last two corners made the engine miss. McKendrick, I'm all right. No one's following me.'

He remained uneasy. 'Listen,' he said, 'we're less than two or three minutes away from you. Just keep rolling.'

Harland interrupted. 'Don't get her hopes up,' he said. 'Might take us a bit longer in this traffic.' He slowed down, cursing the driver of the car that had braked in front of him before he swerved to avoid a cyclist with a death wish who had underestimated the Peugeot's speed.

Hoping they wouldn't run over anyone or hit anything immovable, McKendrick began his own search for road signs, mentally recalculating their arrival time now the road had become more congested.

Despite Harland's best efforts, over the next half-kilometre their speed continued to drop, only stabilizing once they'd entered the outskirts of Zerf itself where the countryside gave way to houses, some of them with children playing in the gardens and with smoke curling from their chimneys, while not far away where west-bound traffic was coming in on the 407 from Kell, McKendrick had a glimpse of a steel bridge over the Ruwer river.

For a second or two he had a better view before he was again forced to brace himself as Harland executed a high-speed manoeuvre that should never have worked, but that somehow miraculously did.

To maintain headway, the American was taking more risks, but driving with such determination that McKendrick was beginning to believe they might just make it in one piece after all. Whether the Peugeot would last the distance seemed more doubtful. The engine was starting to rattle at the higher end of the rev range, and a powerful smell of hot oil had filled the inside of the car.

Harland was unconcerned and showed no signs of easing back on the throttle. 'Better start looking for her,' he said. 'Sing out when you see her and I'll do a u-turn.'

McKendrick used the phone again, this time asking Lucy to keep her eyes open for the approaching Peugeot and explaining that they'd be providing back up while she located a garage where the Mercedes could be refuelled in safety.

'I'm already at a garage,' she said. 'If I see you before you see me, I'll flash my lights.'

He swore under his breath. 'Which side of the road are you on?' he said.

'Left. That means I'll be on your right. I'm sure it's OK. There aren't any other cars here waiting and a man's already come over to serve me.'

'Stay inside the car,' he said. 'If anything happens, just drive off. Never mind about paying.'

Harland glanced at him. 'Has she done what you told her not to do?'

'That's how she operates. She's all right for the minute.'

McKendrick should have reserved judgement. No sooner had he finished speaking than Lucy came on the line again.

'They're here,' she whispered. 'The Audi. It's come and parked in front of me. They must have been following me after all.'

'Reverse,' he instructed. 'Forget the pump hose. Back out. Now.'

'I can't.' She could barely speak. 'Another car's arrived. It's behind me. I think it's the one from last night. I can see bullet holes in the bonnet, and its headlights are broken.'

'Jesus.' He tried to keep his voice level. 'Sit tight. We'll be with you any second.'

There was no answer.

'Lucy,' he shouted into the phone. 'Talk to me.'

'Two men have got out of the Audi. One's forcing the pump attendant back into the office, and I think the other one's coming over. Yes, he is. Oh God.'

'What?' McKendrick yelled.

'He's spraying my car with petrol. I can smell it and . . . .' Her voice tailed off.

By now Harland had become alarmed. 'Is she in trouble?' he asked.

'They've jammed her in so they can torch her car. They're going to burn her.'

'Holy shit. Tell her to use the Uzi. Tell her to shoot the bastards through her windshield.'

'Too dangerous with petrol around.' McKendrick pointed. 'There she is.'

The Audi had been easy to recognize, and now Harland had put the Peugeot into a long slide across the road, the Mercedes and the other car could be seen as well. So could the man at the pump. He was standing at the rear of Lucy's car directing a fountain of petrol over the boot lid and under the wheel arches.

'I'll ram that motherfucker in front of her.' Harland straightened up the Peugeot. 'Hang on to something.'

'No.' McKendrick grabbed at the steering wheel. 'I know about fires, you don't. Do what I say. We only have one chance of getting her out of this. Stop the car. Do it.'

'How the hell's that going to help her?'

He ignored the question, speaking quickly into the phone instead, not knowing how long she might have, and half-expecting to see the Mercedes enveloped in flames before he could issue his instructions.

'Lucy, don't get out,' he said. 'And whatever happens, don't panic if the car catches fire. You'll be fine. All you have to do is push your way past the Audi. Hit it at an angle as hard as you can. Then, the minute you're clear, follow us to the river down the road. It's real close, so you don't have to be scared by the flames – they'll be trailing back behind you, and they'll look a whole lot worse than they are. When you see us stopping on a bridge, try and remember to throw Harland's gun out your window in case we need it, then you stand on your brakes and bail out the instant the car's stopped moving. If your clothes or your hair catch fire, run straight to the edge of the bridge and jump. If that's what you have to do, I'll be going down into the water with you, so we'll both be getting wet together. Promise me you'll do what I've said.'

He didn't have to wait for her answer. The tyres of the Mercedes had already begun to smoke as Lucy started out on her bid to escape the danger.

She'd caught the man at the pump off guard. Dropping the hose, he backed away from the spreading pool of petrol, aware of how easily sparks from her spinning wheels could finish his job for him.

Lucy, though, had no option but to take the risk. With no space in which to manoeuvre, she used the Mercedes as a battering-ram, twice slamming into the rear of the Audi and relying on her traction control electronics to provide grip on the petrol-wetted surface after each rebound.

McKendrick could hardly bring himself to watch, knowing that, even if her luck continued to hold, it would run out with a vengeance when she attempted to scrape her way past the other car.

There was time for him to see the Mercedes break free in a shower of sparks. Then he could see nothing but a wall of boiling flame.

'Go,' he yelled at Harland. 'Don't worry about her keeping up.

Drive like hell.'

On their earlier journey into Zerf, the American's driving had been risky enough but now, to satisfy the need for greater urgency on their high speed run to the river, he'd adopted a new technique, holding the Peugeot in the centre of the road while he sounded the horn and flashed his headlights at all oncoming vehicles.

For the most part, McKendrick was managing to keep his attention on the burning car behind them, trying not to wonder where its fuel tank was located and how vulnerable it might be to heat.

So far, the signs were good. As he'd predicted, the faster the Mercedes travelled, the more the flames were being carried rearwards by the airstream, and where a moment ago smoke had been billowing out of the wheel arches on the left-hand side, now he could see none.

Equally encouraging was the absence of a burning fuel trail, although he knew that once Lucy had come to a standstill, the fire could easily intensify to the point where she might be too frightened to get out.

'Bridge,' Harland shouted. 'Here we go.' Cutting across in front of a truck he executed a left-hand turn on to the 407. 'Any sign of those bastards following us?'

McKendrick had forgotten to check. 'Can't see them,' he said.

'OK. Let's hope she remembers to drop off the gun.' Harland prepared to reduce speed. 'Get ready.'

Now McKendrick could see how high the bridge was above the water, he was reconsidering the wisdom of allowing Lucy to jump. But the time for second thoughts was over.

Through the rear window of the Peugeot he saw the nose of the Mercedes suddenly begin to dip and skitter as she threw out the gun and stamped down hard on her brakes.

For a second the flames appeared to die. Then, as though rekindled by the draft of passing traffic, they swept forwards like a wave.

The Peugeot was still moving when he kicked open his door and hit the bridge running, nearly overbalancing in his haste to reach her before the now stationary Mercedes became a fireball.

But Lucy was already out of the car, stumbling unharmed towards the bridge rail on her one good foot, turning to face him when she heard him call out to her.

He sprinted the last few metres, checking to make sure Harland had gone to collect the Uzi before he helped her limp away from the heat and the flames.

Considering what she'd just been through, she was in fairly good shape, coughing on the fumes and smoke she'd inhaled and glancing apprehensively over her shoulder in case the drivers of the cars at the garage had decided to take up the chase again, but otherwise a good deal less frightened than she'd been last night.

'Lucky we never had to make that jump.' He couldn't think of anything sensible to say. 'Have you seen how far down it is?'

She nodded, either unable to speak after her ordeal, or because she was too busy gulping air.

'Can you make it to Harland's car?'

She nodded again.

'Look, if you're not OK, say so.' He tried to see if she was hurt.

'Why didn't those men just shoot me?'

The question was a give-away, he realized. Of all the things she could've asked him, this was what she wanted to know most – an indication not just of how truly terrified she'd been, but of how long she'd been expecting the worst.

'Same reason they didn't drive you off the road,' he said quietly. 'This way it would've looked like an accident.' He took hold of her arm. 'Come on. Let's get you somewhere warm.'

She was steady on her feet, still limping, but going on ahead of him once they neared the Peugeot.

He opened the door for her. 'You hop in and wait while I make certain we're out of the woods,' he said. 'I'll only be a second.'

At the kerb on the centre span of the bridge, the burning Mercedes was causing a traffic-jam. The fire had grown fiercer, fed now by blazing tyres and by litres of fresh petrol that had finally spilled out of a tank that had lost its battle against the increasingly high temperature beneath it.

Passing drivers were either slowing down to rubberneck or hurrying to get by in the face of an opposing stream of cars and trucks that were being forced to put their wheels up on to the narrow left-hand walkway of the bridge.

Harland was in the thick of it, partly obscured by smoke, holding the Uzi out of sight inside his jacket while he searched for the Audi or the other car, but starting to head back to the Peugeot now he'd seen McKendrick beckoning to him.

McKendrick went to meet him, wondering how far off the police or a fire engine might be, hoping that most of the passing drivers had been too distracted by the fire to notice Lucy getting into the Peugeot.

'Close run thing.' The American was out of breath. 'Doesn't look like those bastards even tried to come after us – probably figured Lucy wouldn't make it. How is she?'

'Hard to tell. We'd better get off this bridge while we still can.'

'Right.' Harland began walking faster. 'If you didn't know last night, you sure as hell know now, don't you?' he said.

'What?'

'That you and Lucy have hit a jugular somewhere. These guys are taking big risks. Whatever Zitelmann's teaching at his institute, you can bet your fucking life it isn't religious tolerance or any other kind of fucking tolerance.'

Not the most astute of observations, McKendrick thought, but nicely put. 'We'll have to stay on the 407 for a bit,' he said. 'We can't turn round here.'

'Leave the driving to me. You look after our passenger.' Harland smiled at Lucy as he climbed back in the car and handed over the Uzi to McKendrick. 'If we're shit out of luck you'd better hope that still works.' He started the engine, then swivelled round in his seat to study her more closely. 'Pity about your boss's car,' he said.

'I don't know how I'm going to tell him.' She was overwhelmed by another bout of coughing. 'Do you think that man who started serving me petrol will have been all right?'

Judging by Harland's expression and the time he took to answer, he'd reached the same conclusion as McKendrick. 'Worrying about other people doesn't get you anywhere,' he said. 'Worry about yourself. How are you feeling?'

'I'm not sure yet. Shaky, and I can't stop being scared. I didn't believe things like this could happen to anyone in Germany – well, not to people like me.' She attempted a smile. 'I suppose that's what I thought after last night, too. Aren't you going to tell me it's my own fault?'

'If this is anybody's goddamn fault, it's mine.' Harland pushed the nose of the Peugeot out into the traffic stream. 'If I had half a brain, I'd have figured things out before you got yourself into this much trouble.'

'What things?' McKendrick interrupted.

'Remember what I said to you over breakfast – about the chance of Zitelmann phoning Lucy's office and pretending to be some kind of businessman so he could find out which hotel you were staying at?'

'We've got that covered,' McKendrick said. 'That's why we didn't go back there.'

'That's about all we did cover. What if the son of a bitch made his call after Lucy contacted her office to say where Linder could get hold of her when he phoned this morning from Chicago?'

'Are you saying that's how Zitelmann knew we were at Emily's – because he was given Emily's number and he traced it back to an address?'

'Think about it. How else would that Audi driver have known where to pick up Lucy on the road? Her call to Zurich made it easy. The bastards knew exactly where you'd been overnight. They were just waiting for one of you to show.' Reaching over his shoulder, Harland handed his phone to Lucy. '091 quick dial,' he said. 'Tell Emily she needs to pack a suitcase and that we'll be collecting her in fifteen minutes. She'll be less worried if she hears it from you. Just say it'll be best if she spends some time with her niece in Bonn. If that's not convenient, I'll arrange for her to go somewhere for a couple of days while I do some sorting out.'

A couple of days to sort out what, McKendrick wondered? Assemble more pieces of the jigsaw, or to search for a couple of hundred missing pieces? Or was Harland being deliberately optimistic, somehow hoping that the puzzle would put itself together?

To avoid attracting attention and unaware of McKendrick's misgivings, the American was driving more carefully, heading east away from Zerf, away from the river and away from the burning Mercedes on the bridge.

The Peugeot, though, was still carrying with it the smell of hot engine oil and smoke – reminders, along with the freshly scratched machine-pistol on McKendrick's lap, of how quickly things could change in the space of two short days, and of how difficult it was going to be to extricate himself from a mess that had just become even murkier and more dangerous that it had been yesterday.

# Chapter 9

After the events of last night and this afternoon, their choice of accommodation had been based on an urgent need for anonymity. At the time, the decision had seemed sensible enough, but over the last quarter of an hour while McKendrick had been standing at the window of his new hotel room staring out at the rain-sodden streets of Trier, he'd begun to wish he'd argued more strongly in favour of crossing the border into Luxembourg where they might have been able to find somewhere less depressing to stay.

Not that Trier or the guesthouse was more depressing than anywhere else would have been on such a miserable afternoon. As German guesthouses went, the Jugendgästehaus was well located, the rooms were warm and all the linen was freshly starched and laundered.

In which case, why was he finding the view from his window so damn dreary, McKendrick wondered?

The building was slap bang in the middle of town, no more than a block away from the Hauptmarket and not far from the gothic Liebfrauenkirche basilica, but in spite of the hustle and bustle of the evening rush hour, he was feeling hemmed in and trapped by the circumstances that had brought him here.

The feeling was familiar, not unlike the let-down he'd experienced after his return to Brussels from Hawaii and Kalimantan, when, for nearly a week, the cold and wet of a European winter had prevented him from thinking himself out of a situation that had been no more of his own making than this one had been – both of them equally intractable and both having their origins in warm countries where the temperatures had been twenty degrees higher than it was outside in the street he was looking down at now.

The rain had begun shortly after they'd collected Emily and whisked her north to the railway station on the Kürenzstrasse, where she'd gone off on the 4.55 train to Bonn clutching a bunch of flowers from Harland. No more than mildly flustered by the speed of her evacuation, she'd been quite happy at the prospect of an enforced visit to her niece, and although she'd realized that Lucy was far from being herself and noticed how wary Harland and McKendrick had been during the drive, she'd asked few questions and been careful not to pry.

The drive itself had been without incident, as uneventful as Lucy's subsequent visit to a department store on the Flieschstrasse in downtown Trier where, this time in the company of McKendrick, she'd been able to buy the shoes and clothes that, earlier today, she'd very nearly paid for with her life.

Since checking into the Jugendgästehaus, he'd been doing his best not to dwell on what could have happened and endeavouring not to think about Lucy either, knowing that if he'd never met her to begin with, he would never have agreed to start out on such a complicated and risky enterprise.

He left the window, intending to see if he could unwind by lying down on the bed for a while, but had no sooner kicked off his shoes than he had to answer a knock on the door.

Lucy was standing outside in the corridor, her hands in the pockets of her new Levis and wearing the cream-coloured, high-necked sweater she'd bought this afternoon.

'Hi.' She gave him the kind of half-smile she reserved for occasions like this. 'Can I come in?'

'Sure.' He stood aside and closed the door behind her. 'Where's Harland?'

'Getting us pizza from a place he saw on the corner of the Brückenstrasse. He doesn't want us to eat out.' She sat down on the edge of the bed. 'I came to say thank you.'

'For what?'

'For telling me the right things to do in the car. You know what I mean.'

By attempting not to sound trite, she'd embarrassed herself, but unlike this morning, he could see no trace of colour in her cheeks.

'Have you phoned Linder yet?' he asked.

'Yes, except that it was one o'clock in the morning in Chicago, so I woke him up.'

'How did he take the news about his car?'

'I couldn't tell. He said he'd organize things with the insurance company himself. Mostly he just kept asking me if I was all right.'

'And are you?'

She nodded. 'I suppose so. I'm not as strung out as I was after last night. I don't know why that is, though.'

'It's because of how your brain works. Compared with being shot at, everyone feels safer inside a car, even if it does happen to be on fire at the time.'

'Is that McKendrick do-it-yourself psychoanalysis, or is it true?'

'I have no idea.' He smiled at her. 'Just thought it might make you feel better.'

'You sound like Harland. If you start patronizing me, too, I'll go home.'

'No you won't, not while Zitelmann's still trying to run you down.'

'He's looking for you as well – or don't you care about that?'

'Yeah, I care, but apart from throwing him into his lake or setting fire to his institute while he's inside it with his Nazi friends, I can't see there's a hell of a lot I can do to stop him. It's not up to me any more. I'll leave it to Harland and Linder.'

'Harland's already explained why the DEA won't do anything to help, and you can't expect Mr Linder to handle a problem as serious as this by himself.'

'He doesn't have to handle it by himself. He's already getting other people to give him a hand. That's what you said.'

'Yes. Other people like you.' She compressed her lips. 'You were happy to take his money before things started going wrong, but now they have, you've decided you don't want anything to do with him or me.'

She was only half right, but McKendrick doubted that she'd included herself in the statement on purpose. On the other hand, she seemed to have recovered enough to argue – a good sign, he thought, even if this was hardly the time to correct what she'd said.

Now the room was getting darker, he went to switch on the lights and draw the curtains, glancing out again at the rain and the sea of flashing neons, hoping that the trapped feeling might have gone away, but discovering it hadn't.

Lucy had fallen silent as though considering her own position, still sitting on the bed, and with her lips clamped together in a tight line, responding to his question about how long Harland had said he'd be with nothing more than a shrug.

'He thinks there's a chance of the DEA investigating Justin Quaid,' she said.

'Because Quaid's a US citizen?'

She shook her head. 'Because of the link between Quaid and Maria Kessel. The DEA know she's trafficking South American drugs into the Middle East, so they have an excuse to see if Quaid's doing something worse than just running his Christian Freedom Party and laundering her money for her. If he is, that might get us more information on Zitelmann, don't you think?'

McKendrick's reply was interrupted by the sound of Harland's voice outside the door.

'I'll go.' Lucy went to let him in.

The American was dripping wet, handing McKendrick three pizza boxes and a six-pack of Salator beer before taking a soggy newspaper from the pocket of his jacket. 'Picked this up on the way,' he said. 'My German's lousy, but if the clip on page four says what I think it says, Lucy's not going to like it.' He gave her the paper. 'You might want to grab a slice of pizza and have a couple of beers before you check it out.'

'Dry yourself off with one of my towels,' McKendrick said. 'There's a clean one in the bathroom.'

'Right. Thanks.' Harland went to get it. 'If I'd known it was going to piss down this hard, I'd have brought a coat from Emily's.'

Lucy had been busy unsticking pages of the paper, unfolding them one at a time on the suitcase stand where she had more light.

'Found it?' Harland came back into the room and helped himself to a beer.

'Yes.' She didn't raise her head.

'How about translating it for us, then? If we're going to have more shit thrown at us, we're better off knowing where it's coming from.' The American opened one of the pizza boxes and took it with him over to a chair by the radiator. 'What does it say?'

'You and McKendrick aren't mentioned. It's about me, and about that man who owned the garage.' She glanced up. 'According to this, he died in the fire, and it's all my fault.'

Harland shrugged. 'More or less what I figured – something about you using a cell phone while he was filling your car with gas. Is that right?'

She nodded, hesitating for a second before she smoothed down the page and began to read out loud:

'*PROPRIETOR OF SERVICE STATION BURNED TO DEATH. Police are searching for the driver of a car that caught fire on the forecourt of a Zerf garage at 1.26 P.M. today.*

*Witnesses confirm that the vehicle was driven by a young woman who was seen to be using a cell phone continuously while her Swiss registered Mercedes was being refuelled by the garage owner, Friedrich Kipphardt, 39, of Zewen.*

*It is thought that volatile petroleum fumes ignited by her phone were responsible for the conflagration, which spread quickly to other parts of the garage.*

*According to staff members from the Weiskirchen Institute of Islamic and Christian Studies who were on the scene, and who unsuccessfully attempted to resuscitate Herr Kipphardt and fight the fire with extinguishers taken from the workshop, the woman driver made no attempt to offer help and drove off at high speed while the pump nozzle was still in place.*

*The Mercedes was subsequently abandoned and destroyed by fire on the east-bound lane of the Ruwer bridge, where the woman was last seen getting into a medium-sized, black car. She is wearing a dark-coloured sweater and mud-stained tracksuit pants and is recognizable by a white bandage on her left foot and by extensive freckling on her face and neck.*

*Police are currently tracing the origin of the Mercedes, which may have been stolen and hope to have more information by tomorrow.*

*Kipphardt is survived by his wife, Margarethe, a 12-year-old daughter and a teenage son.*'

Harland was philosophical. 'Well that's got you stitched up,' he said. 'The good guys come from ICIS, and you're a heartless rich bitch who didn't give a fuck about that poor bastard who got himself incinerated while he was filling up your car for you.'

Lucy was visibly upset, looking at McKendrick for reassurance.

'Well, that's it, then,' he said. 'We'd better get you out of Germany quick smart. It wouldn't have taken the police long to trace the car, so they probably know who you are by now.'

Harland was more pessimistic, speaking with a large piece of pizza halfway to his mouth. 'You'll need to do more than get her out of Germany,' he said. 'That's the easy bit.'

McKendrick could guess what the hard part was going to be. Harland's choice of the word *you* instead of *we* had been no accident – a not so subtle indication of the American's intention to use Lucy as a pawn – distancing himself from a problem he wanted no part of unless McKendrick agreed to the terms they'd discussed over breakfast at Emily's this morning.

Unwilling to commit himself to anything, McKendrick took one of the pizza boxes over to her.

She shook her head. 'You can share mine between you. I'm not hungry.'

'How about one of these?' He opened a bottle of beer. 'Don't get yourself screwed up because of something you've just read in a newspaper. We can ride this out.'

'How? Even if we went to the police now, they wouldn't believe a single thing we told them about Zitelmann and his lake, would they? And if you're more interested in putting out underground fires than you are in Harland's deal, who's going to connect ICIS with Maria Kessel, let alone connect her and Zitelmann to some mad Christian Freedom Party leader in the States?' She paused. 'Aren't you worried about yourself? Have you forgotten what happened to Dean and Bridget Goddard?'

McKendrick hadn't forgotten, nor had he forgotten why he'd decided to visit the offices of Linder International to begin with, even if his reason for doing so had been somewhat overshadowed. 'Look,' he said, 'suppose I start following Maria Kessel around Europe, what good's that going to be?'

'She's not in Europe anymore.' Harland closed the lid on his empty pizza box. 'Sorry to disappoint you. There was an e-mail about her on my computer when I got back from buying us dinner.'

'Where is she?' McKendrick wasn't sure whether this was going to be good news or bad news.

'I'll tell you in a minute. There's something you and I need to get straight first – about how much help I might or might not be willing to give you.' Harland drank from another bottle of beer. 'The way I see it, except for Linder, you and Lucy are pretty much on your own now, so maybe this is a good time for you to reconsider your decision about not giving the DEA a hand. Don't forget you've got an edge that our Maria doesn't have.'

McKendrick couldn't think of one. 'What?' he said.

Harland patted his chest. 'Me. The guy who bought you these nice pizzas you're not eating. Maria doesn't know I exist, and she hasn't the first idea that the DEA have been watching her for the last seven months.'

'What about last night in Weiskirchen?' McKendrick was uncertain. 'Those guys in the car you shot at had a good look at you.'

'They'd have figured I was just some dick with a gun who you'd brought along in case of trouble. It's like I said before, the DEA won't put their balls in a vice for someone we don't know who isn't working for us, but if you want some back up wherever you happen to find yourself, we can put you in touch with people we've done business with before – the same kind of people we can get to handle your little project in Indonesia for you. No guarantees, but that ought to make things easier, don't you think?'

McKendrick was past wondering what to think, convinced that there had to be a better solution, but at the same time aware of the danger Lucy would be in if he were to walk away without making at least some effort to secure her safety and, perhaps, by so doing, secure his own.

Harland hadn't finished. 'Maria never realized we were on her tail before,' he said, 'so she won't be looking over her shoulder for anyone – especially now she believes she's home and dry.'

McKendrick hadn't missed the implication. 'Home and dry where?' he said.

'I'll tell you.' Harland consulted his watch. 'According to the passenger list I've been sent, and if her plane from Munich was on schedule, she's just got off Lufthansa flight 343 in Rio de Janeiro, and she'll be about to transfer to an internal flight that'll take her to São Paulo. In a couple of hours she'll be sitting down in her apartment to count all the money she's made from her little holiday in Germany.'

'So we've missed her.' Lucy went to the window and pulled back one of the curtains to look out at the lights of the city.

'I didn't say that.' Harland smiled. 'I thought I was explaining where McKendrick could find her.'

Lucy glanced at McKendrick. 'You've been to Brazil before,' she said slowly. 'I know you have because you told me.'

'The last time I was there, I ended up spending two weeks chained up in jail. I didn't tell you that, did I?'

'So you won't go?'

'To do what?'

'I don't know.' She fiddled with the buckle of her belt. 'Whatever you think you could do. We're not going to find out much more in Germany, are we?'

Harland waited to discover if McKendrick was going to answer her before he spoke again. 'You need Vicente,' he said. 'He's a cocky young Afro-Brazilian who's worked for us before. He knows every drug-dealer and every back street in São Paulo, he's hard as nails, and if you give him enough of Linder's money he'll get you inside the warehouse where Kessel runs her business.'

'And you just happened to have remembered his name,' McKendrick said.

'You're reading this wrong. I figured it'd be better if you didn't have to work up high without a net – that's all. If you're not happy about going to Brazil, why would I care?' Harland stood up and stretched before he went to the door. 'I'm not being rude,' he said. 'But I need to catch up on some sleep. I'll see you both in the morning.'

McKendrick waited until he'd gone before he wandered over to join Lucy at the window.

'You haven't eaten anything either,' she said.

'I know.' He stared out at the rain. 'You're more worn out than Harland. Why don't you have an early night as well?'

'I don't want to. I don't want to be by myself.' She drew the curtain again. 'Would you mind if I stayed?'

'Be my guest.'

'For the night, I mean. If you have a spare blanket I can curl up on a chair.'

He was surprised. Instead of taking over where Harland had left off, she'd apparently decided to save her breath. 'You have the bed,' he said. 'I'll take the chair. I'm used to sleeping pretty much anywhere.'

'Oh. Thank you.' She studied the cut on his lip. 'I'm sorry I never bought that salve for you.'

He smiled. 'We've had a few other things to do.'

'Mm. Perhaps this will help.' She caught him unawares, standing on tiptoe and kissing him very gently and very carefully on the mouth.

Three days of being incarcerated in the Jugendgästehaus had been three days too many. That it had taken McKendrick less than twenty-four hours to come to his decision had made the waiting worse, a decision that had surprised him almost as much as it had surprised Harland and Lucy.

But the advantage had been lost already, offset by the need to book and co-ordinate his trip to South America first through the Zurich headquarters of Linder International and then, after numerous phone calls and an exchange of e-mails, through Harland's contacts in São Paulo.

The resultant delay had provided McKendrick with plenty of opportunity to regret his haste and to wonder whether the trap he'd fallen into had been more of his own making than that of the young woman who, since kissing him so unexpectedly the other night, had grown progressively more withdrawn and, unless he was imagining it, had recently started avoiding his company altogether.

The change in her attitude was a source of worry he could have done without, particularly when he was about to leave her in the care of the American whom he suspected of being intrigued by more than her freckles and the way she treated his stares, and the stares of strangers whom she encountered in the guest-house lobby where she was waiting to say goodbye to McKendrick now.

Harland was with her, standing by the door with his car keys in his hand. He inspected McKendrick's travel-bag. 'Is that it?' he asked.

'I'll pick up what I need when I get there.'

'Did you arrange for someone in Brussels to send me that stuff we talked about?'

'Should be arriving at your office today or tomorrow,' McKendrick said. 'You're getting a marked-up map showing the track and the fire-front, two sketches of the tattoo and a set of the photos I took of the girl and the old man in case the ministry in Balikpapan can't find their copies. If you need anything else, let me know.'

'OK. Sounds good to me.' Harland turned up the collar of his jacket. 'No need for both of us to get wet. You wait here while I fetch the car.' He pushed open the door and hurried out into the rain.

As though uncertain of herself, Lucy was dislodging a piece of chewing gum from the carpet with the heel of her shoe.

'Have you decided where you're going yet?' McKendrick asked.

'Harland said he'll take me skiing in Austria. He has a friend who owns a chalet up in the Tirol somewhere.'

So that's how things were shaping up, McKendrick thought. Harland had made the first of his moves already, and for all of her smartness and her professionally cultivated independence, she was still naïve enough to believe he was doing her a favour.

'I'll be in touch as soon as I know where I'm staying,' he said. 'I'll contact Linder through your Zurich office to start with.'

'All right. I'll phone there every couple of days to find out where you are.' She continued looking at the carpet. 'I hope things work out.'

Sure you do, McKendrick thought. But for whom? By now it was clear that he'd be lucky to receive as much as a peck on the cheek for a goodbye – proof, if he needed it, of how thoroughly he'd deceived himself, and of how extraordinarily stupid he was to be embarking on another overseas trip to a place he didn't want to go to when the reason for his journey had not only turned out to be imaginary, but downright fucking wrong.

# Chapter 10

In common with most Brazilian rental cars, the Volkswagen Bora had been abused to the point where it seemed perpetually about to fall apart. Yesterday, after McKendrick had made the mistake of driving over a rail-crossing at high speed, the right front shock absorber had all but disintegrated, and earlier this morning on his trip out here to the ugly and decaying Santos waterfront, the air-conditioning system had stopped working altogether.

As a result, he'd spent much of the journey sitting in his own sweat trying to navigate his way around the business end of the island and becoming lost in a six kilometre-long maze of run-down container terminals and dilapidated warehouses.

According to his map, there was supposed to be a car ferry that would have brought him directly from the downtown area of São Paulo, but after wasting nearly half an hour in a fruitless search for the departure wharf, he'd set off to the coast by road, travelling east over a series of viaducts and sweeping bridges until he'd found himself surrounded by giant cranes and the rusty hulls of tankers that were tied up everywhere in the narrow oil-choked channels that served as the port of Santos.

If the road journey here had been something of a contrast after his first-class flight from Munich four and a half days ago, the location of his hotel in the up-market Bella Vista district of São Paulo was in even greater contrast with the distinctly seedy neighbourhood he was trying to get himself out of now.

Until today he'd avoided making contact with Vicente, whoever he would turn out to be, but over the last quarter of an hour or so, McKendrick had come to realize how risky it would be to break into

Kessel's warehouse single-handed when he couldn't even find the street it was supposed to be on, and now that he'd seen the gangs of wharfies and labourers who occupied the district. They were in every alley and on every corner, hard-looking men going about their business in a part of Santos where foreigners and tourists were not only unwelcome, but easy game for locals who would cut your throat for a Rolex watch or for a few grams of heroin or cocaine.

Realizing that the road he was on would probably lead him into another dead-end or to nowhere more interesting than another broken-down wharf, he executed a u-turn and was about to increase his speed to avoid attracting the attention of some men who were unloading a truck when he saw the street sign.

It was attached to the side of a building beneath a bricked-up window and partly obscured by the remains of an old steel fire escape, but the words Rua Sabastião on it were clear enough.

He hadn't seen it before because he'd been coming from the other direction. Nor on his first drive past the intersection had he noticed that the area was rather more prosperous-looking than the others he'd been travelling through, but now he'd swung the Volkswagen into the street he'd been searching for he was able to see why – the buildings here were, in the main, well maintained and, in places, even freshly painted.

On the Rua Sabastião, the warehouses were either owned by multinational companies or by major Brazilian exporters, many of them household names.

But it wasn't just the names that he recognized. Along with the wealth and employment that these companies brought with them came security, insurance and alarms.

Above the doors, the steel-barred windows and the loading bays of almost every building were warning signs and red-painted alarm-bell housings, each of them flanked by motion-triggered floodlights – an indication of how difficult it would be to get inside any one of them undetected.

But would Kessel's be equally well protected, McKendrick wondered? Even allowing for the number of girls she was selling and taking into account her lucrative fish and narcotics business, her company was still nothing like as large as most of these were.

Glad to be away from the smell of fuel-oil and the stench of untreated sewage, he opened all of the windows to get some fresh air inside the car and started searching for the name *Arowana*, driving further inland until, on the left-hand side of the street, he saw a small blue-coloured warehouse on which the name and a logo were prominently displayed.

Like the adjacent premises, the building was reasonably presentable and carried the same security warning signs, but this was not a store for coffee beans or tractors, or for cotton or tobacco. This was Kessel's warehouse, the place where, according to Harland, she kept her aquarium holding tanks and where, presumably, she concealed the drugs that her company was trafficking into the markets of the Middle East.

There was little else for McKendrick to see. No vehicles were parked outside; there were few people about, and no evidence that the place was anything other than just another storage depot for just another company who, for reasons of convenience, had chosen to base their business here.

He drove past it, prepared now to acknowledge that Harland had been right. In the absence of anyone to help him, attempting a burglary would be as difficult as it would be dangerous – which meant his reluctance to telephone Vicente had been all the more unjustified, McKendrick thought; another instance of him believing he could accomplish something by himself when, in reality, he was so far out of his depth that if Vicente was unable or unwilling to provide assistance, he might as well give up the whole damn idea and catch the next flight back to Europe.

Disheartened and disappointed because he'd learned nothing that he didn't already know, he spent another two or three minutes aimlessly exploring the neighbouring streets then, more by good luck than by good navigating, managed to find his way out on to the west-bound lane of the Estrada Velha do Mar and began the 70 kilometre return drive to São Paulo.

By five o'clock he was back in his hotel room, cool for the first time since he'd left this morning and sufficiently relaxed to waste half an hour standing in the shower before he recorded a brief message on Vicente's answering machine and got himself ready to go out for a walk in search of a friendly air-conditioned bar somewhere.

*

Like most *Paulistanos*, the taxi driver had an innate understanding of the morning rush-hour traffic, stopping at red lights only when forced to do so by cars crossing in front of him and ignoring all stop signs if there was the opportunity of beating other vehicles that happened to be bearing down on him from one direction or another.

Having experienced the cut and thrust of Brazilian city driving before, McKendrick was resigned to it, optimistic that he'd arrive at his destination in one piece, but less certain of how he should approach the subject of his impending meeting with someone whose occupation and credentials were rather different from his own.

The phone call from Vicente had come last night, shortly after McKendrick had returned from a noisy bar whose name he couldn't remember. What he could remember was the length of time he'd spent wondering about Lucy and Harland – a concern that, try as he might, he couldn't seem to get out of his mind, and one that had been brought to the surface by a persistent, short-skirted redhead who'd twice asked him to buy her a drink in payment for favours that he hadn't quite understood.

But that had been last night, he told himself, and if he didn't make an attempt to stop thinking about Lucy, he could be at a disadvantage when it came to discussing business with the young man he was about to meet.

The driver brought the taxi to rest by driving up over the kerb and parking behind several other vehicles that were already blocking the sidewalk. 'Please.' He pointed a finger at the meter.

'OK. Thanks.' McKendrick gave him a fifty reais note and climbed out into the heat of the morning, looking for the telephone booth on the Avienda do Estado where he'd been told to wait.

It was nearby, on the other side of the road, forcing him to brave the traffic and to sprint the last few metres to avoid being run over by a girl on a scooter who was overtaking a car on the inside.

The phone booth was unoccupied, and there was no one standing around who McKendrick thought could be Vicente.

He was still looking when a Brazilian youth emerged from a shop doorway to his right.

'*Bom dia*,' the boy said. 'You are Senhor McKendrick?'

'That's me. Are you Vicente?'

'He waits. Please, you will come to the car with me.' He showed McKendrick over to a yellow Ford Taurus and opened one of the doors.

Inside, the young man who was sitting in the rear seat was no more than one or two years older than the youth. He was dark-skinned, not yet out of his teens, and immaculately dressed in an expensive, open-necked pink shirt and a white linen suit.

'I am Vicente,' he said. 'I am pleased to make your acquaintance and ready to discuss this business you wish to do with me.'

'Here?' McKendrick was wary.

'Inside my car it is cool. Outside it is hot.' The young man patted the seat beside him. 'If there is a place you like to visit, my driver will take us there while we talk.'

McKendrick got in and shook hands. 'We don't need to go anywhere,' he said. 'This won't take long.'

'I think it is best if we keep moving.' Vicente waited until the boy had started the car and pulled out to join the traffic before he issued him with some brief instructions and turned to offer his passenger a cigarette.

McKendrick shook his head.

'You receive the package I leave for you at your hotel?'

'Yes. Thanks.'

'Then today you carry the little gun I give you?'

'Why?'

Vicente shrugged. 'I ask only because it is my wish for you to be safe. For foreigners who visit here there can sometimes be danger on the streets.'

'Does that mean you know why I've come?'

'I am told only that you are interested in a woman who has the name of Maria Kessel. But to show my goodwill, already I do some work for you. It is how I learn that in some places she is called the black widow.'

'Why?'

Vicente smiled. 'She has an appetite for well-hung black boys who do not always enjoy what she does with them.'

McKendrick decided not to press for details. 'She runs an import and export company called *Arowana*,' he said. 'It's a warehouse on the

Rua Sabastião in Santos. But the place has security alarms all over it, and it looks pretty hard to get into.'

'You have seen it?' Vicente was surprised.

'Yeah. Can you get me inside?'

'If it is not improper for me to enquire, first I should like to know what it is you wish to steal. In matters of this kind it is always best to be open with each other.'

'I don't want to steal anything. I just need to look around and see if I can find her company records.'

'Because you wish to trace a girl she has sold who was once very kind to you?'

'No.'

'Then perhaps you have been cheated by this woman who has supplied you with bad cocaine?'

'Look,' McKendrick said, 'it's a simple question. Can you do the job or not?'

'Of course, but it will cost much money. To hire people who have the skills to disable the alarms and unlock the doors is not so easy. You must understand that on the Santos waterfront, it is not the police who provide protection, but gangs who operate in the area. If we are not to be disturbed, these men must be paid to be busy in another place.'

'I don't want to know who you have to pay,' McKendrick said. 'All I want to know is how much I have to pay you.'

'When is it you wish to go?'

'How about tonight?'

'It is not possible. I think there is no one in São Paulo who can arrange this for you at such short notice.'

'What about tomorrow night?'

'You offer reais or American dollars?'

'Whatever you like.'

'I see.' The young man blew some cigarette smoke out of his window and thought for a moment. 'For tomorrow night the price will be seven thousand US dollars in cash,' he said.

'Five.' McKendrick was more interested in creating the right impression than he was in saving the odd one or two thousand dollars of Linder's money. 'Three thousand up front, two thousand after the job's done, and you provide the transport.'

'For six perhaps I can do it. But I shall require four thousand by nine o'clock tonight if I am to employ the services of men who may have to postpone their own plans for tomorrow night. It is a good price, I think, and you will find no one else who can help you for so little money. As it is, I offer you this only because of the good arrangement I have with the American DEA in Rio.'

McKendrick grinned. 'You can ease up on the sales pitch. I can manage the four thousand down, but if you screw up, you can forget about any end payment and you won't be getting any more work from the DEA. How does that sound?'

'It is a deal.' Vicente reached across to shake hands on it. 'But I am not accustomed to screwing up, as you call it, so please to bring the other two thousand with you. Now we are to trust each other, it is best for there to be no misunderstanding between us after the job is done.' He threw his cigarette out the window. 'If we have nothing more to discuss, may I deliver you back to your hotel, or do you prefer to call first at your bank so you may arrange for the necessary funds?'

'Hotel's fine,' McKendrick said. 'Don't worry about your money. I'll have it ready for you.'

'I am sure of it.' Vicente leaned forwards and spoke to his driver, giving him the Bella Vista address before pointing out the window at a large equestrian monument in the Parque da Independencia. 'It marks the place where my country's independence is first declared,' he explained. 'But now there are more than five million *Paulistanos* who live in slums and hovels, so I think it is my generation who must make things better for our people.'

Coming from someone like Vicente, the remark was as ironic as it was sad, McKendrick thought. The young man obviously cared about his city, but by becoming involved in the São Paulo underworld at such an early age that he'd be lucky to reach twenty, he was contributing to the very problem he wanted to solve – a situation not dissimilar to the one in Kalimantan where half the damn population were being forced to live outside the law for much the same reasons.

To stop himself from thinking about Kalimantan, for the remainder of the drive back to his hotel, McKendrick kept his mind on the present, agreeing to wait for Vicente's phone call tomorrow and shaking hands for the third time in half an hour before thanking him for the lift and hurrying up to his room in order to relieve himself of the too many cups of coffee he'd drunk before going out.

He was flushing the toilet when he realized someone had been in the bathroom before him.

A previously unopened bar of hotel soap had been stripped of its cellophane wrapper, and a towel on the rail was in the wrong place – a sloppy job by one of the maids, he told himself. Or maybe someone from room service had taken a quick leak and washed their hands when they'd come to collect his breakfast tray.

Conscious of over-reacting because of his experiences in Germany, he reached into his pocket for the gun Vicente had given him, a tiny .25 calibre Bauer automatic that was not much better than a toy, but better than nothing if he'd interrupted an intruder by returning early from his appointment.

But if he'd caught them unawares, where the hell were they now, he wondered? Had they taken the opportunity to slip away while he'd been busy in the bathroom? Or were they waiting for him in the other room? And if so, how many of them were there?

To find out, after turning on the washbasin taps to disguise the sound of him chambering the first round in the Bauer, he checked that he'd moved the safety catch in the right direction, and very cautiously eased open the bathroom door.

No one was outside. The hallway was empty. But a few metres to his right, sunlight from the bedroom window was being blocked by something or by someone.

For a second or two he waited, endeavouring to summon up his courage, then launched himself along the corridor, skidding to a halt when he saw who was in the room.

Lucy had evidently been hoping to surprise him. Instead he'd frightened her half to death.

She was standing wide-eyed in front of the window, one hand clamped over her mouth, the other held up to ward off her attacker.

'Shit.' McKendrick started breathing again.

She lowered her hands, but continued looking nervously at the gun. 'Are you going to shoot me?' she said.

He threw the gun on to the sofa, too confused and too relieved to answer, staring at her as though she was someone he'd never seen before, and uncomfortably aware of how easily he could have squeezed the trigger.

'Don't I get a hello?' She remained apprehensive, realizing the mistake she'd made, but not knowing how to recover a situation that had backfired badly on her.

His relief turned to anger. 'What in God's name are you doing here?'

'I thought you'd be pleased.' She spoke so quietly that he could hardly hear her. 'I'm sorry if you're not, and I'm sorry I surprised you.'

'You didn't answer my question. Whose idea is this?'

'Mr Linder's – well, and mine too. He thought you could use my help – you know, because of my languages, and because he wasn't sure you'd be able to manage everything by yourself.' She paused. 'And because he decided it'd be best if I left Europe for a while.'

'Wasn't he worried about you getting yourself arrested at the airport before you left?'

She shook her head. 'He called the German police from Chicago and swore I was in Zurich on the day his car caught fire. He told them he knew I was there because he'd spoken to me twice while I was at the office.'

'So the police have decided the car must have been stolen? They believed him?'

'I don't know. But I didn't have any trouble leaving Europe.'

Almost as glad to see her as he was to find she hadn't gone to Austria, McKendrick was beginning to calm down. 'What was all that crap about you going skiing with Harland?' he asked.

'I only said he'd take me; I didn't say I was going. Why would I? He was just being polite. Why would he want me to go anywhere with him?'

If she didn't know, McKendrick wasn't about to enlighten her – particularly now he'd had a chance to have a better look at her.

She was wearing flat-heeled shoes and a plain, long-sleeved summer dress that he imagined was intended to cover up her freckles, but which, if anything, seemed to exaggerate the effect of the ones that were still in view.

'When did you get in?' he said.

'The middle of last night. I caught a flight from Zurich to Santa

Cruz, and then took another one straight here. I was going to phone you when I arrived, but it was too late last night, and when I tried this morning you'd already gone out.'

'Who let you into my room?'

'A nice man in reception.' She smiled slightly. 'I told him I was your sister.'

'And he believed you?'

'He did after I gave him a hundred reais note.' She went to the bureau and picked up an envelope. 'He gave me this for you. Someone left it at the desk. Do you think it's from that man Vicente who Harland wants you to contact?'

'No. I've just been talking to him. Where are you staying?'

'Here. On the fourth floor. Room 402.' She held up the envelope. 'Aren't you going to open it?'

'It'll only be junk mail from some local tourist attraction.' Relieved though he was to see her, McKendrick couldn't help wondering why her boss had sent her all this way when there were plenty of other places in the world where no one would have thought of looking for her.

'What is it Linder figures you can help me with?' he said.

'I've brought some up to date photos of Zitelmann. I copied one from an ICIS brochure and I turned up a couple that were in a magazine that shows him winning a prize for exhibiting some kind of exotic fish. I think it was an African cichlid, but I'm not sure that's right. Shall I go and get them?'

'They don't sound like a good reason for a trip to South America.'

'You didn't let me finish. I've had special link-cables made for my laptop, and I found some clever software that'll allow us to download Kessel's computer records.'

'If she has a computer.'

'You know she has. All that information the DEA have on her comes straight from her computer files – things like her tax returns and her customs applications for importing and exporting her fish.'

'If she has files she doesn't want anyone to see, fancy software isn't going to help,' McKendrick said. 'She'll have them protected with a password. Maria Kessel's a smart operator.'

'She isn't smart enough to know that Mr Linder's been in touch with the Simon Wiesenthal Centre, though, is she? Have you heard of them?'

McKendrick thought he had. 'Is that the Jewish outfit that hunts down Nazi war criminals?'

'Yes. They know more about Hitler's Third Reich and the Nazis than anyone does, so they were able to give Mr Linder a list of passwords for me to try. I don't know if any of them will work, but if there really is a Nazi connection between Zitelmann and Kessel and these weird Christian Freedom Parties, we might be lucky.'

Although she was less ill at ease now she was talking about her own area of expertise, he'd seen how often her eyes were straying to the sofa where the gun was lying.

He went to retrieve it, working the action to unload the rounds before he put it away in a drawer.

'Why did you buy that?' she asked.

'I didn't buy it. It's part of a welcome to Brazil present from Vicente. One gun, twenty rounds of ammunition, a cell phone, a street map of São Paulo and a couple of grams of what looks like cocaine in a plastic bag.'

She raised her eyebrows. 'I can't wait to get mine.'

McKendrick smiled. 'It'd probably be earrings and perfume. Vicente doesn't exactly come across as your neighbourhood bad guy. If you didn't know better you'd pick him for a rich kid just out of college.'

'Have you been talking to him about breaking into Kessel's warehouse?'

'I had a quick drive past it yesterday. I don't think anyone could get inside it without a fair bit of help.'

'How much help?'

'Six thousand dollars worth of Linder's money. You'd better hope he's set up that account with the Banco do Brasil he promised me. I'm going to need the up-front payment by tonight.'

She looked at him. 'I've arrived just in time then, haven't I? I wasn't expecting you to organize things so quickly.'

'And I wasn't expecting you to turn up here.'

'Do you wish I hadn't come?'

McKendrick took the easy way out and changed the subject. 'Did Harland get that stuff I sent him about Kalimantan?' he asked.

'I don't know. He didn't say anything about it, but I've only spoken to him once on the phone since you left. He went back to Bonn the day after you came here.'

Wondering whether it would be worth asking her to e-mail Harland so he could check, he went to open the envelope she'd left on the bureau, assuming it would contain nothing more than another free invitation to another night-club or another strip-joint.

He could not have been more wrong. Inside the envelope was his second surprise for the day.

'What's the matter?' She'd seen his expression change. 'What is it?'

'Our friend Maria knows we're here. It's a note from her.'

'It can't be from her.' Lucy appeared to be equally disconcerted. 'She doesn't know either of us are here.'

'Yes she does. Listen to this. "Dear Senhor McKendrick, to avoid any further misunderstanding, I believe a meeting between us would be of mutual benefit. So, if you are not otherwise engaged, and if your friend is sufficiently recovered from her jet-lag, my assistant and I would be pleased to have coffee with you both tomorrow morning at the San Michel restaurant which you will find on the Rua 13 de Maio near the basilica of Achiropita. It is within easy walking distance of your hotel, and a very public place, so I hope I have chosen well. If I have not, or if you would prefer to meet elsewhere at another time, please phone me at my office. Maria Kessel".'

'Someone's told her,' Lucy said. 'Vicente.'

'He didn't know you were coming. Even I didn't know. Remember what you told me about you finding your way around Germany better than I could?'

'What do you mean?'

'This is the same thing. Kessel's on her own ground. If Harland's people can get hold of airline passenger lists, it'll have been ten times easier for her.'

'That doesn't explain why she wants to talk to us, though – not unless it's a trap.'

The possibility had already occurred to McKendrick. 'I'll check out the restaurant when I go to collect the money from the bank this afternoon,' he said. 'If it's where she says it is, I can't see her trying to pull anything on a busy downtown street – not even in São Paulo.'

'You can't collect the money by yourself.' Lucy spoke quietly. 'I'm supposed to countersign any withdrawals you make over five thousand dollars, and for all you know I could pick up something about the restaurant that you don't.' She paused. 'I also happen to know more about computers than you do.'

Which meant she had every intention of accompanying him tomorrow night as well, he thought, a complication that was unlikely to be met with much enthusiasm by Vicente's men, who would doubtless be as unprepared for the company of a young woman as McKendrick himself had been half an hour ago when he'd found her standing in his room with the sun in her hair like some half-imagined pixie.

The San Michel was more a relic of old São Paulo than it was a restaurant, a tiny but ornate lean-to squashed between two equally old but much larger buildings on the same side of the road as the basilica.

Yesterday afternoon, when they'd carried out their surveillance of the place, all of the outdoor tables had been taken, and the coffee counter had been too crowded for them to have a proper look around inside.

But this morning, even viewed from this far away, McKendrick could see that there were fewer people queuing at the counter, and that many of the outside tables were unoccupied.

What he couldn't see was any sign of Maria Kessel.

Lucy couldn't see her either, squinting in the bright sunlight and using a hand to shield her eyes. 'Do you think it's safe?' she asked.

'Who knows? I thought we were safe when we went to Weiskirchen. I don't want to make that mistake again.' He consulted his watch. 'She's late.'

'No she isn't.' Lucy pointed. 'That's her, isn't it? I recognize her from the photos in Harland's file.'

McKendrick's recognition of Maria Kessel was based not on photos, but on his first-hand encounters with her five weeks ago in the bar and the lobby of his Waikiki hotel. She was more than fifty metres away from him, but he could have picked her out of a crowd at twice the distance.

She'd emerged from the building carrying a cup of coffee and a folded newspaper and was speaking to a man by her side who was less easy to identify.

McKendrick guessed it was Meyer, although if it was, he'd materially changed his appearance since the DEA had taken their photos of him. Unlike Kessel who was well groomed and smartly dressed in a coloured skirt and matching blouse, her male companion looked more like a scruffy European skinhead than a suave cosmopolitan *Paulistano*.

'OK.' McKendrick gave up trying to assess the risk. 'Let me do the talking.'

'That won't get you far if she only speaks Brazilian Portuguese.' Lucy didn't smile. 'Are you still worried?'

He was, almost wishing that he'd asked Vicente to come with them, but unwilling to admit that he could have overlooked the potential for hidden danger.

For her part, Lucy had either decided there wasn't any, or she was making another attempt to demonstrate her newfound confidence, although he hadn't yet decided whether the confidence was in him or in herself, or simply because he'd agreed to let her accompany him tonight. Whatever the reason, she'd been on her best behaviour since yesterday afternoon, enjoying their guarded evening out on the town together as much as he had and showing no reluctance to spend the night alone in her hotel room.

That her confidence could be displaced at any minute had apparently not occurred to her. No longer favouring her bruised foot, she walked with him towards the restaurant, leaving McKendrick to watch out for fast-moving cars and for male pedestrians who exhibited anything more than normal interest in the pretty European girl at his side.

Meyer saw them first. Alerting Kessel, he stood stiffly to attention, waiting for them to approach the table. He was about thirty, as coarse-looking as Kessel was refined, a shaven-headed man who had the red-rimmed eyes and pallor of a heroin addict. In spite of the climate, he was wearing a flight-jacket from which the arms had been cut off, and his tight-fitting jeans were rolled up to reveal the white laces of his combat-boots – the accepted dress code of neo-Nazis who wanted to announce who they were and what they stood for.

Why Maria Kessel would choose to be associated with someone like him was hard to imagine – especially now McKendrick had been able to study her more closely and see how elegantly and expensively dressed she was. She was a striking woman, not just because of her figure or the colour of her skin, but because of her eyes. They were unusually large and almost as dark as her hair, a feature about her that he particularly remembered after Goddard had wrongly identified her as a thousand-dollar-a-night Hawaiian whore.

'Mr McKendrick,' she said. 'How nice that you've brought Ms Mitchell with you.' She allowed herself time to inspect Lucy. 'Do please sit down while I introduce my assistant Jürgen Meyer. Jürgen will be happy to order coffee for you if you'd be kind enough to tell him the kind you'd prefer.'

'We haven't come for coffee.' McKendrick moved a chair up for Lucy and sat down to face Meyer across the table. 'Whatever it is you have to say, just say it. I've got other things to do today.'

Kessel smiled. 'In Brazil we are more polite,' she said. 'But if you are so anxious to discuss business, allow me first to say that I find it difficult to understand why an expert in the field of underground fires should wish to follow me to Europe and now here to Brazil. Why is it you interfere in my affairs?'

'What affairs are those?' McKendrick said.

Kessel's face showed no expression. 'I think you are an intelligent man who is as good at his job as I'm sure Ms Mitchell is at hers, but you are meddling in things which do not concern you.'

'Does that mean we're being more trouble to you and your friends than Dean and Bridget Goddard were? Have you come up with a better solution this time?'

'You may decide for yourself.' Unfolding her newspaper, she removed some photographic prints and slid them across the table. 'I imagine you know who this is.'

Maria Kessel had made a fundamental error. Unaware of what McKendrick had been through in Kalimantan before any of this had started, she'd misjudged his mind-set as badly as she'd underestimated who she was dealing with. Lucy could have told her. And Harland or Linder could have told her. But she hadn't bothered to find out, and as a result she had made a very serious mistake indeed.

On the table in front of McKendrick now were four photographs of his son, two of them taken while Andrew had been on holiday with him in Hawaii, and another two showing the boy leaving the gate of his school in San Diego.

McKendrick was dangerously close to making a mistake of his own. But so hard was Lucy gripping his arm that he was able to remain seated while she gathered up the photos in her other hand and gave them back to Kessel.

'I don't think we need these,' she said quietly.

'As you wish.' Kessel slipped them back inside her newspaper. 'Today is Wednesday,' she said. 'May we agree that you will leave my country before the weekend? Shall we say Sunday at the latest?'

'If we can get on a flight.' Lucy answered the question, realizing that McKendrick was not yet trusting himself to speak.

'Very well.' Kessel stood up. 'And of course, at the same time you are guaranteeing to stop these foolish enquiries you've been making.'

Lucy nodded.

'Then I think our business is complete. I'm sorry you haven't tried the coffee here. It really is very good. If you intend staying on for a while, I recommend the *cafezinho* rather than the *café com leite*, but do ask them not to put too much sugar in it. For Europeans, the *cafezinho* can sometimes be too sweet.' She turned to leave, beckoning to her assistant and glancing briefly at McKendrick before she walked away.

Throughout the meeting, Meyer had uttered not a single word. But now, as he left the table, he made a silly mewing noise and reached out to draw his finger across a line of freckles on Lucy's forehead. 'Like a pretty cat,' he said.

She didn't move. Instead she stared him down, looking at him with such disdain that he couldn't meet her eyes – a response that did more to humiliate him than the direct action McKendrick had been about to take.

McKendrick, though, was still in trouble, struggling to contain his fury and his increasing sense of helplessness, instinctively wanting to lash out, but knowing that there was only one real way to protect his son from a threat that he should have seen coming long ago.

But from here on, protecting Andrew could be nothing more than a first step, he realized. If there had been occasions when he'd doubted his commitment to a cause that had seemed to have less to do with him than it had to do with Linder's hunt for retribution, by introducing Andrew into the equation, Kessel had personalized a fight which McKendrick could never afford to let her win. In Hawaii he had seen Goddard blown to pieces, he'd been shot at in Weiskirchen and he'd nearly been forced to watch Lucy being burned to death in Zerf – reasons enough to harden his resolve. But now the stakes had suddenly and irrevocably become much higher.

Lucy was shaking him. 'McKendrick,' she said, 'listen to me. It'll be all right. No one's going to hurt Andrew. You can phone his mother while I try and contact Harland. We can be back at the hotel in fifteen minutes.'

'I know.'

'And we don't have to break into the warehouse. We won't go tonight.'

'Oh yes we will.' He'd never been so certain of anything. 'We've got this one chance to find out what these sick bastards are up to. If we walk away now, the minute they hit trouble they're going to blame us – and you don't want my son on your conscience any more than I'm ever going to let that happen.'

# Chapter 11

Vicente was not happy. He was standing on the steps outside the hotel, pressing his hand hard against McKendrick's chest. 'This is not part of our agreement,' he said.

'What difference does it make?' McKendrick had expected resistance, but not quite this much.

'There can be more danger if we are to take the girl.'

'She's not a girl. She's older than you are. And her name's Lucy.'

'If there is a problem, she will make things more difficult for us.' Vicente stood his ground.

'No she won't.'

'Then for the additional risk, I require more money – one thousand dollars more.'

Which by a remarkable coincidence just happened to bring the price up to the original figure, McKendrick thought.

'You pay?' Vicente asked.

'Yeah, yeah, I'll pay, but all I have with me is the two thousand you'll be getting at the end of the job. You'll have to wait until tomorrow for the extra thousand. I'll need to get it from the bank.'

'It is OK. I trust you.' Taking Lucy by the arm, Vicente escorted her to the waiting car. 'This is not usual,' he said. 'Last night when I send my driver to collect my down-payment, why did you not introduce yourself and say you are a friend of Senhor McKendrick who wished to accompany us?'

'Senhor McKendrick wasn't certain he needed my help until I explained some things to him.' She slid into the back seat. 'We had a little problem to work out between us first.'

'Ah. You are like me. In my business too, always there are problems.'

Vicente waited for McKendrick to join Lucy in the car, then closed the door and went to sit beside his driver in the front. 'But tonight I promise you there will be none. We travel first by road, then by boat before we go again by road.'

'Why the boat?' McKendrick asked.

'It is a precaution only. On our return journey, if we are to be followed it is always best to have a choice of transport. But please, you must not concern yourself. I have my job to do as you have yours.' Vicente turned his attention back to Lucy. 'You are the close friend of Senhor McKendrick?'

She smiled slightly. 'We're working together. I know about comput-ers.'

'I have seen the one you carry with you. It is very thin.' After check-ing his watch, Vicente instructed his driver to move off. 'At the warehouse I have arranged for us to be undisturbed for one half of an hour,' he said. 'This time will be sufficient for you?'

'We'll see when we get there.' McKendrick had no real idea of how long they'd need. He was finding it hard to concentrate on what he was supposed to be doing, knowing that his efforts to safeguard Andrew had been as thorough as he could possibly make them, but conscious of having to rely on the actions and goodwill of other people.

Lucy had sensed his unease. 'As long as we leave by Sunday, Kessel won't do anything,' she said. 'She'll think she's frightened us off.'

'These people didn't try to frighten off Dean and Bridget Goddard, and those weren't warning shots they fired at us in Weiskirchen.'

'Once Andrew's somewhere safe, no one's going to find him, are they?'

'I don't know. They found out where he goes to school. It depends where Gina's decided to take him.'

'Is Gina the name of your wife?'

'Ex-wife.' He wished he'd taken the time to speak longer to her on the phone. 'Somehow or other, Harland's going to have to sort this out,' he said. 'I can't see how the hell I can fix it by myself. This whole thing is getting way out of hand.'

'Harland will sort it out. He promised he would. I told you what he said on the phone.'

'All he said is that he'd get in touch with Gina and do what he could.

That doesn't necessarily mean he'll involve the DEA. They aren't exactly in the same line of business as the Simon Wiesenthal Centre, are they? Why would the DEA care about any of this?'

'You know why – because of Dean Goddard. Anyway, Harland said all he needs is hard evidence and that's what we've come here to get.'

He was in no mood to remind her that neither of them would be here if it wasn't for her damn boss. Not that it was really Linder's fault, McKendrick thought. Blaming him was about as pointless as blaming Zitelmann's father for being a commandant at the Dachau concentration camp where Linder's grandparents had been gassed to death. History was history, and this was now.

Or was it, he wondered? Was the present being influenced by some lingering legacy from the past? Could people like Quaid and Meyer really be attempting to rekindle the Nazi flame, and if they were, what the hell for, and where did Kessel and Zitelmann fit into things?

At this time of night, the traffic was heavier than it had been during the day, but like the São Paulo taxi drivers, the boy at the wheel had a thorough understanding of the city, avoiding all the main arterials and threading the Ford through a warren of poorly lit back streets while he headed east between the fingers of estuaries and waterways that extended inland from the coast. He was a smooth driver, keeping a watchful eye on his mirror, and only once hesitating when an approaching car braked suddenly ahead of him at an intersection.

McKendrick had long since lost his sense of direction, uncertain of how far they had travelled, and he'd given up trying to guess where and when they would be transferring to the boat.

Lucy seemed similarly confused, peering out into the darkness more and more often in an endeavour to find out where they were. 'Isn't the warehouse in São Paulo?' she asked.

'Depends who you ask.' It had taken McKendrick the best part of two days to appreciate that *Paulistanos* tended to regard the port of Santos as a coastal suburb of their city. 'It's an hour's drive from downtown.'

Vicente wanted to reassure her. 'For us it will not take so long,' he said. 'We lose nothing by splitting our journey. We use a very fast boat that belongs to a friend of mine.'

'Is he taking us?' McKendrick asked.

'In the streets, I know my way; on the water he is better.' Vicente punched a number into his cell phone. 'I tell him we are coming. In less than five minutes we shall be on board. Please to be patient.'

McKendrick wasn't impatient: he was concerned – not so much about the arrangements, but because he was uncertain of what to do if tonight's exercise turned out to be a waste of time.

If it did, it wasn't going to be the fault of Vicente's transport.

Moored halfway along one of the narrower estuaries at the end of a concrete pier, a seven-metre-long, gleaming, glass-hulled launch was waiting for them, its engine idling with the deep-throated throb of a marine V8.

The boy parked the car on the pier itself, opening the door politely for Lucy while Vicente unloaded two Kalashnikov assault rifles from the boot.

'You wish to be armed?' He offered one of the guns to McKendrick.

'Why do we need these?'

'They are in case we are to cross the paths of men who make a night delivery of cocaine to one of the big ships, but we use them only if they fire upon us first.'

'I'm paying you good money,' McKendrick said. 'If we run into trouble, I expect you to get us out of it.'

'Of course. The chances are very slight.' Vicente helped Lucy on board the launch and introduced her to a swarthy dark-skinned man who was standing at the helm. 'This is Claudio,' he said, 'but you may call him Cacão.'

Unlike Vicente, Cacão was a man of few words. After showing Lucy to a seat on the port side and exchanging pleasantries with the car driver who was apparently remaining behind to guard the Ford, he shook hands with McKendrick then cast off, checked his instruments and switched on a powerful halogen lamp that was mounted on a hatch at the bow.

Vicente went to stand beside Lucy. 'You will enjoy this, I think,' he said. 'If the mosquitoes are bothering you, I promise they will not be able to keep up with us.'

He was right. McKendrick had been in fast boats before, but not at night and never in one that had anything like this level of performance.

Once the launch had cleared the pier and was free of the areas of matted weed that grew along the edges of the estuary, Cacão spun the wheel and opened the throttles wide.

For a second, as the big V8 began to roar, the bow rose up. Then, just as suddenly, the hull flattened out and started to accelerate, gathering speed at a rate that not only left the most determined of the mosquitoes behind, but everything else as well.

In places, the estuary was no wider than forty or fifty metres, flanked by sandbanks and the remains of old wharves and rotting piles, hazards that in daylight would have been easy enough to see, but which, at night, seemed to swim out of nowhere without warning, illuminated only briefly before they were swallowed up again in the darkness to be battered by the swell from the bow wave and from the rooster tail that was fountaining up behind them.

It took McKendrick several minutes to become accustomed to the speed, by which time he'd decided that it was to some extent an illusion created by the restricted width of the light beam and by their proximity to the shore.

But the experience was still exhilarating, and despite a disgusting smell from the churned up water, Lucy had a broad smile on her face.

After travelling for nearly twenty minutes within the confines of the estuary, they at last reached open water where, instead of sandbanks and wharves, the hazards were fewer but much larger, most taking the form of tankers and freighters riding at anchor without lights.

The smaller ships were the easiest to see, looking less like lumps of headland in the patchy moonlight, but Cacão was still being forced to rely on his light, swinging it from side to side in order to pick out the odd dinghies and row boats that were going about their business quietly in the darkness.

He'd reduced speed substantially, heading for a block of rectangular shadows that McKendrick imagined were buildings on the Santos waterfront, although none of them seemed to be familiar, and as yet he had no idea at which end of the waterfront they might be landing.

Cacão, though, knew exactly where he was, edging the launch closer to the shadows until he could see clearly enough to switch off his light.

The jetty where they disembarked was in one of the heavily industrialized districts that McKendrick thought he recognized.

There were cranes everywhere, a forest of them towering over the jetty, their steel girders casting criss-crossed shadows across a concrete apron upon which stood hundred upon hundreds of shipping containers.

Not far from the jetty, between two container rows, their second car was parked.

'I am sorry not to have provided a better vehicle.' Vicente ushered them over to it. 'But since we have only a short distance to travel, I think you will not be too uncomfortable.' Taking McKendrick's Kalashnikov from him he placed it beside his own on the front seat. 'Please to get in.'

The car was a five year-old Chevrolet, well used and smelling powerfully of fresh marijuana and damp carpet. The interior trim had been removed to reduce weight and create more space, a rev counter and a state-of-the-art radar detector were screwed to the dashboard, and a pair of nitrous-oxide cylinders occupied the passenger-side footwell at the front.

McKendrick waited until they'd pulled away from the container terminal before he asked Vicente how far they had to go.

'We could have walked, but at night in this part of Santos it is not always so safe on foot. There.' Vicente pointed at a street sign. 'You see?'

The sign was not the one McKendrick had come across yesterday. But it had Rua Sabastião written on it, which probably meant they were entering the street from the other end, he decided. 'Do we just drive up to the warehouse and let ourselves in?' he asked.

'I shall enquire.' Vicente used his cell phone again, slowing the car to walking pace while he checked with someone.

Since leaving the boat, Lucy had said nothing and by now the smile had faded from her face, presumably because she, too, was apprehensive, McKendrick thought, although for her own reasons. Like him, she'd be wondering how successful they were going to be, but she'd also be aware of her surroundings and have realized the kind of neighbourhood she was in.

'We are early.' Vicente put away his phone. 'So you will have seven minutes more than the half an hour that first I promise you.' Swinging the Chevrolet into an alley beside the warehouse, he switched his head-lights to high beam.

'What are you looking for?' McKendrick asked.

'We are to use a side entrance. The other doors stay locked. It is that one over there, I think.' He let the car coast to a halt and turned off the ignition. 'You see now how well I spend your money?'

'Are the alarms off?'

'I shall see.' Kalashnikov at the ready, Vicente went on ahead, confidently opening the door and disappearing inside.

Giving McKendrick her laptop to hold, Lucy started coiling the link-cables around her arm to make them easier to carry. 'Are you going to bring the other gun?' she asked.

'Not unless Vicente wants me to. He's supposed to be looking after us. I don't want to spend all my time keeping watch for you.'

Vicente had completed his investigation and was standing in the doorway with his rifle held loosely at his side. 'You may come in,' he said. 'Everything is clear.' He pressed a button on his watch. 'Please remember that in thirty-five minutes a security patrol car will return, so by then you must have finished and we should be gone from here.'

McKendrick had brought two flashlights with him, expecting the interior of the building to be in darkness. But it wasn't.

High above each aisle between the rows of fish tanks, low-wattage fluorescent tubes were bathing the whole warehouse in an eerie blue light. The place was also far from silent.

A background hum from the air-conditioning system was being overlayed by the whirring of electric motors that were driving a multitude of aerators, filtration units, protein skimmers and recirculating pumps.

The set-up was both sophisticated and extensive, a fully automated, climatically controlled environment that was as spotlessly clean as any hospital. The aquariums were equally impressive. There were dozens of them; tanks containing fresh-water fish, tanks for salt-water fish, small tanks, large ones, some as long as five metres, and all filled with crystal clear water and so cleverly aquascaped that they gave the impression of being three dimensional paintings of a brightly-coloured underwater world.

Vicente showed no interest in them; evidently anxious for his clients to get on with the job they'd come to do. 'I am told you will find the office at the top of some wooden stairs on the north side of the building,' he said.

'I can see them.' Lucy took her laptop from McKendrick.

'Do you want a hand?'

'No.' She headed off by herself.

'Hang on a second. I'll have a look around before you try to find out where Kessel keeps her computer.' He went up the stairs ahead of her and opened the door to a small, whitewashed room.

Locating the computer was easy. In a corner of the office, standing on a desk was a PC, still switched on and displaying a coloured *Arowana* logo on its screen.

'How about some more light?' McKendrick checked for windows.

'It's all right. There's enough coming from the monitor.' Lucy placed the cables and her laptop on the desk, but instead of sitting down, she walked over to inspect some shelving at the rear of the room.

'Come and look at this,' she said.

The shelving occupied an entire wall and was crammed from floor to ceiling with the most unlikely junk.

Stacked untidily on the top three shelves was a huge selection of disposable paper cups, plastic cups and cardboard cups. There were throwaway coffee cups from Starbucks, cups from McDonald outlets in America, Canada and Mexico; polystyrene versions from Eastern and Western Europe, and dozens more bearing the names of soft drinks from almost every country in the world.

Alongside them, and on the lower shelves were scattered small unopened sachets of salt, pepper, sugar, artificial sweeteners, coffee whiteners, mustard and tomato sauce, together with boxes overflowing with teabags, beer mats, table napkins and even plastic airline cutlery.

'Maria Kessel's a kleptomaniac.' Lucy examined the contents of a box. 'She must keep everything from every trip she goes on.'

'Unless she gives it away to a local school or something.' McKendrick couldn't imagine anyone hoarding such worthless stuff.

'I know what they're for.' Lucy held up a teabag. 'This is how she smuggles her drugs.'

'It's pretty hard to hide cocaine in the rim of a cardboard cup or in the handle of a plastic spoon.' He checked his watch. 'You'd better see what you can dig out of her computer. We haven't got that long.'

'I don't want you watching me. I work better if I'm alone.'

'OK. Let me know if you need a hand.' McKendrick returned to the ground floor and went to join Vicente who had been exploring by himself.

'She is successful?' he enquired.

'She's just starting. Is there anything to see except fish down here?'

'There is a tank for octopus, and one for some spotted frogs. And I find another for land frogs whose name in English I do not know.'

'Toads?'

Vicente shrugged. 'I am not so familiar with the names of these animals. But I see little lizards in a glass box that has a sign to say it contains California rough-skinned newts. You understand what a newt is?'

'More or less. You didn't trip over any drums with phenol written on them, did you?' The question was so stupid that McKendrick wished he hadn't asked it.

Vicente shook his head. 'You go to look,' he said. 'I shall remain here to make sure no one comes to interfere with your work.'

Over the next ten minutes, McKendrick was able to satisfy himself that, at face value at least, Kessel was operating nothing more and nothing less than a well-run aquarium fish business.

Apart from an alcove housing an octopus tank and some landscaped terrariums for the toads and newts, the rest of the building was given over entirely to fish of every conceivable size, colour and kind.

How many of them there were, he couldn't begin to estimate. For every tank of cyprinids, anabantoids, oscars, killifish, shubunkins, veil tails, bubble eyes and characins, there were an equal number containing varieties that McKendrick had never heard of, and had certainly never seen, some fiercely coloured, others with long feelers or wonderful fan-like tails.

But nowhere was there a scrap of evidence to connect *Arowana* to either Günter Zitelmann in Germany or to Justin Quaid in Alabama. Which meant that, rather as he'd thought, everything was going to depend on Lucy.

Conscious of how quickly the time was ticking away, he went to see how she was getting on.

He should have stayed downstairs. Instead of her being busy at her computer keyboard, she was sitting with her hands on her lap, and the cables she'd brought were strewn across the floor where they'd been discarded.

'Problems?' McKendrick stepped over them.

'My software doesn't work. It won't interrogate the hard drive.' She consulted a piece of paper on the desk beside her.

'What are you doing, then?'

'I've put my floppy disk into Kessel's PC. If I ever get through to the confidential files we want, I can send the information straight to that.' She glanced up. 'But my passwords aren't working either.'

'Have you found anything at all?'

'Only her fish transaction records. I've already transferred those, but they aren't going to help us.' She entered another password.

'Any good?' McKendrick asked.

'No.'

'How about translating your German passwords into Portuguese?'

'I'd be better off translating them into English. Kessel keeps her records in English, but I don't think she'd protect her files with a translated password. How much time do I have?'

'About twelve minutes. How many words do you have left to try?'

'All of these in the second column.' She showed him on the sheet of paper. 'I don't think any of them are going to get me in, though.'

'You don't know that.' He could almost see her confidence draining away. 'Just take it easy and keep going.'

She keyed in a word from the head of the column, then slammed her hand down on the desk in frustration when the rejected sign appeared on the screen again.

McKendrick intervened, choosing a word at random. 'What does *Nibelungen* mean?'

'It's a Wagnerian opera that's supposed to have been one of the sources of Hitler's inspiration.' She tried it without success.

'How about *Schutzstaffen*?'

She entered it. 'That's just the German name of the Nazi SS, but I don't think it'll be any good.'

It wasn't. Nor were the next three, by which time Lucy was red-faced, and McKendrick had stopped looking at his watch, believing now that they could indeed have come here for nothing.

Knowing it wasn't her fault and wanting to show her that it wasn't, he leaned over her shoulder, selected the longest word on her list and keyed in the letters SICHERHEITSDIENST.

There was no reason for the gamble to have paid off. But against all his expectations, it had.

In place of the flashing reject sign, suddenly the screen was displaying a new menu altogether:

## PROTECTED FILES

- Kessel 1. Middle East Recruitment
- Kessel 2. Ya-ba methamphetamine, Cocaine, Ecstasy, Heroin
- Kessel 3. Christian Freedom Party

The titles of the first two files were self-explanatory, and the third one could hold some promise, McKendrick thought. But he remained cautious, hoping Lucy would be able to transfer the data to her disk, but not yet sure that she could.

She had no such doubts, quickly repositioning herself at the desk and clicking on to each of the headings in turn before she hit the send key. 'Tell me that was a guess,' she said.

'What?'

'*Sicherheitsdienst*. It's the name of the Nazi SS Political Intelligence Department. I should've tried it first, shouldn't I?' She was more relieved than he was. 'Is there time for us to see what we've got?'

'Only if you're certain it's on your disk.'

She smiled at him. 'Don't you trust me?'

'Just do a quick scroll through,' McKendrick said. 'Vicente's going to be dragging us out of here at any second.'

The first of the files was little more than a list of names, medical records and the US dollar prices Kessel had received for hundreds of the infected girls she'd sold to brothels and private clients in the Middle East.

The second file was longer, a comprehensive record of her narcotics business, showing that she was making nearly five times more profit

from drugs than she was from girls, although several entries were anno-
tated with the words 'purity contamination' and highlighted losses, one
of them to the United Arab Emirates for an eye-watering $300,000.

As well as being unlike the other two, the third file was more interesting. Instead of listing the purchase and selling prices of
Brazilian-sourced girls or drugs, this one was some kind of manifesto
– a statement of purpose for an organization called the Coalition of
Christian Freedom Parties.

McKendrick had barely read beyond the introduction when Vicente
appeared in the doorway.

'Please, you must stop now,' he said. 'It is not good for us to stay here
longer.'

He walked over to find out what they were looking at, but Lucy had
seen him coming and had already removed her disk and reset the
computer to bring up the *Arowana* logo on the screen again.

'So you have finished?' Vicente asked her.

'Not quite, but it's all right.' She fastened the catches on her laptop
and stood up to show she was ready to leave. 'I'm sorry I've taken so
long.'

'It is not such a problem, but we should hurry now.' Vicente helped
her gather up the cables from the floor, then set off down the stairs.
'You prefer to return by boat, or will I drive you back to São Paulo in
the car?'

'Doesn't that depend on whether anyone decides to follow us?'
McKendrick said.

'For the moment I am told that the area is safe for us, so you may
choose.'

'Which is quicker?'

'Because we make good time coming here, I think the boat is faster.'

'OK.' At the foot of the stairway, McKendrick stopped to take a
final look around. 'I need you to make sure your people relock every
door and reactivate the alarm system,' he said.

'Of course. Just as there can be some risk for you if this woman
Kessel learns that someone has been here, so for me and for those I pay
for their work tonight it is better if no one is to know.' Vicente opened
the door for Lucy and walked with her to the car. 'I wish to apologize
for my rudeness when first we are introduced,' he said. 'You must

forgive me. I am not accustomed to doing business with young women, but tonight it has been my pleasure.'

'You weren't rude.' She smiled at him.

'I think the Santos dockyard is not such a pleasant place to visit, so if you and Senhor McKendrick have the time to spare, on another day I would be most happy to show you the more beautiful parts of my city. Perhaps tomorrow, when you bring me the extra money I ask for looking after you, I may take you to the Ibirapuera, or drive you to Atibaia in the mountains.'

Lucy smiled again. 'That's very kind, but I'm not sure we'll be able to. If we can, though, that would be really nice.'

'Then I shall wait for your telephone call in the morning so we may arrange to meet somewhere.' Vicente lit a cigarette. 'But first I must return you safely to your hotel tonight.' He entered a number on his phone. 'I shall tell Cacão he should prepare the boat ready to receive us.'

Hoping to speed things up, McKendrick had already installed himself in the car, aware that the whole exercise had gone rather too smoothly, and anxious for them to leave the area before something could go wrong.

But as long as nothing did, this had been a pretty damn good night's work, he thought. If he was right – if the last of Kessel's private files was truly what it seemed to be, as well as solving the problem of Andrew's safety, it looked as though he'd found the best possible way of protecting Lucy too.

He was only partly right.

Two hours later, sitting beside her on the sofa in her hotel bedroom, McKendrick was staring at the screen of her laptop in disbelief, reading and re-reading the most profoundly chilling document he had ever seen.

# Chapter 12

As though she couldn't believe what she was reading either, Lucy was skipping from one part of the document to another, searching out individual paragraphs to make certain she understood the implications and scrolling through the text too rapidly for McKendrick to keep up.

'Stop it.' He blocked her keyboard with his hand. 'Go back to the beginning. Bring up one section at a time.'

'Not until we've e-mailed the whole thing to Mr Linder. I don't like us being the only two people who are looking at this. It's giving me the creeps.'

'You'd better e-mail it to Harland too, then, Can you do that?'

She nodded. 'It'll only take a second.'

'OK.' He tried to clear his mind, wanting to persuade himself that his interpretation of the document could not possibly be correct, but already knowing they'd stumbled on something he'd never dreamed existed.

This wasn't simply the justification for Linder's suspicions, he realized – not just the reason for the threat to Andrew, or an explanation for the events of the last five weeks – but something of such wide-ranging significance that he could no more come to grips with it than he could come to grips with the frightening insight it provided into events that were apparently already starting to be played out on an international stage.

'All done.' Lucy pressed a key on her laptop. 'If you want to go through it section by section, you can do the scrolling.'

Displayed on the screen again now was Kessel's File 3, the document that McKendrick was beginning to think looked more like a declaration of war than a statement of purpose from an organization that claimed to have Christian roots.

This time he read the text more slowly, endeavouring to distance himself from the rhetoric in order to more accurately analyse its meaning:

### Coalition of Christian Freedom Parties

### INTERNATIONAL MANIFESTO
(Numbered copy 0140)

*This document should be kept in a safe place by senior party leaders and may be disclosed in its entirety only to active members of covert cells for the purposes of recruitment or motivation. At your discretion, the contents of Section 1 may be released to the media or to organizations sympathetic to the concept of the New Crusade. Disclosure of information from all other sections is prohibited, and as a holder of this referenced copy, you are accountable for maintaining an adequate level of security when accessing its contents outside the US or European headquarters of the CFP.*

### 1. THE FIVE PILLARS OF TRUTH

- Islam is a religion in which Allah requires you to send your son to die for Him. Christianity is a faith in which God sends His son to die for you.
- The Prophet Muhammad is dead. Jesus Christ arose from the dead and is alive.
- The Muslim practice of mutilating female genitalia (circumcision) is a barbaric violation of human rights.
- Islamic Shari'a law permits public executions, the stoning of adulterers and the amputation of human limbs for offences as slight as minor theft.
- By declaring their willingness to conduct a Holy War or Jihad by any means (chemical, biological, nuclear or conventional), Islamic extremists pose a threat to global peace on a scale the world has never seen before.

*Note: Pamphlets illustrating this section are available for public distribution from Christian Freedom Party offices in your country and in your language.*

## 2. BACKGROUND PERSPECTIVE

In spite of continuing efforts to combat atrocities executed by terrorist groups such as al-Qaeda and Jemma Islamiah, the inter-national Christian community has failed in its attempts to stem the rising tide of Islamic fanaticism and, as a consequence, has begun a futile search for diplomatic answers.

Experienced theologians who have been studying this problem for the last nine years are unanimous in their conclusions and state unequivocally that no reduction in the level of threat can or will ever come from initiatives of a diplomatic kind.

Instead, the solution lies where, historically, it always has done – in the hands of Christian people themselves. In the twenty-first century, they alone can influence the political landscape to the degree that is necessary to meet the challenge of Jihad, but only if Arab nations are first made weak, and only if Christians are suffi-ciently aroused by what are *perceived* to be acts of extreme malevolence perpetrated against them and their children in the name of Islam.

## 3. STRATEGY

In accordance with the Rosenberg Principle therefore, the Coalition of Christian Freedom Parties is committed to:

- Establishing worldwide political organizations to promote the Five Pillars of Truth and to draw public attention to all fresh acts of Islamic violence.
- Undermining Muslim society by the distribution of addictive drugs throughout the Middle East, and by the introduction of sexually transmitted disease which Arab nations are tradi-tionally slow to recognize and ill-equipped to handle.
- Implementing the TTX Programme in order to inflame anti-Islamic sentiment to a point where public demand for a New

Crusade will force western governments to crush Arab aspirations for the next two decades.

*Note: To avoid the political backlash that accompanied the 2003 invasion of Iraq, Coalition members should be made to understand that the TTX Programme has been developed to generate a precisely opposite effect whereby governments will be incapable of ignoring the resultant public clamour for international military action.*

## 4. THE TTX PROGRAMME

| Date | Country | Co-ordination | Target |
| --- | --- | --- | --- |
| Nov 22 | France | Partie Chretiénne de Liberté | Fallièrs |
| Nov 23 | USA | Christian Freedom Party | Bowden |
| Nov 24 | Spain | Partido Christiano De la Libertad | Pattullo |
| Dec 5 | Germany | Christliches Frieheit Beteilgtes | St Catherine's |
| Dec 5 | Italy | Partito Christiano Di Liberta | St Gabriel's |
| Dec 12 | UK | Christian Freedom Party | To be advised |
| Dec 12 | USA | Christian Freedom Party | To be advised |
| Dec 25 | Await further CFP instructions | | To be advised |

*Note: For reasons of authenticity, false 'Claims of Responsibility' for each target must appear to come from appropriate Islamic terrorist groups, and should be posted on the internet or supplied to the media from non-traceable Middle East addresses and be in Arabic only.*

## 5. THE FUTURE

For the sake of your children and the children of those who share your values, your morality and your faith, over the next two years the Coalition will greatly expand its influence.

Using the lessons of political and public coercion learned from the TTX Programme, a powerful stage two strategy will be launched that will leave the governments of predominantly Christian countries no choice but to remobilize and refocus the already established forces of the New Crusade in order to forever rid the world of the Jewish scourge, and in so doing, at last fulfil the vision of our forebears. May God bless us and be with us in this cause, and may He rejoice in our success. Amen.

## 6. DISTRIBUTION

Those CFPs listed in Section 4 plus:
- Partido Christian Da Liberdades, Portugal and Brazil
- CFP Canada and CFP Australia
- Partido Christiano De la Libertad, Mexico

Lucy leaned back in the sofa and put her hands behind her head. 'Well,' she said, 'now we know.'

'No we don't.' The longer McKendrick considered the Section 3 strategy, the more insidious it seemed to be. 'We don't know what the Rosenberg Principle is,' he said. 'We don't know what TTX stands for or what the targets are, and there's not a single thing in here to connect Zitelmann or ICIS with this Coalition of Christian Freedom Party outfit.'

'I mean that we know what we're dealing with now.' Lucy shivered. 'Whoever wrote this has to be really sick. I didn't realize there were people who thought this way.'

'It hasn't been written by any one person,' McKendrick said. 'It's been written by a bunch of fanatics, and they haven't just been thinking about it. This is a hard plan. If those November dates are right, the first three TTX targets have already been hit.'

'I can check on the Internet to see what they were. If Arab terrorists are being blamed for things that happened last week in France, America and Spain, there'll be reports on websites everywhere.' She paused for a moment. 'But none of the claims of responsibility will be true, will they?'

'No, but everyone in the West is going to believe they are. That's how this thing works. The Coalition choses the targets. They organize the hits – then they make damn sure that Islamic extremists get blamed for what's happened.'

'It still doesn't mean thousands of people are going to start pressuring western governments to launch some kind of crazy new crusade against the Arabs, though, does it?'

McKendrick hoped she was right. 'Depends what the targets are,' he said. 'If they're anything like the Twin Towers or the Madrid trains or the Bali nightclub, Quaid will have his crusade up and running in a couple of months. He'll have more rednecks wanting to join up than he'll know what to do with.'

'And get even more once the CFP start nudging public opinion against Israel and the Jews.' Lucy stretched her arms. 'I don't even want to think about that.'

'Think about this, then.' He pointed to the first paragraph of Section 3. 'Establish worldwide political organizations. That's what Quaid's busy doing.'

'So what?'

'Bear with me. If that's Quaid's responsibility, then this next bit is the job description for our friend Maria.' He moved his finger down the screen. 'Undermine Muslim society by distributing addictive drugs and by introducing sexually transmitted disease into Arab countries. According to her receipts, that's what she's been doing for the last six years with her drugs and the HIV infected girls she's selling into the Middle East – which leaves us with the last paragraph and with one more major player to place.'

Lucy looked doubtful. 'Are you saying Zitelmann's running this TTX Programme, whatever it is?'

'Somebody's running it.' Scrolling back to Section 2, McKendrick read part of it out loud. 'Experienced theologians who have been studying this problem for the last nine years are unanimous in their conclusions. Doesn't that sound like Zitelmann to you?'

'Only because the nine years is right.' She studied the paragraph for herself. 'I know that's how long ago he started up ICIS, but I don't think it proves anything.'

'Proof isn't going to make any difference one way or the other,' McKendrick said. 'It's public perception that matters. Who the hell's going to believe a religious institute could be mixed up with a plan to infect the Arab world with AIDS?'

Instead of answering him, Lucy had begun reciting the first of the *Five Pillars of Truth* under her breath. 'Harland read this out to us when we were at Emily's,' she said.

'He'd have seen it in one of those pamphlets the CFP say they hand out. It's a load of crap – just a way to make people think all Muslims are raving extremists. If you sat down with a copy of the Old Testament you'd find enough quotes to make you wonder why anyone would want to be a Christian. This isn't about religion: it's just a new twist to the old Aryan racial garbage the Nazis came up with sixty years ago.'

She smiled at him. 'I'm not going to sit down and do anything. I'm going to have some breakfast sent up for us. What would you like?'

So quickly had the time been passing that he hadn't realized it was morning. 'I don't care as long as the coffee's fresh and there's plenty of it,' he said.

'You don't have to worry about coffee being fresh in Brazil.' She left the sofa and was about to call room service when the phone began to ring.

McKendrick guessed it might be Harland, but he was wrong. Lucy had answered in English, but had already switched to German.

She beckoned to him. 'It's Mr Linder. He wants to talk to you.'

'Has he read the e-mail?'

'Yes.' She gave him the receiver.

'Hi,' McKendrick said. 'Looks as though you were right all along.'

'So it seems, although it's hard to take much pleasure from it. On the other hand, I suppose we should be glad to find ourselves in a position where we finally know what's going on.'

'Which is why you're calling,' McKendrick said.

'Indeed. I'm leaving Chicago within the hour, and I've already been in touch with Craig Harland in Bonn, so I'd like you and Lucy to be back in Zurich for a meeting with us on Monday afternoon. Can you manage that?'

'We need to leave here before tomorrow night anyway,' McKendrick said. 'I don't want Kessel thinking we've overstepped her deadline. We'll book our flights this morning. Did Harland mention Andrew?'

'Forgive me. I should have dealt with that first, shouldn't I? As I understand it, the American DEA have assigned someone to look after your son and his mother who, as far as I know, are both safe and well.

I'm sorry I don't know the exact details of where they've been taken, but I imagine Harland will be able to tell you.' Linder coughed discreetly. 'Unless of course you prefer not to know until we've refined our thoughts about the Rosenberg Principle and learned more about this TTX Programme, so we can do something about it.'

'Have you any idea what TTX is?' McKendrick asked.

'Not yet, but by Monday I'll have more information on the deaths of Father Fallièrs, Senator Bowden and that Spanish newspaper editor, Pattullo. I'm hoping that will help us. Have you or Lucy had any thoughts about what TTX could be, or what it stands for?'

'No.' McKendrick made the effort to catch up. 'We hadn't even got as far as figuring out that the first three targets were people.'

'I expect you've had rather less opportunity to watch TV than I've had. They were definitely people, I'm afraid. Fallièrs, Bowden and Pattullo were well-known public figures who shared a dislike of all things Islamic. They made no excuses for their views, which made them ideal victims, I suppose. As I'm sure you can guess, there's an international outcry over their deaths. CNN are screening back to back stories in Europe and the States about how claims of responsibility have been received from three different Muslim terrorist groups in three different countries, but most of the coverage is being generated by people like Quaid and his supporters.'

'Is Quaid shouting about his new crusade yet?'

'No, but I guarantee he will soon. He's either waiting for the pot to boil over, or for December 5th when the CFP are scheduled to bring down their next two targets.'

'What's the reaction been?' McKendrick asked.

'Nothing too serious so far. Some mosques in France have been fire-bombed, and a couple of Spanish policemen were injured while they were trying to stop a crowd from pulling down a fence outside the Saudi Embassy in Madrid, but that's about all. It's getting worse, though.'

'What's it like in the States?'

'Quiet enough here in Chicago, but there's been a bit of trouble in Los Angeles and New York. Arab shopkeepers have had their windows smashed and late last night some of the TV channels were running a story about five members of a Muslim family who were killed when a truck driver deliberately ran his rig into their car outside a gas station in Minnesota somewhere.'

'Are any terrorist groups denying they were responsible?' McKendrick could guess what the answer was going to be.

'It wouldn't do them any good if they did. The public doesn't know the claims are fictitious. Once people read something on the Internet or in the papers they want to believe it, and after all the propaganda they've been fed since September 11, Americans tend to regard all Muslims as potential terrorists.' Linder paused. 'Which could present us with a problem. I don't think people are in a mood to believe in an anti-Islamic conspiracy, let alone in one that has an anti-Semitic component built into it.'

'So how are you going to stop this thing from growing more heads?'

'If I knew how to do that, I wouldn't be seeking your help. Harland has some ideas, but I'd rather not discuss them until we're all together. I presume I can count on your support?'

'I'll let you know on Monday.'

'Mr McKendrick, you don't have to remind me that you're your own man. If I thought otherwise I would never have asked for your assistance to begin with, and I certainly have no wish to coerce you into anything. Whatever you decide is entirely up to you, but I'd still like you to know how grateful I am for what you've done – and for looking after Lucy, too. I tried my hardest to dissuade her from joining you in Brazil, but I imagine you've already found out for yourself what a strong-willed young woman she can be at times. Now, is there anything more we need to talk about before I go and catch my plane?'

'Nothing that can't wait.' McKendrick was thinking of something quite different. 'Have a nice flight. I'll see you in Zurich.' Wondering how much of the conversation Lucy had overheard, he replaced the receiver and tried to see if she was looking uncomfortable.

'What's the matter?' She returned his stare.

'Nothing – only that Linder wants us back in Europe right away.'

'We can book our flights when we go to pick up Vicente's money from the bank. What was all that about Fallièrs, Bowden and Pattullo?'

'I'll tell you after you've ordered our breakfast. If I don't get some coffee inside me, my brain's going to stop working altogether.'

'Don't you want to go through the manifesto again?' She smiled.

'Once more and you ought to know the *Five Pillars of Truth* off by heart.'

'There aren't any *Five Pillars of Truth.*' He went to her laptop and unplugged it. 'Remember me saying how you were so busy trying to be smart that you might have started believing you were?'

She nodded. 'Now you know how clever I really am, is this where you apologize to me for being rude?'

'No.' He put his hands on her shoulders. 'This is where you stop playing games. Linder said he tried to talk you out of coming here, but that you wouldn't listen to him. I want to know why?'

'No you don't.' She wriggled free, picked up the phone and pushed the button for room service. 'I don't have to explain myself to you. I don't work for you: I work for Linder International. Anyway, this isn't the right time to talk about it, is it – not when we have so much to do?'

The way things were going, there wouldn't be a right time, McKendrick thought, which, judging by her expression, seemed to be fine by her – unless she was simply annoyed at being found out, or maybe warning him off by pretending to have misunderstood his question.

After a return trip to Santos in the dark, and after spending too many hours peering at the screen of Lucy's laptop, being out in the sunshine of a bright São Paulo morning was allowing McKendrick to review what they had learned from something of a fresh perspective.

What last night had seemed to be a document so shot through with hate and echoes of the Nazi past that, like Lucy, he'd begun to wonder how people could have ever written it, seemed in the light of day to be less monstrous.

But the manifesto was still the key, he thought. If there was any truth in the cliché about knowledge being power, then maybe Linder now had the means to prevent the Christian Freedom Party movement from duping the public into believing in the threat of an imminent Islamic Jihad.

Lucy had been equally glad to get out in the sunshine. Despite her lack of sleep, she'd been in good spirits during their drive to the bank, doing her best to navigate until McKendrick had finally driven the Volkswagen up over the kerb and parked outside the glass-fronted

Lufthansa office that had taken them the best part of half an hour to find.

She'd gone in to buy the tickets by herself, but that had been ten minutes ago – long enough for him to start wondering if he should be looking for somewhere less inconsiderate to park.

There was no need. She was coming, hurrying over to get back in the car.

'Any problems?' he asked.

'No. I booked us business class. I thought that would be all right.'

He grinned. 'Are you trying to save some of Linder International's money?'

'That's not fair. Even Mr Linder doesn't always travel first class. I didn't think you'd mind.'

'I don't. What time's our flight?'

'Eleven thirty tonight. Check in at ten.' She waited for him to reverse out into the traffic, then settled back in her seat. 'We ought to go back to the hotel before we find out where Vicente wants us to drop off his money.'

'Why?'

'In case Harland's left a message, or there might have been another call or an e-mail from Mr Linder.'

McKendrick had a better idea. 'Why don't we take Vicente up on his offer to show us around?'

'Do you mean it?'

'Sure. Of course I mean it. I don't see why you and I should spend the rest of today worrying about something we can't do a hell of a lot about. Anyway, we deserve some time off, don't you think?'

'Mm. Yes I do. It's still early too, so we might have time to go up to Atibaia.'

'Give him a call, then. Did you bring that cell phone he gave me?'

'It's here.' She took it from the glove box. 'What's the number of his mobile?'

'It's on the back – written on a piece of tape. Tell him we've got his thousand dollars and say that, if it's OK with him, we'd like him to drive us up to the mountains.' McKendrick wound down his window. 'At least we'll be in an air-conditioned car instead of this heap of junk.'

'It'll be cooler in the mountains anyway.' She punched in the

162

number. 'Atibaia's supposed to be the strawberry capital of Brazil. It says so in one of those brochures in the hotel lobby. You didn't know that, did you?'

He didn't reply.

'Did you hear what I said?'

'Yes, I heard. Is his number ringing?'

'There's no answer. He's probably still in bed.'

McKendrick didn't think so. 'Listen,' he said.

'To what?'

'Just listen.'

'I don't know what you . . . . Oh.' Her voice tailed away.

'Can you hear it?'

She nodded nervously.

'Redial the number.' He wound up his window to block out the traffic noise.

This time there was no mistaking the muffled sound of a phone ringing from somewhere inside the car.

Lucy had gone pale and was biting her lip. 'It's coming from the boot,' she said quietly. 'We have to look.'

'We can't. Not here.' Telling himself he was jumping to conclusions, he began searching for an alley or a lay-by where it would be safe to stop, driving without thinking about where he was going until he pulled into a small service road at the rear of a derelict factory.

'I'll go.' Lucy opened her door.

'No you won't.' He stopped her. 'I'll do it.'

Vicente's body was lying in a foetal position, a note pinned to the lapel of his jacket, his knees drawn up against his chest, his feet wedged against the side of a wheel well.

There was no blood on his face and his left eye was wide open, but where his other eye should have been, the shattered bone of an empty socket showed where the bullet had entered his skull.

After removing the note, McKendrick forced himself to search for powder burns, leaning over in the boot, but recoiling at the sight of the exit wound.

Vicente had been shot with a hollow-point, a soft-nosed bullet that had blown half the back of his head away, taking his life from him as swiftly as Jusaf's bullet had taken Kalyem's life from her.

Another fucking execution, McKendrick thought, and another unnecessary death, although, mercifully, he hadn't been a witness to this one, and unlike Kalyem, Vicente wouldn't have suffered or known much about it.

The click of the passenger door warned him that Lucy was coming to see.

Quickly he slammed down the boot lid and turned round.

'It's Vicente, isn't it?' she said. 'Tell me. Tell me he's not dead.'

'He's been dead for a while. Someone shot him in the head.'

'Oh God.' The remaining colour drained from her cheeks. 'Why? He didn't know anything about the manifesto. Why in God's name would Kessel want to kill him?' She looked at the note in McKendrick's hand. 'Is that from her?'

'It's signed by Meyer.' He read it out. '*If you have not yet booked your return flights to Europe, perhaps this will serve as a small reminder.*'

'They found out you hired Vicente.' Lucy leaned back against the car. 'He'll have told them we've been to the warehouse.'

'If Vicente had done that, it wouldn't just be him in the boot; we'd be in there along with him. It doesn't look as though anyone tried to make him talk before he died. He wasn't shot at close range.'

'He didn't have to be shot at all. They could've shot us instead.'

'They didn't have to,' McKendrick said, 'not when threatening Andrew and scaring the shit out of us is a whole lot easier and a whole lot safer for them. No one's going to miss Vicente, but a couple of dead Europeans could cause a fair bit of trouble even in São Paulo. Kessel didn't want to make the same mistake she made with the Goddards.'

'And you don't have to make everything sound so matter of fact. That's what you did in Germany. Whenever something dreadful happens, you think you have to insulate me from it. Well you don't. It's patronizing, and I don't like it. I'm not a schoolgirl.'

This was hardly the time to tell her he already knew she wasn't a schoolgirl. Nor in the present circumstances was he inclined to bother. With too many hours of daylight ahead of them before it would be sufficiently dark to dispose of Vicente's body, and with a hotel bill to settle, a rental car to return and a late-night, long-haul flight to catch, McKendrick had enough on his mind.

He spent the remainder of the day hoping nothing else would go wrong or take them by surprise, endeavouring to rid himself of the words of a manifesto that was beginning to haunt him and, right up until nightfall – just as he had done after the deaths of Kalyem and Jusaf at the fire-front – wondering if he could have somehow prevented the death of the young man whose body they committed to the still and oily waters of a Santos estuary before they started out on their drive back to the bright lights of the international air terminal in São Paulo.

# Chapter 13

Harland had shown little surprise at the news of Vicente's death. Linder, though, had been less philosophical, returning to the subject more than once during the afternoon, and evidently more concerned about it than he was letting on.

He was standing in front of his office whiteboard waiting for a reply to his last question, seemingly unaware of how tired McKendrick and Lucy were from a night without sleep in Santos and their long flight back to Zurich.

'We can't be a hundred per cent sure,' McKendrick said.

'But you don't believe Kessel or Meyer know you managed to copy the manifesto?'

'I don't think Lucy and I would be sitting here if they did, do you?'

'Probably not.' Linder cleaned the whiteboard. 'I suppose we'll have to proceed on that assumption. In which case, if Harland has no more questions, I suggest we get on with this.'

Harland was too busy writing notes to look up. Like Linder, he was being professional, interrupting only when he had something to add, or to seek clarification on a point in which he had some particular interest.

'Right,' Linder said. 'Harland and I spent half of last night and most of this morning coming up with what we think is the best way to expose the Coalition before they attack their next two targets on December 5th. That means we have six days to get ourselves organized and to put everything in place.'

'You're going too fast,' McKendrick said. 'This time yesterday, Lucy and I were in Brazil – remember? There are a whole bunch of things we don't know. I don't even know if Andrew's OK.'

'Your son's fine.' It was Harland who'd answered. 'He's in a safe-house north of San Diego at a place called San Elijo.'

'With his mother?'

'Yeah. The DEA haven't told her much – just enough to get her really pissed off with you. But she won't have to be there long. Now we know what these Christian Freedom pricks are up to, she should be able to get Andrew home in a few weeks.'

McKendrick didn't think so. 'What makes you think you can stop something like this in a few weeks?' he said.

'How about the Rosenberg Principle?' The American leaned back in his chair. 'The Coalition's relying on public support to get their new crusade up and running, but two can play at that game. As long as this manifesto document isn't just a load of crap we can use the Rosenberg Principle as well as they can. If we can prove Islamic terror groups are being made to take the blame for every target the Coalition hits, and if we can make the public realize they're being manipulated and lied to, it won't be the Arabs who get into trouble; it'll be Quaid and his Nazi friends who'll wind up getting themselves crucified.'

The explanation hadn't helped McKendrick. With no real idea of what the Rosenberg Principle was, he was no further ahead than he'd been five minutes ago, and judging by Lucy's expression, neither was she.

Unlike him, she'd managed to snatch a few hours' sleep on the plane, but if anything, she was more tired than he was, having fallen asleep in their taxi from the airport, and over the course of their debriefing session this afternoon, gradually losing the battle to keep her eyes open.

Linder had recognized the symptoms, and seemed to have realized he needed to slow things down. 'How about a history lesson?' He smiled at Lucy. 'I can make it short if you can stay awake long enough to listen.'

'Oh, I'm sorry.' She tried to appear more attentive. 'I'll be all right in a minute.'

'Alfred Rosenberg was an intellectual,' Linder said, 'a man of his time who came from fairly humble beginnings. His father was a German shoemaker, but even when Rosenberg was a young man he had the kind of shrewdness that eventually allowed him to drag himself up to the position of *Reichsleiter* of the Nazi party. It's how he did it that's interesting. It came about after he managed to present Adolf Hitler with a copy of a Russian manuscript he'd got hold of called the *Protocols of the Wise Men of Zion*. Rosenberg knew it was a forgery, but he also knew it was just what he'd been looking for – a completely fictitious record of what was claimed to be a meeting of The World Congress of Jews held in Basle in 1897. Have either of you ever heard of it?'

McKendrick hadn't, and Lucy was shaking her head.

'If you were Jewish you would have,' Linder said. 'At the time it was dynamite, the most subversive anti-Semitic document anyone had ever seen – not unlike a nineteenth-century version of the Coalition's manifesto although, of course, there was nothing like Quaid's *Five Pillars of Truth* in it.'

'Because it was only anti-Semitic,' McKendrick said, 'not anti-Islamic as well.'

'Yes. It outlined what was supposed to be a plan for world domination by Jewish Zionists – a scheme for a secret international network of Jews to take control of the world's capital so they could dominate the governments of just about every major nation. The entire concept was a fabrication, but Rosenberg knew the German public would swallow every word of it. For the Germans, it was the reason why they'd been defeated in World War One, and the explanation for why so many brave Aryan soldiers had been stabbed in the back while they'd been fighting for the Fatherland on French soil – proof of a vile and loathsome Jewish conspiracy that was being hatched out right on their doorstep.'

By now, Lucy was awake. 'And Hitler believed it?' she said.

'I don't think anyone knows whether he did or not, but it didn't matter. Once Rosenberg had gained Hitler's confidence, he spent months converting the *Protocols of the Wise Men of Zion* into a blueprint for the Nazi's own master plan. To do that, he rewrote the *Protocol* document from one end to the other, turning it inside out until it became the definitive guide for the racial policies of the whole Nazi movement. It was Alfred Rosenberg who pioneered the principle of gaining power by exploiting racial hatred, and by frightening tens of millions of people into believing their religious beliefs and their way of

life are under such a threat that they start searching for stronger leaders and rioting in the streets for a change of government.' Linder
glanced at McKendrick. 'Which is precisely what happened a year ago
after the train bombings in Spain, and why six million Jews came to
lose their lives during the last World War.'

'And why the Coalition believes it's worth using the Rosenberg
Principle again.' Now McKendrick had a better idea of what Harland
had been talking about, he could see how the aims of the Christian
Freedom Parties could perhaps be made to work against them in the
long-term. What he didn't understand was how Linder proposed stopping them from going through with the next stage of their programme
in six days' time.

But Lucy did. She was still pale, but ready to offer her solution to
the problem. 'We can go to the media with the manifesto.' She looked
at Harland. 'That's what you meant by playing the Coalition at their
own game, isn't it?'

The American shook his head. 'Nice idea, but if you're in the
propaganda business, you need more than a few sheets of paper to
grab the hearts and the minds of the public. This manifesto might look
like the next best thing to a smoking gun, but the media aren't going
to give two shits about it. By itself it doesn't prove a goddamn thing.'

'Yes it does.' She turned a page on her copy. 'The proof's right here
in Section 4, where the TTX targets are listed. The European media
already know something's going on, so this will show them why Fallièrs
and Pattullo were killed, and it'll show the Americans why one of their
senators was murdered last week. What better proof do we need?'

Harland's face was expressionless. 'OK,' he said. 'Try this then.
Soon as we're done here, you trot off and introduce yourself to an
editor of a big Zurich newspaper. Tell him you can prove Fallièrs,
Pattullo and Bowden weren't assassinated by Islamic terrorists like
everyone thinks they were. Say you've got a document that proves
there's an outfit called the Coalition of Christian Freedom Parties
running around killing people and blaming their deaths on Islamic
terrorists to whip up hate against the Arabs and the Jews. What do you
figure the editor's going to do?'

'Ask to see the manifesto.'

'Wrong. First off he'll want to know who wrote it. And if he's as smart as he should be, he'll think you did. Maybe your husband got himself killed in Iraq, and you're starting up a crusade of your own to see that the Muslims get what they deserve. Anyone with a grudge could write something like that manifesto. If I was running a newspaper, I'd have you out the door so fast your feet wouldn't touch the ground.'

'Because of what you said about the manifesto not proving anything by itself?'

'And because no journalist is going to risk having his hands cut off for taking a hard stand on racism or religion unless he can back up what he prints.'

Patches of colour had appeared on Lucy's cheeks. 'You're making it sound as though McKendrick and I went all the way to South America for nothing. Vicente died because he helped us get this information. Have you forgotten that?'

Linder intervened. 'You're missing the point,' he said. 'All Harland's saying is that now we know what we're dealing with, we have to be more careful. We can't afford to lose any credibility we might have by leaking the manifesto without evidence of its authenticity.' He paused. 'And it's important none of us falls under suspicion, or becomes accidentally incriminated ourselves. So, as I said, we have six days to secure the proof we need, or in the worst case, do what we can to prevent whatever is scheduled to take place on December 5th.'

'How?' McKendrick asked. 'It's going to be pretty damn hard when we don't know what the targets are, or what TTX is.'

As though uncertain of how his comments were being received, Linder had started pacing round his office. 'I think the why is more important than the how,' he said. 'I know you and Lucy will have discussed this together, and I have no wish to overstate the danger of us doing nothing, but it seems to me that if history is anything to go by, once the Coalition's allowed to get a foothold, half the world could be facing the kind of instability no one's seen since the end of the last War.'

McKendrick knew Linder was being deliberately circumspect. And he knew why. By not mentioning the Coalition's ultimate aim of eliminating what they called the Jewish scourge, Linder was either distancing himself from the proposal he was about to put forward, or hoping to obtain maximum help from Harland's masters in the States by focusing only on the Coalition's campaign to pour petrol on the fire the Americans had ignited in the Middle East.

Whatever the reason, and whatever form Linder's proposal was going to take, McKendrick was ready to reject it if it was going to further complicate his own problems – one being what else he ought to be doing to protect Andrew; the other being what, if anything, might happen between him and Lucy now they were on more familiar ground.

Almost from the moment their plane had landed, unconsciously she'd slipped back into her office role, making little effort to maintain the relationship they'd developed in Brazil, and throughout the afternoon, meeting his eyes only when she'd been forced to answer questions about Vicente's execution, or when she'd needed help to remember what they'd seen in Kessel's *Arowana* warehouse.

On the whole, though, she'd been more distant than unfriendly, McKendrick told himself, probably because she was so damn weary that all her energy was going into putting on a good front for her boss.

'Right.' Linder stopped his pacing and went to sit down. 'Time to see what you think about our ideas. I'll let Harland explain. He knows more about TTX than I do.'

'Have you found out what it stands for?' McKendrick was surprised.

'See what you think.' Harland took his notes with him to the whiteboard. 'You'd better hope we've got this figured out, because if we haven't we're going to be shit out of luck.' He printed the letters TTX at the top of the board and began to write down a list of names:

## TTX

TEXAS TRACK X-RAY CORP.
TETRAXON
THOMAS TIPTON XEROX
TOKYO TYRE EXPORT (TTX)
TETTIX
TAMPA TERMITE EXTERMINATORS (TTX)
TRANS-TASMAN EXPRESS (TTX)
TETRODOTOXIN
THAILAND TRAVEL EXPERIENCE (TTX)

'OK.' He turned around. 'There are dozens of companies that use the initials TTX. Mostly, if they're not in the X-ray business or Xerox photocopiers like the two I've written down, they use the letter X as an abbreviation for words like export or express. You can see what I mean.'

'So what are the other three?' Lucy asked.

'I'll tell you.' Harland drew rings around the words tettix, tetraxon and tetrodotoxin. 'A tettix is a kind of cicada, or a cicada-shaped orna-ment that women wear in their hair. A tetraxon is supposed to be a spike or a prickle on a deep-sea sponge and, according to my guys in Washington, tetrodotoxin is a new kind of poison – so new and so nasty it makes anthrax and ricin look like talcum-powder.' He held up a hand to prevent Lucy interrupting. 'Let me read you something. This is a quote from an article in *New Scientist*: *Last year, American federal offi-cers intercepted a suspicious package while it was* en route *to a private address in the US. The package contained vials of a white crystalline powder which was first thought to be heroin. But subsequent tests revealed that the powder was no narcotic. It took a while for scientists at the Lawrence Livermore National Laboratory to identify a sample, and what they found was alarming. The powder was tetrodotoxin or TTX – one of the deadliest poisons on Earth for which there is no antidote and which, gram for gram, is 10,000 times more lethal than cyanide.'*

Although Harland had evidently concluded that the letters TTX referred to this new form of poison, McKendrick could see no real reason why they should.

Lucy couldn't either. 'It's a guess,' she said. 'How do you know TTX stands for tetrodotoxin?'

'Well, let's see.' Harland read from another sheet of paper. '*TTX has a terrifying* modus operandi. *Twenty-five minutes after exposure it begins to paralyse its victims, leaving the brain fully aware of what's happening. Death usually results within hours from suffocation or heart failure.*' He looked up. 'Which, as far as we can make out, is exactly how Fallièrs, Bowden and Pattullo died.'

McKendrick remained unconvinced, reluctant to accept the idea on the evidence he'd heard so far. 'It'll be easy to find out if they died of TTX poisoning,' he said. 'The autopsy reports will tell us.'

The American shook his head. 'No they won't. Once this stuff's been swallowed or ingested, there aren't any tests to detect its presence in the human body. That's one of the neat things about TTX if you're a hairy-arsed terrorist who doesn't fancy being a suicide bomber.'

Lucy was beginning to lose her doubt. 'How hard is it to buy tetrodotoxin?' she asked. 'Where does it come from?'

'That's the good bit.' Harland looked as though he'd been waiting for the question. 'It's officially termed a symbiotic biotoxin. In tiny quantities it's found in the ovaries and livers of certain living things.' To add emphasis to what he was about to say, he stood back from the board. 'But if you're a hot-shot scientist, you can use a technique called biosynthesis to manufacture tetrodotoxin artificially in a laboratory. All you need is a real good brain, some super-fancy equipment and a way of extracting the natural base biotoxin from specific varieties of fish.'

Lucy might have been avoiding McKendrick's eyes before, but she wasn't now.

He was as stunned as she was. 'Jesus,' he said slowly. 'Fish. Kessel and Zitelmann.'

'Right.' Harland nodded. 'You can get TTX from a few other animals too, but it mostly comes from fish. In its natural form it's produced by bacteria that operate a kind of biowarfare factory in the guts of puffer fish, globe fish, harlequin frogs, Atelopus toads, Californian newts and blue-ringed octopi, or octopuses or whatever the hell you call them. They use it to kill their prey or to fight off predators in the wild. The problem is that you'd have to grind up hundreds and hundreds of their goddamn livers and ovaries to get any useful quantity of TTX. As long as you can figure out how to do it, culturing the bacteria in a lab is the only practical way to get enough of it to kill people.'

'People like Fallièrs, Bowden and Pattullo,' McKendrick said.

'Sure, and anyone else the Coalition feels like knocking over.'

'What's the name of the bacteria?'

'You'll wish you hadn't asked.' Harland consulted his notes. '*Pseudoalteromonas*. You any the wiser?'

'No. How new is it?'

'First identified in 1997, but there's no record of anyone successfully isolating it or culturing it artificially on any sort of scale – well, not up to now there hasn't been.'

'But it can be done?'

'Sounds like it. Researchers in South Korea and Japan are having a go, and there's a fair bit of information coming out of the University of South Carolina. My guess is that the Pentagon's suddenly decided tetrodotoxin could be the next big terrorist threat. They might even have got it right this time.'

McKendrick was still putting together pieces of the puzzle, endeavouring to remember whether he'd seen anything resembling a laboratory in the *Arowana* warehouse. 'If Kessel's manufacturing TTX, I don't think she's doing it in Santos,' he said.

Lucy interrupted. 'It's not her,' she said. 'Günther Zitelmann studied biochemistry when he was a young man. It's him. He's making TTX at the Weiskirchen institute. That's what Kessel was doing there, and why he's paranoid about security.'

Linder shook his head. 'Sorry,' he said. 'Zitelmann isn't running a tetrodotoxin laboratory either.'

'How do you know he isn't?' McKendrick said.

'Because while you and Lucy have been away, I did what I said I'd do. I arranged for an associate of mine to attend one of Zitelmann's religious courses at ICIS.'

'Did he go right through the place?' McKendrick was trying to recall the layout of the buildings.

'She, not he.' Linder smiled slightly. 'Yes she did. It wasn't very hard. Apparently the Weiskirchen estate isn't just an internationally accredited institute for Christian and Islamic studies. Because the manor house is so old, it's also a registered German National Heritage site, which means the public have access to it on selected weekends and public holidays. Last Sunday, my associate had the full guided tour. She even took photographs, so I'm as certain as I can be that Zitelmann isn't manufacturing TTX in Weiskirchen – well, at least as certain as you are that Maria Kessel isn't making it in Santos.'

'What about fish tanks?' Lucy said. 'Did she see any of those?'

'Several. There are aquariums in the main hall, two in Zitelmann's study and a number of small ones in the dining room – none of them containing any of the tetrodotoxin-producing fish on Harland's list. Do you want to see the photos?'

'No.' Lucy hadn't given up. 'Did she smell the phenol from the lake?'

Linder shook his head. 'She didn't smell anything unusual at all while she was there. I did say it would be helpful if she could take a look at the lake, but she'd been asking so many questions about other things, she thought it wasn't a good idea to start wandering around an area that has keep out signs all round it.'

'So we still don't know why he's poisoning the water,' McKendrick said. 'And if he's not operating a bioweapons lab, where are the Coalition getting their TTX from?'

'I was hoping to hear it was coming from South America.' Linder stretched. 'But never mind. We're not going to solve everything in one afternoon, and I can't see that holding up our plans for the coming weekend.'

'You mean your plans,' McKendrick said. 'Why's the weekend important?'

'You know why. On December 5th the *Christliches Freiheit Beteilgtes* have something or someone in their sights at St Catherine's in Germany, and in Italy, the *Partito Christiano Di Liberta* have the same brief for their St Gabriel's target. So, we either have to make sure German and Italian counter-terrorism squads can catch Coalition activists in the act, or we ourselves have to acquire evidence to back the information we already have.'

'Too risky,' McKendrick said. 'If we start warning people about what might happen and we're wrong, who's going to believe anything we have to say afterwards? And I don't think it's a smart idea for us to be contacting counter-terrorism organizations either – not when they're just as likely to believe we're defectors from the Coalition who've changed sides or lost their nerve.'

Linder was unconcerned. 'Which is precisely why Harland's flying back to Washington tonight,' he said. 'He thinks he can persuade his agency to issue the warnings for us.'

'I thought the DEA didn't want to get their hands dirty.'

'They don't.' Harland pointed to Linder's copy of the manifesto. 'But if the DEA gets some solid evidence to prove that's authentic, they'll be earning themselves a bucketful of points from the White House. There isn't a bureaucrat in Washington who'd pass up the chance to lift the image of the US in the Middle East right now. Think how grateful the President's going to be when he hears how the DEA choked off a conspiracy to brainwash the public into demanding a crusade against our Arab friends.'

While Harland had been talking, Linder had been using magnets to secure a map of Europe to his whiteboard. 'Irrespective of what the Americans choose to do, we can't afford to sit on our hands,' he said. 'At the very least we have to force the pace.' He glanced at McKendrick. 'I think you appreciate that better than any of us.'

McKendrick could have done without the reference to Andrew. The remark had been unnecessary, particularly when it had been so transparent. 'It's going to be pretty damn hard to force the pace if we don't know what the targets are. St Catherine's and St Gabriel's could be anything.'

Linder nodded. 'Indeed they could. There's a bronze statue of St Catherine somewhere in Germany, and we could probably find one of St Gabriel in Italy if we look hard enough. Statues hardly fit the bill, though, do they?'

This time McKendrick kept his mouth shut.

'Our first thoughts were hospitals,' Linder said, 'but once the date is factored in, the field becomes narrower.' He paused. 'You see, December 5th happens to be a Sunday – which we think raises flags over religious institutions like churches and convents.'

'Christian targets,' Lucy said.

'Yes. Imagine the outcry once the public have been misinformed about Islamic terrorists poisoning nuns or murdering people in a church.'

Harland had a more pragmatic view. 'Not just Christian targets,' he said. 'Nice soft ones with a nice high profile and with great media impact. Beats the shit out of blowing up trains and buildings.'

Lucy went to study the map. 'Are there convents and churches with the right names in the right countries?'

Linder pointed. 'A St Catherine's convent where I've marked it there just east of Frankfurt, and a St Gabriel's church in Italy.'

McKendrick joined Lucy at the whiteboard. 'Whereabouts in Italy?' he said.

'On the Adriatic coast.' Linder moved his finger downwards on the map. 'We haven't a street address yet, but it's listed as being here somewhere, near Giulianova. I'm afraid that's all the information we have at the moment. We'll know more once someone's had a look.' He gave McKendrick an envelope and handed another one to Lucy. 'Details in there. Travel arrangements, accommodation, contact phone numbers and names of people I've been in touch with who can help you while you're there. Your flights aren't until tomorrow night, so you have a day to yourselves before you leave. I know that's not long, but in the circumstances, I think it's best for you to be where you have to be in plenty of time.'

Irritated but too worn out to argue, McKendrick didn't bother to open his envelope, presuming Lucy had drawn the convent and already resigned to spending an unwanted long weekend in Italy by himself. 'You don't mess around, do you?' he said.

Linder compressed his lips. 'I don't expect you to be happy about this. I know I'm being unreasonable and I'm sure you think I'm push-ing too hard, but unless someone learns how and when this TTX material is going to be used on Sunday, God knows how many people could die this time.'

Lucy had stopped inspecting the map and had swung round to face McKendrick. 'I know how it's used,' she said. 'So do you. Cups – throwaway cups, paper plates and things like those sachets of salt and the little tubes of sugar we saw – remember?'

He hadn't forgotten. But it had been Lucy, not him, who'd made the connection and found the reason for Maria Kessel's extraordinary collection of disposable drink containers, airline cutlery and cardboard plates – not the hoard of a kleptomaniac: not the trash he'd discounted as being unimportant, but product samples to determine which of them would most easily carry an invisible, lethal dusting of white powder.

Linder was waiting for an explanation. 'I'm afraid I'm being slow,' he said. 'I don't understand.'

McKendrick enlightened him, describing what had been stacked on the shelves in the upstairs office of the warehouse and apologizing for failing to appreciate the significance of what they'd seen.

'The main thing is that we know now.' Linder went to his desk. 'At the very least it adds weight to our case. I'll see if I can find out how much TTX we ought to be looking for.'

'Not worth the bother.' Harland snapped shut the catches on his briefcase as though to indicate he was ready to leave. 'One single milligram is enough to kill an adult stone dead. That's less than half the amount you can put on a pinhead. A couple of sips from one of our Maria's cups and you'd be gone. If you're unlucky, you might hang on for a few hours, but seeing as how you're going to be wide awake but paralysed, you'd be better off finishing your drink to hurry things along a bit.'

'Which I think is probably a frightening enough note for us to end the day on.' Linder handed Lucy a slip of paper. 'Could you call those people for me please, just to say I'll be unavailable for the next few days. I know you're anxious to get home, so do it from there if you like. Do you mind?'

'No, of course not.' She sat up straighter. 'Is there anything else?'

'Not unless you'd care to order a taxi and make a hotel reservation for Mr McKendrick. I'm afraid I forgot he'd have nowhere to stay tonight.' Linder picked up his phone. 'Right then. Except for me wishing you all good luck, we seem to be finished here for the day.'

Harland was in a hurry. Nodding a casual goodbye to Linder, he smiled at Lucy and headed for the door, walking so quickly that McKendrick had to sprint to catch him up.

'I know what you're going to say.' The American continued walking until he reached the foyer where the receptionist was leaving for the night.

'Well?' McKendrick said.

'Our people in Indonesia have got that stuff you gave me, but I haven't heard anything back from them yet. It's too early.'

'It's over a week.'

Harland frowned. 'Look, I know how you feel about what happened to the girl, but there isn't any quick fix for something like that.'

'You don't know how I feel. You weren't there. If you had been you'd know it was my fault and you'd know why I want a quick fix.'

'OK. So it was your fault. That's fine. All I'm trying to say is that you need to give the *Kopassus* some time. Just because that mother-fucker with the tattooed hand told you his men use the same fire-trail through the forest every month, it doesn't mean the *Kopassus* are going to sniff them out overnight. No one's let you down yet, and I haven't forgotten you and I have a deal.' Harland peered out through the glass

178

doors. 'How about having a drink with me somewhere? I'm not in that much of a rush; I just wanted to get out of here: Linder wears me out.'

'I don't think so.' McKendrick wasn't in the mood. 'Listen, I should've said before – I'm sorry as hell about Vicente.'

'Not your fault either. You sure about that drink?'

'Yeah, I'm sure. Thanks anyway. I need to talk to Lucy.'

'Ah.' Harland grinned. 'If you figure all she needs is a talking to, you'd better start putting Viagra on your cornflakes.' He stuck out his hand. 'Let me know when you find out how far down those goddamn freckles of hers go and take care of yourself in Italy. I'll be in touch.'

For several minutes after Harland had left, McKendrick remained alone in the foyer, looking out into the street while he endeavoured to reconcile what was supposed to have been a research trip to Indonesia with everything that had happened to him since, no less conscious of his guilt for the deaths of Kalyem, Jusaf and Vicente than he was for putting Andrew at risk, and now more worried about who was going to take care of Lucy in Germany than he was about taking care of himself.

Wondering whether he should mention his concern to Linder, he turned round to find her standing behind him.

'You off?' he asked.

'Mm.'

'Did you fix me up with a hotel?'

She shook her head. 'None of the hotels in Zurich are full on Mondays, so you can choose for yourself where you want to stay – unless you'd rather do something else.'

'Like what?'

'Well, there's a restaurant near where I live, so if we had dinner there together, I thought you could come back to my place afterwards.' She stopped abruptly. 'Only if you want to, of course – you know, in case you're sick of staying in hotels.'

Caught wrong-footed by her invitation, he was slow to reply.

'Here's your taxi.' She opened one of the glass doors for him. 'You'd better decide what you want to do.'

It was like being asked if he'd prefer to spend the night drinking in a bar with Harland. Taking her by the arm, he walked her over to the waiting cab. 'Two conditions,' he said. 'Neither of us talk about what we've been talking about all day, and instead of me spending the evening with Linder's personal assistant, it'd be a whole lot nicer if I could spend it with Lucy Mitchell. Do you think you could arrange that?'

'I'm not sure.' There was no change in her expression. 'It depends what you mean. You'll have to explain over dinner.'

# Chapter 14

Their dinner at the restaurant had been largely unsuccessful. Neither of them had been sufficiently hungry to do justice to the meal, and the bottle of wine they'd shared had made them both so drowsy that, to avoid falling asleep at the table, they'd been forced to leave early.

The short walk to Lucy's apartment and the night air had freshened up McKendrick a little, but that had been twenty minutes ago, and despite drinking two cups of coffee he was beginning to wonder how much longer he'd be able to keep awake.

'Turn up the thermostat if you're still cold,' she called to him from the shower. 'And put some music on. The CDs are in that wooden box beside the player.'

He wasn't cold any more, and he didn't want to hear any music. What he wanted was a chance to unwind and time to think, although how much time he should waste thinking about tonight remained unclear.

Over dinner, particularly after the wine had taken effect, Lucy had become more like the Lucy of the last few days, skirting around the subjects they'd agreed not to mention, but happy enough to talk about herself, even to the point of explaining how close she'd come to turning down her job at Linder International once she'd realized it would provide no outlet for her continuing interest in the world of art.

If her apartment was anything to go by, she'd made the right decision, McKendrick thought. As well as it being located within walking distance of Zurich's desirable lakeshore, the whole place had been expensively furnished by someone who was making enough money to indulge their tastes.

More out of curiosity than because he knew anything about art, he went to look at the collection of paintings that were hanging on the wall above her bookcase.

Illuminated by lights hidden in the ceiling, the majority of the paintings were reproductions: an enigmatic work by Paul Klee; a modernist oil by Chagall called *Lovers in the Red Sky* which showed a ghostly couple flying through the air against a strangely arresting red background and, taking pride of place, several smaller framed pictures by Lee Bontecou and Julian Schnabel.

Lucy's selection of books was just as varied. She had books on art, a shelf full of language reference works, biographies of people McKendrick had never heard of and, standing on the bottom shelf, sandwiched between some paperbacks, a collection of well-used *Winnie the Pooh* books.

He was glancing through one of them when she returned to the lounge.

Wearing a thin white housecoat and fresh from her shower, she had a towel round her head as if to remind him of the night they'd spent at Emily's two weeks ago.

'Well,' she said, 'what have you decided?'

'About what?'

'Me. Aren't you supposed to be able to tell what people are like by the kind of books they read?'

He held up the *Pooh* book. 'This one's making it hard.'

She smiled. 'Family bible. My parents grew up on *Winnie the Pooh*, so I had to as well. Didn't you want to listen to music?'

'Go ahead if you want to. I don't mind.'

'I'll put on something then. It might stop me going to sleep.' She slipped a CD into the player and came to sit beside him on the sofa. 'Did Harland have news for you? That's what you were asking him at the office, wasn't it?'

'Yes it was, and no he didn't. He thinks I'm being impatient.'

'He probably doesn't understand why it's important to you.'

'He understands better than you do.' McKendrick wished she'd gone to sit somewhere else.

'Only because I don't understand how you think. Most of the time you're too complicated for anyone to understand.'

182

'You shouldn't have asked me back here then, should you? Or are you feeling the same way you did in Trier when you wanted to stay the night in my room at the Jugendgästehaus?'

'No. I told you why I asked you back.' She hesitated. 'And I suppose I thought it was about time you told me the truth about that Indonesian girl.'

'I did.'

'Why don't you ever use her name when you talk about her?'

'It's not a secret. Her name was Kalyem.'

'Was she pretty?'

He nodded. 'Yes, she was.'

'Had you been sleeping with her? Is that why you can't forget her?'

'I never slept with her, and the reason I can't forget her is because no one should have to go through what she went through before she died, and because it was my fault she did. I've already explained all that.'

'I'm not trying to interfere.' She unwrapped the towel from her head. 'What about the old man who shot her? Don't you feel the same about him?'

'Jusaf made his own decision. He had a choice: Kalyem didn't.' McKendrick was wondering how much longer this inquisition was going to last.

'Do you really think the *Kopassus* will catch the men who raped her?'

'I don't know.' He was surprised she'd remembered the name. 'Depends on how many days they're prepared to stay at the fire-front. It's not the kind of place anyone would want to hang around.'

'Because it's so dangerous?'

'Not just that. It's everything.'

'Like what?' She snuggled up to him and took one of his hands in hers. 'Tell me.'

He didn't want to, but for some reason or another, found himself answering her question. 'You really need to look at photos,' he said. 'But even photos don't give you that much of an idea. A big underground fire is the nearest thing to Hell you're ever going to come across. Once a coal seam starts burning its way under a forest, every living thing above it on the surface dies, the air's so hot you can't breathe it, and all you can smell is sulphur – that's before you start worrying about what's going on beneath your feet.' He stopped talking, thinking she'd fallen asleep, but discovering she hadn't when she released his hand and made herself more comfortable by stretching out on the sofa with her head resting on his lap.

'Go on,' she murmured.

He couldn't. Light-headed from the wine, the fragrance of her hair and his lack of sleep, so distracted had he become by the open front of her housecoat and the swell of her breasts, that he was temporarily no more capable of talking about fires than he was able to take his eyes off her.

For a while he did nothing. Then, without any clear idea of how she might respond, but unable to resist the temptation any longer, very slowly he slid his hands inside her housecoat and brushed his fingertips across her nipples, growing bolder when she welcomed his caress by arching her back and pushing her breasts upwards against his palms.

'You've forgotten your manners,' she whispered. 'You could at least kiss me while you're doing that.'

As eager to kiss her as she was to be kissed, he was bending forwards, anticipating the touch of her lips on his when, almost without him knowing, something flickered through his mind.

The thought had been fleeting, but it had lasted just long enough for Lucy to sense his hesitation.

Forcing his hands away, she quickly pulled her housecoat together and sat up. 'It's all right,' she said. 'You don't have to explain.'

'Explain what? What's the matter?'

'Don't pretend you don't know.' She scrambled to her feet. 'I have to look at myself in the mirror every day.'

'For Christ's sake.' McKendrick managed to grab her before she could walk away from him. 'Listen to me,' he said. 'It's about time someone straightened you out. You've got things all back to front. Men don't stare at you because of your damn freckles. They do it because they can't help it any more than I can help it. I don't know whether it's your figure, your legs, your mouth or the way you walk. If I knew, I'd tell you. But it sure as hell has nothing to do with your freckles. That's an excuse you've invented for yourself – a way to insulate yourself from something you don't like.'

'Let me go.' She attempted to free herself.

'If Harland was here, he'd be saying the same things I'm saying. Most women would give their eye teeth for what you have.'

'I don't believe you. The minute you saw more of me than you'd seen before, you weren't so certain you wanted to kiss me after all.'

'Take your housecoat off then – right off. Now. Then we'll both find out.'

'No.' She tightened her belt. 'Stop trying to embarrass me.'

'Have you thought how I might feel?'

'I don't care. You're the one who's spoiled the evening, not me.'

'It's as much your fault as mine.'

She raised her eyebrows. 'Really.'

'If you hadn't asked me about Kalyem, I wouldn't have had things like fire-fronts messing up my head at the wrong time. Something just happened to cross my mind. That's all it was.'

'While you just happened to have your hands on my breasts?'

'Yes. What else do you want me to say?'

'Nothing – although if whatever you were thinking about was more important to you than what we were doing, I suppose I should find out what it was. Then I'll know if you're lying or not, won't I?'

'It's something we agreed not to talk about tonight. It can wait until tomorrow.' Hoping to regain lost ground, he pulled her towards him.

She didn't resist, but made it obvious that she had no intention of continuing from where they'd left off. 'If you won't tell me, I'm going to bed – by myself.'

'OK,' McKendrick said. 'If you're not going to believe me about your freckles, try this instead. I know where the tetrodotoxin laboratory is.'

'No, you don't. It's just an excuse you've thought up.'

'It's under the lake in Weiskirchen – inside what's left of the old coal seam.'

'In the burned-out tunnel?'

'I've been in enough of them to know how big they can be. Zitelmann will have all the space he needs down there, and who's ever going to think of looking for a bioweapons laboratory in a place like that?'

If the information had come as a surprise to Lucy, she was either still too upset or too discouraged to show any interest. She hadn't tried to remove McKendrick's hands from her shoulders, but neither were there any signs of her thawing out.

'How could anyone build a laboratory under a lake?' she said. 'How could you ever get into it?'

'Probably through that derelict power station we broke into – the same route the hot combustion gases took when they were brought up to the surface. We never had a proper look around. We saw the camera, but we never did figure out why Zitelmann would have his implement shed fitted out with surveillance equipment. Now we know.'

'And you think that's the reason why he keeps topping up his lake with chemicals – to keep people away?'

'Yep. Except that after Bridget Goddard arrived all bright-eyed and bushy-tailed with her video camera, the idea backfired on him. The lake was probably polluted for years after the power station was bombed or closed down, but it wouldn't have been hard for Zitelmann to work out that a lakeful of phenol is a hell of a lot better protection for his laboratory than any kind of fence.'

'Well, aren't you clever?' Lucy shuffled her feet. 'I suppose you want me to call Mr Linder for you – or do you want to tell him yourself?'

A clear enough hint that she considered the evening beyond recovery, McKendrick decided. 'Call him in the morning. I can't see there's much anyone can do about it until you and I get some proof about the Coalition's plans for Sunday.' He released his grip on her. 'Look, I know things have got kind of screwed up for us tonight. It's because we're both so damn tired.'

'Is that a way of saying you've changed your mind about taking me to bed?'

He gave up, no closer to reading her thoughts than he had been five minutes ago and unable to tell if she was teasing him.

To show him she wasn't, she suddenly stepped forwards, wrapped her arms round his neck and kissed him open-mouthed, pressing herself against him so hard he nearly overbalanced.

Despite all of his previous preoccupation with her, his imagination had failed to prepare him for the moment, and he was overwhelmed by her need to prove he had neither misunderstood nor misread anything.

They could have chosen their time better. With her mouth fastened on his, Lucy was swaying while she endeavoured to slip out of her housecoat, relying on McKendrick to support her, but without appreciating that he wasn't much steadier on his feet than she was.

He managed to pick her up and had her halfway to the bedroom when the phone rang.

Lucy broke off their embrace. 'Put me down,' she whispered.

'No. Leave it.'

'What if it's important?'

'It isn't.' Because this was an interruption that had not been of his own making, he was more confident than he had been earlier.

'Read me out the number on the caller display, then. The phone's behind you on the desk.'

Resisting the urge to smash the thing to pieces, he did what she asked, realizing his mistake when she told him it was Linder who was placing the call.

'I'd better answer it,' she said. 'He knows I'm here.'

'Does he know I'm here with you?' McKendrick lowered her to the floor.

'I don't think so.' She took a deep breath. 'Don't go away.'

He wasn't planning to, although after an evening spent lurching from one lost opportunity to another, he was learning how short-lived his plans were turning out to be.

Lucy picked up the receiver, listened briefly then immediately put it down again.

'Quick call,' McKendrick said. 'What did he want?'

'Justin Quaid's on television.' She switched off the CD player and fumbled with her TV remote. 'He's being interviewed right now on CNN.'

'So what? You don't work for Linder twenty-four hours a day. Take your phone off the hook and tape the programme. We can watch it in the morning.'

'I don't think that's going to be a terribly good idea, do you? You know – not now – because of what you said before.'

'About our evening being screwed up already?'

'Mm. It didn't even start out well for us, did it? And it's been getting worse ever since. I don't want to watch TV any more than you do, but we have all day tomorrow, and we won't be so worn out once we've had some sleep.' She tried to smile. 'And I won't be so shaky and dizzy in the morning – well, I hope I won't be. I can wait if you can.'

Frustrated though he was, by now he was ready to admit defeat, guessing that, after yet another false start, it would be as difficult to recapture what had been happening between them as it would be to keep awake or start again.

'OK.' He led her back to the sofa and sat her down. 'If you'd rather look at Justin Quaid, that's fine.'

Her second attempt at a smile was more successful. 'You can look at the interviewer. Her legs are nicer than mine.'

The woman addressing Quaid was a typical American TV presenter, an immaculately groomed blonde who was perched on a studio chair with her legs crossed. Her legs weren't any nicer than Lucy's, but she was displaying them on camera to her best advantage.

Not that it was doing her much good, McKendrick thought. She might fancy herself as another Katie Couric, but she wasn't smart enough to realize she was being used.

Quaid was out-manoeuvring her. By being unflinchingly polite he was not only drawing attention to her naivety, but also making his own opinions on Islamic terrorism sound more informed, more insightful and remarkably reasonable.

To add gravity to his views, he'd adopted a low-key approach and was dressed accordingly in a business suit, a crisp white shirt and a statesman-like silver-patterned tie. Unlike the blonde, he was also completely relaxed, leaning back in his chair while he considered the point she'd just raised.

'No.' Quaid shook his head. 'I'm simply saying that, in the present climate, turning the other cheek is not the way to guarantee the security of the American and European public. I think we're all well past the crossroads where half-measures are an option.'

The woman feigned surprise. 'I don't think many people would be willing to accept that,' she said. 'The US occupation of Iraq and the removal of the Taliban from Afghanistan hardly amount to turning the other cheek or half-measures, surely?'

'In the context of an imminent Islamic Jihad or a Holy War, yes, I believe that's exactly what they are. Have those actions made the Christian world a safer place than it was before? Are Americans and

Europeans sleeping more peacefully in their beds than they were a year ago? I think not, nor do I think western governments are developing adequate policies to combat the worldwide upsurge in Arab terrorism.'

'I see.' The woman picked up a coloured brochure. 'This is a multi-language publication put out by an international organization that calls itself the Coalition of Christian Freedom Parties, of which I understand you are a founding member. Is that correct?'

'Indeed.'

'Its purpose seems to be to promote what are termed *The Five Pillars of Truth*, which many people regard as being inflammatory and overtly anti-Islamic. I won't read them out on air, but perhaps you'd care to explain how this leaflet is supposed to contribute to the fight against terrorism.'

'Certainly.' Quaid smiled at her. 'As I'm sure your researchers have told you, *The Five Pillars of Truth* represent some of the more distasteful and disturbing principles of the Islamic faith. By distributing those leaflets, the Coalition of Christian Freedom Parties is doing what it can to make people understand that Islamic fundamentalism is not something that will eventually go away. You and I both know that isn't the case, and I'm pleased to say that in almost every Christian country, more and more ordinary people are coming to precisely the same conclusion.'

Mistakenly, the woman sensed an opportunity. 'You haven't answered my question,' she said. 'How can a leaflet like this possibly contribute to America's security?'

'Oh, I am sorry.' Quaid was apologetic. 'You should have told me I was going too fast. It's to do with the democratic process and with the right of the public to elect their own governments. You see, for those of us fortunate enough to live in Christian democracies, it's information and raised awareness that allows us to decide which political leaders we need, and how best we should protect ourselves and the lives of our children. The leaflet you're holding is simply a means of alerting people to the threat of Islamic fundamentalism in its worst and most extreme form. Does that make things clearer for you?'

It did to McKendrick who'd started hearing echoes of the manifesto in almost every one of Quaid's pronouncements.

Lucy had a different perspective. What she'd noticed most was the manner of the man himself. 'Do you remember what Harland called him?' she said.

'Finest Alabama white-trash.'

'Not that – about him being as dangerous as a cottonmouth snake. But I don't think he's either of those things. His act's too smooth. He doesn't look anything like he did in those photos Harland showed us, does he?'

'Good job for him that he doesn't, now he's getting all this media coverage. If he wants the public to get behind him, he knows he can't afford to come across as a redneck or an evangelical Bible-basher. That's why he's reinvented himself.' McKendrick stopped her from speaking. 'Wait a second. Listen to this bit.'

Having unwittingly provided Quaid with a platform for his views, the blonde had wisely changed the subject by asking him what policies he thought the US should be following.

'Well, in the short-term, clearly not the policies we're following now.' Quaid put his fingertips together. 'You don't pacify a rabid dog by patting it on the nose, and the West would be incredibly foolish to confront a Jihad with anything other than a large, internationally co-ordinated force of the strongest kind. After that, though, I think we have to realize that the same commitment will be needed if we're to address the real reason for Islam's historical hatred of the Christian world.'

'The reason being what, in your opinion?'

'What a strange question.' Quaid's face was expressionless. 'The Jews of course. Your viewers already know that the longer Israel is allowed to continue slaughtering Palestinians, the worse the Middle East situation will become. Regrettably, the whole problem of Islamic terrorism has its roots nowhere else but in the arrogance and in the uncompromising intransigence of the Jewish people. If it wasn't for the Jews, you and I wouldn't be discussing terrorism of any kind, and the world would be a very much safer place than it is today.'

Too late to extricate herself from an interview that should never have been screened to begin with, the woman was either receiving urgent instructions from her programme director, or embarking early on her wind-up to try and save her job.

McKendrick had stopped listening, not so much concerned by the racial messages, but worried by the ease with which Quaid had been able to announce the Coalition's stage two strategy.

He'd laid it out pretty damn well, McKendrick thought. First, generate hate by blaming the Muslims for acts of violence for which they were not responsible, then, to satisfy the aims of a reborn Nazi Reich, use the tried and true Rosenberg Principle to so distort public opinion that the Jewish race would once again be made to pay a dreadful price for being Jewish.

Doubting that Lucy would want to carry on watching, he reached for the remote. 'You don't want to see any more of this crap, do you?' he said.

He needn't have asked. Without him knowing, during the last few minutes she'd fallen fast asleep, leaning comfortably against him and breathing far more regularly now.

For the second time this evening, although for more restrained reasons than before, he wondered whether he should carry her to the bedroom, or at least make the effort to help her get there by herself.

In the end, apart from switching off the TV, he did nothing, staying where he was with his arm round her, reluctant to disturb her, half-anticipating tomorrow, but drifting off to sleep while he was still imagining what tonight would have been like had they been able to consummate it in the way they both had wished.

During the week he'd spent in Brazil, on two consecutive mornings McKendrick had woken up from dreams in which Lucy had played a part. But on neither of those occasions had he awoken to find her on his lap.

She was facing him, kneeling on the sofa with her legs immodestly straddling his, trying not to spill a distinctly un-dreamlike mug of coffee while she shook him.

'OK. You can leave off.' McKendrick was more awake than she thought he was.

'Drink this,' she said.

'How do you expect me to drink anything with you kneeling there like that?' He took the mug from her.

'Oh.' She rearranged her housecoat. 'It's getting late, so you ought to call Mr Linder.'

'You do it – unless you want him to know I spent the night on your sofa.'

'He won't know. You could've told me about your theory yesterday before we left the office – or you could've phoned me this morning.'

McKendrick's attention was elsewhere. 'You call him while I take a leak and have a shower,' he said. 'If he won't believe there's a bioweapons lab under Zitelmann's lake say you'll arrange for me to call him later.'

'How much later?' She slid off his lap and went to the phone. 'After your shower, or after you've thanked me for letting you stay the night?' She placed the call before he could reply and began speaking quickly in her customary German.

Thinking she might want him to remain in the room until she'd finished talking, he took his time finishing his drink, recognizing the odd German word, but only listening properly when he saw her expression change to one that looked suspiciously like dismay.

'What?' He mouthed the word.

She shook her head, continuing to talk for a further two or three minutes before carefully replacing the receiver. 'You're not going to believe this,' she said.

'Don't tell me. He'd already figured it out for himself.'

'No.' She was unable to conceal her discomfort. 'He was really pleased to hear what you think about the tunnel. It's not that.'

'What's the matter then?'

'He's sending a taxi for me – so I can collect his new car for him. It's come down from Germany on a transporter overnight.'

'To where? Where is it?'

'At the Mercedes dealer in Schaffh'ausen. I can't very well not go – not after what I let happen to his last one. He sounded really sorry about having to ask, but he thought I wouldn't mind.'

McKendrick minded. He minded a lot. 'Go this afternoon,' he said. 'We can both go.'

'No we can't. We're expected for lunch at Mr Linder's home at one-thirty. He wants us to meet a Catholic priest who's going to tell you what to look out for at the church and explain what I need to do when

I get to the convent.'

By now, too resentful to care any more about churches and convents than he did about Linder's replacement car, McKendrick could almost believe a more personal conspiracy was at work somewhere.

Lucy was equally unhappy. She'd remained standing awkwardly by the phone as though still hoping to find a solution to a problem neither of them had foreseen. 'Your plane doesn't leave until six,' she said quietly. 'And I don't have to check in before eight-thirty. We'll have part of the afternoon.'

He wanted her to be right. With their day already reduced to a few, short hours, and after their less than rewarding night together on her sofa, McKendrick was willing to believe there was still a chance their luck could change.

It was wishful thinking.

Just as Lucy had interpreted his reaction to her freckles wrongly last night, so had she overestimated the time they would have together.

The pre-delivery checks on the Mercedes turned out to take longer than expected, the Catholic priest was late to arrive and late to leave, and Linder had so many questions about the burned-out seam that by four o'clock McKendrick had written off the day and become resigned to not having Lucy to himself again until they'd both returned to Zurich after the weekend.

Though she drove him to the airport and waited there with him until his flight was called, because they'd avoided discussing what needed to be discussed, he was more uneasy about leaving her than he had been yesterday – the reason, he told himself, why long after she'd kissed him goodbye and his plane had taken off into a particularly bleak and starless night, he remained conscious of the taste of her on his lips, and why, for the next half-hour, he fancied he could still detect the last, faint, lingering vestiges of her perfume.

# Chapter 15

Giulianova was the kind of place no one could dislike. Even at this time of year, with not a tourist in sight, the waterfront and the old medieval town centre were always crowded with Italians going noisily about their business and, rain or shine, on every one of the four days McKendrick had been here, there had been people strolling along a beach that was claimed to be one of the most beautiful on the whole of the Adriatic coast.

This morning, because it was Sunday, the waterfront was comparatively quiet, and except for some hardy joggers braving the cold, there were fewer people on the seafront than he'd seen before.

He hadn't intended leaving his hotel until after breakfast, but having slept only fitfully, he'd persuaded himself that an early start would help overcome his jitters and allow him to review the arrangements at the church before the young Italian officer once again assumed control of the operation.

He went to his car, but instead of getting in, decided to delay his departure to avoid alarming the parish priest by turning up at the church before he did.

Not that Father Moreti could be alarmed much more than he was already, McKendrick thought. The arrival of the five-man Italian counter-terrorism team had seen to that. Despatched from Rome in response to an urgent communication from the Pentagon, they'd appeared at the church shortly before midday on Wednesday, and by Wednesday evening had not only succeeded in frightening the wits out of the priest, but wasted much of the afternoon seeking the reason for McKendrick's presence and establishing that his role extended no further than offering advice in the unlikely event of him being asked for any.

Until this morning he hadn't minded. In unfamiliar surroundings and with few intelligent suggestions to make, he'd been in no position to prevent the Italians from running the operation in whatever manner they wished. But now, with morning Mass less than an hour away, McKendrick's nerves were on edge and he was starting to wonder if he'd been too hasty to dismiss the church as a worthwhile Coalition target.

His doubts had surfaced the minute he'd seen the place. The St Gabriel's church wasn't just small: it was tiny, an unprepossessing seventeenth century chapel located about ten kilometres inland from Giulianova itself in a village called Comi near one of the bridges over the Tordina river.

In common with most of the other buildings in the village, the church was picturesque, but otherwise unremarkable. It had the correct name and it was in the right country, but its profile as a potential target could hardly be lower and, as a consequence, each time McKendrick had visited it the more doubtful he'd become – so much so, that yesterday he'd finally mentioned his reservations over the phone to Linder and, later on, discussed them with Lucy during the somewhat strained evening calls she'd made to him from her mobile.

Although at first reluctant to admit it, she'd confessed to having reached much the same conclusion about the St Catherine's convent, which according to her, appeared to be a no more probable target than the little church of St Gabriel's.

So had Harland and Linder made a mistake, McKendrick wondered? Or had the *Partito Christiano Di Liberta* and the *Christliches Frieheit Beteilgtes* chosen these targets because of their unobtrusiveness? Was that the whole idea? Did the Rosenberg Principle work best when the public saw how easily terrorists could strike at ordinary people in the most ordinary of places?

He wasn't certain. What he did know was that if the congregation of St Gabriel's was really at risk of being poisoned today, he'd better be damn sure he'd done all he could to avoid adding another mistake to all the others he'd made in recent weeks.

He got into his car and started the engine, waiting for the windscreen to demist before he set off on the short drive to Comi.

Like his rental car in São Paulo, this one too was a Volkswagen – a late model Golf which, having spent its life being abused by enthusiastic Italians, was not at its best on a frosty morning while its engine was still cold.

McKendrick wasn't comfortable in the cold either. With Christmas only three weeks away, even here on the Adriatic, winter was beginning to take hold – the time of year when normally he'd be pressuring the UN into finding him an assignment somewhere further south.

But with Lucy and Andrew on his mind, and now he'd almost certainly lost his job at the UN for being away so long, thinking about another assignment was about as practical as imagining he could avoid a situation that, ever since the day he'd walked into Linder's office, had become progressively more involving, more convoluted and more frightening.

To stop himself from trying to solve an insoluble problem, he concentrated on where he was going, driving slowly and taking the road to Mosciano Sant'Angelo that ran parallel with the river until he reached the church.

In spite of his good intentions, he'd still arrived too early. There was no sign of Father Moreti's car, but parked discreetly in the narrow cobbled street that flanked the east side of the churchyard were two vehicles that hadn't been here on any of the previous days – both of them ambulances or what McKendrick thought were supposed to look like ambulances.

The one nearest the bridge seemed normal enough, but mounted on the roof of the other one were several microwave or satellite dishes and a cluster of radio aerials of varying shapes and sizes.

Standing at the rear of the vehicles was Geovanni, the leader of the counter-terrorism team. Geovanni wasn't his real name because he'd told McKendrick it wasn't – which, although he spoke good English, was more or less all he had said, either about his job, or about the information that had brought him and his men here to the Comi church.

He was a slightly built man with thick curly hair and dark-brown eyes, not much older than Vicente had been, but fit, well-trained and, if his manner was anything to go by, more hard-bitten and quick-thinking than he looked.

Today, to ward off the cold he was wearing a coat over his civilian clothes and, as usual, he was speaking into his cell phone.

He waited until McKendrick had finished parking the Volkswagen then came over to say good morning.

'You're early,' McKendrick said.

'As are you.' The young man shook hands. 'We are both a little nervous, I think. For me it would be easier if my work today was more like that to which I am accustomed. Even so, I hope our arrangements will still be good.'

'Did you bring the wine and the wafers?'

'I have them. Also I have the cardboard cups, all of which have been sterilized and locked in sealed containers. One of my men will be stationed in the vestry where he will give them to the priest at the right time.'

'Did you have to twist Father Moreti's arm to stop him using his silver chalice for the wine?'

Geovanni nodded. 'But not too much. He will say the cup is away for repairs, or to be reconsecrated, or whatever excuse he chooses to make. Perhaps this experience will show him we live in an age when it is no longer wise for many people to drink from the same vessel – even in a house of God.' He smiled slightly. 'I myself would not exchange saliva with anyone except a pretty girl. Is it your intention to attend the service?'

'If it's OK with you.'

'You believe you will see a problem that we do not?'

'I don't know.' McKendrick had already spent too long thinking about it. 'If you and I have missed something, those ambulances of yours aren't going to do you any good. You know that, don't you?'

'I am told that for victims of this toxin it may be possible to reverse neurological complications by administering a drug called Neostigmine. The science is not proven, but if the destruction of acetylcholine by acetylcholinesterase can be slowed down by only a little, then I understand this will help patients to transmit their impulses across what is called their myoneural junctions.'

McKendrick was impressed. 'Where the hell did you find that out?'

Geovanni grinned. 'I learn these difficult words only last night from data the Americans send to us. It is from research carried out by the University of South Carolina. A small quantity of the drug we have brought with us today, so if we are unlucky, we shall find out if it works soon enough.'

'What about the inside of the church?'

The young man shrugged. 'Since four this morning we have searched for traces of white powder. We have swabbed and inspected the candles, the cross, the altar, the hymnbooks and even the pews and the kneeling pads. My men are very thorough, but like me they are better at finding bombs and guns.' He checked his watch. 'Please to forgive me. It is necessary for me to radio my first report. Once the people are seated, I shall join you inside before the doors are closed.'

Hoping he might yet think of an aspect that had been overlooked, McKendrick went for a walk, making his way over to the weed-filled graveyard at the rear of the church where it was easier for him to observe the people and the odd cars that were beginning to arrive.

Except for one or two families with children in tow, most of the congregation was elderly and on foot with their collars turned up against the cold. None of them seemed out of the ordinary, they all appeared to know each other, and despite McKendrick's efforts to pick out someone who looked as though they could be a stranger to the district, by the time the service was ready to start, out of the thirty-eight people he'd counted, he'd failed to identify a single suspect.

Telling himself that he'd done everything he could do, he went to find a seat inside, choosing one in the back row near the door where he had an unobstructed view of the altar and the people in front of him.

Although the morning had dawned fine and clear, the thick stone walls of the chapel were holding in the overnight cold, and it was more like being in a deep-freeze than in a church – an impression shared by Geovanni who, having come to sit beside him, was trying to silently stamp his feet.

'Have you got someone outside the door?' McKendrick asked.

'Two men, another on the bridge and one armed man in the vestry who is making sure the good father can recognize each member of his flock.' Plugging a tiny radio receiver into his ear, Geovanni pulled the lapels of his coat together to conceal his throat microphone. 'You are of the Catholic faith?'

'No.' McKendrick shook his head.

Whether Geovanni was a Catholic himself was impossible to tell. Over the next three-quarters of an hour he remained unmoving, occasionally flicking his eyes from one side of the church to the other while the priest laboured his way through yet another traditional morning Mass.

After a hymn, a greeting and what McKendrick imagined was a penitential rite, an epistle was followed by the chanting of the Holy Gospel by the standing congregation – all conducted with a marked lack of enthusiasm by the elderly and portly Father Moreti who, long before he'd embarked on his homily, seemed to have forgotten what he'd been planning to say, or finally succumbed to the numbing cold.

To McKendrick, able only to comprehend one or two Italian words, most of the service was a mystery. Like Geovanni, he'd been endeavouring to keep his wits about him, but now the priest had delivered his eucharistic prayer and had finished consecrating his freshly sterilized wafers and his carefully sealed bottle of sacramental wine, McKendrick was alert to the point where his nerves were getting the better of him.

Were his doubts about to be proved correct, he wondered? Or was this going to be the moment of truth when he found out he'd been in the right place all along?

Uneasily aware of how long it could take for the initial symptoms of TTX to manifest themselves, he watched as one by one the people of Comi dutifully received the blood and the flesh of Christ, holding out their cups for the wine and accepting the innocent wafers of unleavened wheat that with one thousandth of a gram of toxin on them would be more deadly that any bullet or any bomb.

Geovanni was similarly on edge. Throughout the proceedings he'd said not a single word to McKendrick, listening to reports he was receiving from his earpiece and speaking quietly into his microphone only when he had to.

But during the past minute, the exchange of communications had grown more frequent.

'Is something happening?' McKendrick asked.

'I must leave at once.' Geovanni stood up. 'If you wish, you may come with me.'

'Where to?'

'So we do not disturb these good people before they have completed their Mass, it is best we pretend not to hurry.'

McKendrick followed him outside. 'Don't you think one of us should've stayed?'

'It is no longer necessary.'

'Why isn't it?'

'I show you.' Geovanni headed off across the churchyard, taking a short cut to the ambulance that carried the aerials and the satellite dishes. 'Please wait.' He knocked on the rear door and spoke briefly to the man who opened it before standing aside to let his visitor climb in.

Rather as McKendrick had suspected, the vehicle wasn't an ambulance at all. It was a full-blown, mobile communication centre, crammed from floor to ceiling with cables and electronics and equipped with its own auxiliary power supply unit that was humming away somewhere beneath his feet.

Illuminated in the light from a battery of glowing television monitors, two members of Geovanni's team were waiting for his reaction to what was on their screens. The men were wearing microphones attached to radio headsets, but even in the semi-darkness, McKendrick could see how grim their faces were.

Three of the screens were carrying the same picture – coming from what he guessed was a hand-held camera. As well as being jerky, the pictures were grainy and of poor quality, showing what appeared to be the interior of a compact, stripped-out theatre somewhere. It had a high, vaulted ceiling and a stage that was flanked by curtains and a pair of freestanding, coloured floodlights.

But, scattered haphazardly on a floor of polished wood where the seats should have been, all McKendrick could see were the pitiful bodies of dead and dying children.

It was a scene from hell; one so ghastly and of such unspeakable horror that for several seconds his mind refused to accept the truth of what his eyes were telling him.

Even after he forced himself to look again, he found it impossible not to turn away.

'What you see comes not from any church,' Geovanni said quietly. 'Nor are these pictures from this area. They are being transmitted to us from a Catholic school – from one that is near the centre of Milan.' He pointed to a man who had separated himself from the swarm of paramedics, doctors and nurses who were attending to the few children who were still able to move their limbs. 'This is the man who leads the Milan terrorist response team. His people have much experience, but I think even they will not have witnessed anything so bad before.'

'What's the name of the school?' McKendrick could hardly bring himself to ask.

'You already know, I think.'

'St Gabriel's,' McKendrick said slowly. 'It's called St Gabriel's, isn't it?'

Geovanni nodded. 'The intelligence we receive from the US tells us only of this little church. So, because Washington makes no mention of a school in Milan of the same name, we are 500 kilometres from where we should have been, and now we can do nothing but watch these children die from the poison they have swallowed.'

This time, McKendrick couldn't answer at all, no more capable of coming to terms with the awful reality of what was occurring than he was able to believe that Linder, Harland, Lucy and himself could ever have been so stupid, so negligent and so desperately wrong.

Geovanni steadied himself against one of the benches. 'You have seen the stage?' he asked.

'What?' McKendrick made himself look at one of the screens. 'What do you mean?'

'At Christmas time in Italy it is customary for schools to put on a play to celebrate the nativity. According to the reports I am receiving, these are children who each Sunday in December come to rehearse with their teachers. That is why on the stage they have painted scenery to show the manger where the baby Jesus is to be born.'

201

It was hard for McKendrick to think of an explanation that could have been any worse. 'How many children?' he said.

'So far, six girls and two boys are confirmed dead. Seven more children are not expected to survive, and there is also a music teacher who is too paralysed to speak.' Geovanni adjusted his earpiece. 'We are about to lose our feed,' he said. 'Milan is worried about their signal being intercepted by television networks who may have the technology to broadcast live pictures that the public should not be permitted to view.'

'Do your people in Milan know they're dealing with tetrodotoxin?'

'I have told the forensic experts they have there, but they do not believe me because they can find no evidence of such a poison. In one hour from now, I shall enquire again.'

Before McKendrick could suggest it would be crazy not to assume it was TTX, one of Geovanni's men interrupted, pointing to another screen which was displaying a far less graphic picture – not of the school hall, but of a brief, typed statement of some kind.

Although the words were in Arabic, and the notes and the hand-written translation beneath it had all been scribbled in Italian, McKendrick knew exactly what it was.

In case he didn't, Geovanni read it out in English. *'Just as we have destroyed your palaces of Satan in New York, your commuter trains in Madrid and your immoral night-club in Bali, so shall we target your children and the children of your children. See now for yourselves how great is the wrath of Allah.'* Geovanni glanced at McKendrick. 'It is signed by a terrorist cell called *Assirat al-Moustaquim.*'

Mercifully, in the last few minutes the other three screens had gone blank. 'How genuine do you think the claim is?' he asked.

Geovanni shrugged. 'Who can know? According to our translator, the *Assirat al-Moustaquim* form part of the *Saafia Jihadia* in Morocco who are known to us. He says here in his notes that the same claim is reported to be already on the Internet, and that in the last hour, my government has been contacted by the *Al Quds al-Arabia* newspaper in London who have received a copy of the claim by e-mail.'

Too sickened by what he'd seen to ask if something equally hideous had taken place in Germany, McKendrick was struggling to make decisions, conscious of his helplessness in the face of evil on a scale that not even Linder had foreseen. 'I need to get some air,' he said. 'I'll be outside if you need me.'

Being out in the open made no difference. Instead of the smell of stale sweat and cigarette smoke, the air was fresher and cleaner, but to McKendrick, unable to rid himself of one particular image, the brightness and the chill of the still-cold morning seemed no more real than the shocking pictures he'd just seen.

The image was appalling: that of a slim nine or 10-year-old girl, a golden-haired Virgin Mary lying on her back on the floor of the school hall. She was dead, her costume still padded out with a cushion to simulate a pregnancy that had given birth to the Christian faith – a faith whose principles were so far removed from those of the men who had killed her that, at this very moment if McKendrick could have had his way, every single member of every Christian Freedom Party would have paid with their lives for the horror they had brought to the children of St Gabriel's today.

It took him nearly five minutes to regain any sense of normality and to realize that Lucy could be caught up in events that might not only be just as bad, but possibly even more repellent.

To find out, he called her on his mobile, discovering that she either had her phone switched off or that she was outside the Frankfurt receiving area somewhere.

Linder, though, was in his office and, judging by the concern in his voice, was expecting McKendrick's call, and aware of what was going on.

'How bad is it in Italy?' Linder asked.

'One teacher and fourteen children – eight of them already dead. 'How did you hear?'

'From Lucy. I had a quick call from her about twenty minutes ago. She's up to speed on what's happening in Germany, of course, but she said all the information she's been getting from Italy has come through the German police who are stationed at the convent with her. We're not much better off here, although Swiss TV are beginning to screen what they're calling a breaking story, and a couple of local Zurich radio stations have direct links to reporters in Milan and Cologne. Didn't Lucy call you too?'

'No,' McKendrick said. 'That's why I'm phoning you. Was there a

St Catherine's school in Cologne?'

'I'm afraid so. The children are all young boys – 11-year-olds at their Sunday morning soccer practice. Some of the parents are in a bad way too, and Lucy said the coach is already dead.'

The concern in Linder's voice wasn't concern at all, McKendrick realized. The man was thoroughly shaken, suffering from a crisis of confidence for the first time in his life and speaking too precisely in an attempt to cover it up. 'Did Lucy sound OK?' he asked.

'She was upset, but apparently the Germans have asked her to help them with a lead they have, so perhaps she won't have time to worry too much about how wrong we all were.'

'What lead?' Even without knowing what it was, he didn't much like the idea. 'Have they found TTX at the school in Cologne?'

'No, unfortunately they haven't – which is why we're in danger of losing every shred of credibility we have. If there's no evidence of TTX in Milan either, the manifesto won't just sound like a conspiracy theory: people will either assume we're playing a sick joke, or think we're trying to sell them a fairy tale.'

'What's Lucy been asked to do?' McKendrick was still waiting to hear.

'She was in a hurry, so I haven't got the details. The police were flying her from the convent to Cologne by helicopter – that's why she won't be answering her phone. All I know is that a matron at the school remembers seeing the driver of a van that delivers catering supplies to the school every Friday morning. Apparently she only noticed him because he wasn't the usual driver, and because she saw the same man and the same van again today.'

'At the school?'

'Yes. At about the time the principal received a claim of responsibility note that's supposed to have come from a terrorist organization who call themselves the *Groupe Islamique Armee*.'

'What the hell's any of that got to do with Lucy?'

'As far as I can make out, it's because of the matron's description of the van driver. She remembers that he was a skinhead wearing combat boots.'

'With white laces,' McKendrick interrupted. 'It was Meyer. Jürgen bloody Meyer. He was there – to make sure everything had gone to plan.'

'That's what Lucy thinks. The catering company reported the van stolen on Wednesday night, so I think we can assume half the police in Germany will be out looking for it by now.'

'And they want Lucy to talk to the matron?'

'Presumably. They've promised to fly her straight to the airport afterwards so she'll be back in Zurich sometime this evening.' Linder coughed discreetly. 'I know this sounds like another imposition, but if you can get on an early flight from Rome, I don't suppose you could call round and see her at her home, could you? In the circumstances, I think she might be grateful for the company. I'd go myself, but I have to decide how on earth we're going to handle this mess we're in, and I'm expecting a call from Harland later on.'

'From Washington?'

'No. He's back in Bonn. He flew back to Germany last night – something to do with his bosses believing the White House will be more impressed if Harland is seen to be the DEA's local man in Europe. God only knows what they'll be thinking once they hear about these Italian and German children.'

'OK,' McKendrick said. 'Leave Lucy to me. If you hear from her before I do, tell her I'm on my way.'

'I'm sure she'll be pleased. If you have something to write on, I'll give you her address.'

'Don't bother. I know where she lives.' McKendrick hesitated for a second. 'Do you want her to call you when she gets in?'

'No, no. I'll be in touch first thing tomorrow. By then we'll know how successful the Coalition have been, and we can see whether Harland believes there's anything sensible we can do to recover the situation.'

McKendrick had his own ideas about what ought to be done, but since none of them were sensible, he said his goodbye and ended the call still unwilling to believe that any of this was really happening and anxious now to be gone from a place where he should never have been to begin with.

Geovanni and his men were preparing to depart as well. The Italian came over to shake hands. He too seemed preoccupied with his own thoughts, either unable to forget the images on his monitors, or perhaps because he wrongly believed he'd witnessed nothing more sinister than Islamic terrorism in its most repugnant form. 'I promise you we will destroy the *Saafia Jihadia*,' he said. 'We shall hunt them down, we will find them and we will kill them. In the meantime I wish to thank you for your help.'

'I didn't give you any.'

'In these matters it is never possible to do more than one can do.' Geovanni handed over his business card. 'Should you obtain better information about this tetrodotoxin poison I would welcome a phone call from you. Until then, I am sorry your visit to my country has been attended by such atrocity.' He pointed to the families who had begun emerging from the church. 'I think they are better people than you and I. For men like us it is hard to forgive and to believe in the goodness of God, is it not?'

It wasn't hard for McKendrick: it was utterly impossible – a thought that continued to haunt him long after he'd started out on his drive back to Rome.

To save time he took the E2 Autostrada from Mosciano Sant'Angelo, turning on to highway 5 just south of Pescara before heading inland across country, gradually increasing his speed until the Volkswagen would go no faster, half-willing the engine to explode so he could use the breakdown as an excuse to phone Geovanni and tell him the truth.

But just as the Volkswagen stubbornly refused to expire, so did McKendrick come to realize that the truth would no more bring the children back to life than it would bring justice to the organization that had planned their deaths.

Even if Geovanni could be made to believe that, instead of hunting down the shadowy terrorists of the *Saafia Jihadia*, he should be raiding the Italian offices of the home-grown *Partito Christiano Di Liberta*, what guarantee was there of him uncovering the evidence he needed? And if there was none, and once a major European Christian Freedom Party had been cleared of any suspicion or wrong-doing, what then would there be to stop the Coalition from implementing the rest of their awful strategy?

The dilemma was the same one McKendrick remembered discussing a week ago in Linder's office – a dilemma brought into such sharp focus by the events of today that from here on he knew that nothing less than a solution of the severest kind could ever hope to stop them from happening again.

For the remainder of his journey he continued wrestling with the problem, only managing to put it aside when he reached the outskirts of Rome where the traffic made it impossible for him to drive too fast and where, to his relief, he found his thoughts of Lucy once again beginning to occupy his mind.

# Chapter 16

She wasn't home yet. The lights were on in the adjoining apartments, but Lucy's was still in darkness.

McKendrick paid the taxi driver, then used the key she'd given him to let himself in and went straight to her answering machine, hoping she might have left a message for him.

She had four waiting for her, two from a French-speaking woman who was querying a clause in a contract for the erection of wind turbines at a place called St-Gilles-Croix-de-St-Vie, and the two messages McKendrick had left while he'd been waiting to board his flight in Rome.

He wasn't altogether surprised to have arrived before her. At this time of year with Christmas round the corner, just about every weekend flight was overbooked and, if the congestion at the air terminal in Rome was an indication of how bad things were in Cologne, she'd be lucky to get on any kind of flight, let alone an early one.

After trying unsuccessfully to find out where she was by calling her on her mobile, he went to the fridge to get himself a beer, then sat down and switched on the television.

He hadn't been sure how long it would take for the news to hit the headlines, but after watching for less than a minute, he understood what had prompted the unsolicited outburst from the taxi driver who'd brought him from the airport − a large, articulate man who, after criticizing the Americans for not yet having turned the Middle East into a nuclear wasteland, had declared himself ready to do his bit by running over anyone in Zurich who looked remotely like a Muslim or an Arab.

Every channel was screening the story, either in the form of newsflashes between programmes, or through hastily arranged studio interviews with politicians, commentators and experts on Islamic fundamentalism – every one of them offering opinions based on a flood of misinformation that was coming in from so many different sources that the Coalition could not have hoped to have done a better job themselves.

In more than one instance, commentators were mixing up the names of the terrorist cells who were supposed to be claiming responsibility, and by some means or other, an English-language channel had got hold of a video clip showing children's bodies being carried out on stretchers from the German school.

To the credit of the Italians, who seemed more wary of creating racial tension on the streets, the information coming out of Milan was either being censored by the networks themselves, or had fallen under government control.

Censorship or not, the consequences of today's events were already more far-reaching and alarming than McKendrick had been anticipating.

In the fight for ratings, the media was feeding on itself, revealing more and more information in more and more lurid detail as the story gathered momentum and now that people on the eastern seaboard of North America had switched on their TVs and radios for the evening news.

He'd forgotten about his beer, too busy surfing channels to bother with it. He'd temporarily forgotten about Quaid too, but he should have guessed the Coalition would be quick to capitalize on their work.

So far, only CNN were being brave enough to air an apparently impromptu interview with Quaid – one that seemed to have been recorded several hours ago before the American public and the US media had been fully aware of what was going on.

The leader of the Coalition was being restrained, drawing the inevitable parallel with other less-newsworthy examples of Islamic terrorism, but at pains to point out that, in comparison with the Twin Tower disaster, the body count at the schools was extremely low – although in this case, as he was being careful to emphasize, there was, of course, a difference because most of today's victims had been innocent, young Christian children.

If not quite a masterstroke, it was a brilliant piece of propaganda,

McKendrick thought. With public revulsion already running at a level that was out of all proportion to the number of actual deaths, any reminder of how very innocent and of how very young the children had been was as good a way of fuelling the Coalition's cause as reminding people about September 11.

McKendrick didn't want to be reminded about anything. During his flight from Italy, by making a conscious effort to do so he'd been able to erase the worst of the St Gabriel's images from his mind – mostly, he'd decided, because images were all they'd been, ill-defined, black and white pictures on Geovanni's bank of television monitors – the reason, perhaps, why unlike his memories of what had happened in Kalimantan, the events at the school, fresh and terrible though they were, somehow already seemed less vivid to him.

He watched for a few more minutes, then switched off the television, disgusted by a plea for calm that was being broadcast by the very channel that, only five minutes ago, had been displaying the pictures of the children's bodies.

The whole fucking world was sick, he thought, so riddled with racial and religious hatred, and so poorly served by a media that was incapable of separating fact from fiction, that Linder might as well let the Coalition get on with their crusade in the vain hope that someone else might find a way to snuff it out before it got even more out of hand.

Instead of drinking his beer, McKendrick tipped it down the sink and went on a hunt for something stronger, searching through the cupboards in the kitchen and the lounge until, in a cabinet beside the bookcase, he found some soda water and a nearly full bottle of Black Label. The Scotch made him feel less edgy, but did little to stop him wondering about how much longer Lucy was going to be, and by midnight his concern was growing fast.

To occupy the time, he went for another aimless wander around the apartment, on this occasion deciding to inspect her bedroom where, if things had turned out differently last week, he would have spent the night with her.

There was an abstract painting hanging on the wall above a small teddy-bear that was propped up on the bed, but otherwise, except for half a wardrobeful of designer clothes and several pairs of expensive shoes there wasn't a great deal to see – or so he thought until he noticed a folder lying on her dressing-table.

Inside the folder were photocopies of a two-year-old magazine arti-cle he'd written about the reignition of underground fires by lightning strikes – a dull, dry treatise that would be of interest only to another specialist in the field, or maybe to someone who wanted to find out more about the person who'd written it.

Unable to decide whether he was pleased or not, and feeling guilty for poking around in her bedroom uninvited, he left the folder undis-turbed and returned to the lounge where, no sooner had he begun to pour what he promised himself would be his last drink, than he heard her at the door.

Knowing she'd have seen the lights on in the apartment, and more than a little relieved, he went to let her in.

It wasn't her. It was Linder – standing outside in the corridor, hold-ing his briefcase in both hands and peering into the apartment as though he was hoping to see Lucy.

'Evening,' McKendrick said. 'What are you doing here?'

'Is she back?'

'No. Why?'

Offering no explanation and without waiting to be asked in, Linder pushed past and went straight to the lounge.

'Are you as worried about her as I am?' McKendrick said.

'I'm more than worried. That's why I've come over. I've just had a call from Cologne to say she's gone missing.'

'What the hell does that mean?' A knot had formed in McKendrick's stomach. 'Gone missing where?'

'After the police had taken her to see the matron at the school, they assigned one of their men to drive her to the airport. But it's beginning to look as though she might not have got there. They've located the car, but they can't find Lucy.'

'What does the driver say?'

'He's dead.' Linder slumped down in a chair.

'Oh Jesus.' McKendrick couldn't handle this. 'How? Where?'

'He'd been shot through the eye. His body was found inside a run-down boarding-house somewhere in the south of the city near the Rhine – the same place they found the catering van.'

'The van Meyer was seen in?'

211

'The German police don't know who Meyer is. They only have the matron's description of him, and however much Lucy's told them. All they've said is that the minute they received a sighting of the vehicle they issued an all-cars alert which they think Lucy's driver could have picked up on his radio.'

'And to see if she could identify Meyer, he took her there without any fucking back up?'

'No one knows. Apparently, if they'd made a detour to the boarding-house it wouldn't have taken them much out of their way, but it's possible the driver dropped her off at the airport first and then went back there by himself.'

McKendrick wasn't taking the chance. 'Give me your car keys,' he said.

'What for?'

'What do you think? I can be in Weiskirchen in four hours.'

'Why should she be there for God's sake?'

'Where the hell else would Meyer have taken her? The minute the bastard saw her he'd have guessed things were going wrong. He'd have been in touch with Zitelmann and Kessel right away. By now they'll have talked to Quaid about putting some kind of damage control in place, but they can't do that until they find out how much of a threat we are.' McKendrick paused. 'And they know Lucy can tell them. You haven't forgotten Bridget Goddard, have you?'

'No. I haven't forgotten.'

'Give me your keys then.' He was prepared to take them if he had to.

Linder remained sitting in his chair. 'What if you're wrong?' he said. 'We were wrong about the church and the convent, and now there's no evidence of TTX showing up at the schools it looks as though we were wrong about that too. So what makes you think you're right about this? If all you're prepared to offer are guesses, you're being irresponsible.'

'If you want to talk about irresponsibility, you listen to me,' McKendrick said. 'Ever since this started you've been treating Lucy as though she's in some kind of private fucking army of yours. If I'd lost my family at Dachau, I might feel the same way you do about neo-Nazis, but that has nothing to do with Lucy, and it never will have. So I don't give a shit what you think, and I'm sure as hell not going to waste my breath arguing with you while she's in the kind of trouble she could be in right now.'

'Have you finished?' Linder said.

'Not yet, no. I'll tell you when I have. Are you really such a self-centred bastard that you don't care any more about her than you care about what the Coalition's going to do next? You're happy to risk her life and see a whole lot more children die, are you?'

By endeavouring to exert more pressure, McKendrick had gone too far.

Linder's expression had hardened. 'You underestimate my concern for Lucy,' he said coldly. 'And you underestimate me. I'm simply trying to ascertain how sure you are about where she is so I can decide how best to do something about it.'

'Neither of us are going to do that by sitting around here, are we?'

'It depends on whether Harland's right.' Linder got to his feet. 'He has a theory none of us had thought of before.'

'About what?'

'The manifesto refers to three more unspecified targets: one in the UK and one in the US on December 12th, and another somewhere else on Christmas Day. But after what's happened in Milan and Cologne, Harland believes the Coalition might not need to go through with any of them.'

'Why not?' McKendrick failed to follow the logic. 'They're doing pretty damn well up to now, aren't they?'

'1996, Dunblane, Scotland: sixteen children shot dead at their school. 1999, Columbine High School in Colorado: twelve students and a teacher similarly gunned down. And then, in 2004, there were those 156 children killed in the Beslan school siege in Russia. Three massacres that created such a devastating public outcry that no one's ever going to forget them.'

'So what?'

Linder contained his annoyance. 'If you'll give me a chance, I'll tell you. Now the Coalition have demonstrated the effectiveness of targeting school-aged children, Harland believes they should be able to sit back and let genuine Islamic terrorists take over their job for them. He thinks al-Qaeda will have learned a useful lesson from the Coalition today. I hope he's not right, but he might be.'

'How does any of that help Lucy?'

'It buys her some time, and it buys us time. If the Coalition think they can afford to scrap or postpone the rest of their TTX programme, no one at ICIS is going to be in that much of a hurry to question her, so she should have a better chance of staying alive over the next few hours.' Linder looked directly at McKendrick. 'Rushing off into the night by yourself isn't going to solve anything. If you end up in Zitelmann's lake with a bullet through your head, you won't be much use to Lucy or anyone else. We need proper support, and we need plenty of it.'

'And you can arrange that?'

'Yes. I don't think I have to explain how many other European Jews lost their families at places like Dachau. The surviving children and grandchildren of those families certainly don't form part of what you term a private fucking army, but I know a number of people who can be relied on in an emergency like this. It'll only take me a couple of hours to arrange for them to meet us somewhere in Germany tomorrow night.'

'What about Harland?' McKendrick said.

'I'm sure we can count on him. He's fairly unhappy. The Pentagon are accusing the DEA of supplying incorrect intelligence about the church and the convent, and since no one can find any traces of TTX, the Americans think the manifesto is a fabrication.'

'And Harland's taking the blame for it?'

Linder nodded. 'Which means he'll be as anxious as we are to prove we haven't been on a wild goose chase. He'll be upset to hear about Lucy too.'

'Didn't you tell him?'

'I hadn't received the call from Cologne when I spoke to him.' Linder opened his briefcase and took out a videocassette. 'I'll start making phone calls,' he said. 'You have a look through this.'

'What is it?'

'Infrared surveillance coverage of the lake. While you've been in Italy an associate of mine spent two nights parked in the lane along the south boundary of the Weiskirchen estate. The tape isn't very clear and it doesn't help us a great deal, but you'll see how much night time activity there is at that derelict power station – which tends to reinforce your view about it being the access point to Zitelmann's laboratory.'

McKendrick had long since stopped thinking about the laboratory. Instead, all he could think of was Lucy, knowing that any attempt at a single-handed rescue would be as futile as imagining she was going to be all right, but desperately willing himself to believe that she somehow would be.

It was a wasted effort.

For the remainder of the night, as his plan began to take shape and as one after another the responses to Linder's phone calls started to pour in, he struggled to overcome his apprehension and his fears. But by dawn he'd lost the battle, no closer to believing he could save her than he was able to believe she was still alive, and only managing to get a grip on himself when, at the end of the longest day he'd ever spent, they at last set off in Linder's new Mercedes, heading north into the darkness towards Saarbrücken and to the grim uncertainty that lay beyond.

# Chapter 17

The bridge at Zerf had turned out to be a less than ideal place for a rendezvous. McKendrick had suggested using it because of its proximity to Weiskirchen, and also because, like Harland, he'd been here before and knew how to find it. But there was more traffic on the bridge than he'd expected for this time of night, and the line of parked cars was attracting the attention of passing drivers.

Altogether there were five cars, with Harland's black Peugeot bringing up the rear. Linder parked behind it and switched off his engine.

'You brief Harland,' he said. 'I'll explain things to the others. Is that OK?'

'Fine.' McKendrick nodded. 'Make it as quick as you can.' He got out and went to meet the American who'd seen them arrive and was already coming to say hello.

The DEA agent was well insulated against the cold, wearing a black leather jerkin over a thick woollen sweater. 'Hi.' He shook hands and pointed to a patch on the road. 'Better not let Linder see that.'

It was the place where Lucy had abandoned the burning Mercedes, a scorched area of bitumen that had melted and resolidified, a reminder of what had happened here seventeen days ago, and a warning of how uncompromising Zitelmann's men were likely to be tonight.

'Will you do something for me?' McKendrick said.

'I thought I was.'

'Something else. I don't want anyone except you and me going down into the tunnel.'

'Because that's where you think they've got Lucy?'

'I don't know. But if Zitelmann's still scheduling courses at ICIS, he

216

might not want to have her locked up in the house.'

'You don't know what shit we could run into down there. What if we get ourselves boxed in?'

'We won't. Linder's giving us two of his men. They can make sure no one jumps us from behind.'

'What about head on? If you're right about where the laboratory is, what if the tunnel's connected to the house?'

'It isn't.' McKendrick injected more confidence into his voice. 'Linder's got tapes showing people going between the house and the power station. They wouldn't be doing that unless they had to. And the fence round the lake wouldn't need a gate in it, would it?'

'Just asking. Don't get your balls in a knot. If that's how you want to play things, that's what we'll do. You never know, even if it's a rat's nest down there, we might still get lucky.'

'Lucky enough to find Lucy in one piece?'

Harland looked uncomfortable. 'That's not what I meant. I just figure we might be able to rope up Zitelmann, Kessel and Meyer in one hit.'

'Do you think Kessel's there?'

'Why wouldn't she be? According to our guys in Brazil, Meyer flew out to Cologne last Wednesday morning, and Kessel was right behind him on a flight to Rome. You don't have to be too smart to figure out why that was.' Harland spat out a wad of gum. 'Looks like we're ready to rock and roll.'

Linder had finished issuing his instructions and was walking back along the bridge in the company of someone else – a slim, young woman wearing an unzipped ski jacket and a rolled up balaclava.

'Hello.' She smiled. 'I'm Zoe. It's me you'll be hearing over your radio, so I thought I'd better come and introduce myself. I know this'll sound silly, but if you have cell phones, you can either give them to me, or switch them off and put them in your car. That way they won't start ringing at the wrong time.'

Wondering who she was, and surprised by her directness, McKendrick gave his to Harland who tossed it into the back of the Peugeot.

Linder was quick to offer an explanation. 'I'm afraid I haven't been entirely truthful with you,' he said. 'Zoe's my sister. She won't thank

me for telling you this, but in another life she spent nine months working for Israeli Intelligence. That's why she volunteered to attend the
course at Zitelmann's institute, and why she's come along tonight.'

She smiled again. 'That's not the real reason. I was asked to.'

'Because you know the inside layout of the buildings,' McKendrick
said.

'And where to cut the phone lines and how to disable the alarms and
the security cameras.'

Zoe Linder was younger than her brother with similar features but
with much darker hair that was spilling out from beneath her balaclava. She seemed relaxed and was making sure they could see the gun
inside her jacket.

Harland was unimpressed. 'This isn't Israel,' he said. 'You're not
going to be up against a bunch of stone-throwing Palestinian kids
tonight.'

'I know that.' She pulled up her zip. 'And I know what I'm doing.
Or don't you think that fourteen men with stun grenades and automatic weapons can do the job?'

'Ask McKendrick. When he and Lucy were out at the estate, they
got themselves hunted down like rabbits.'

Linder put an end to the conversation. 'That's not going to happen
tonight,' he said. 'We're wasting time. Zoe says there's a field about a
kilometre and a half from the main gates where she thinks the ground
will be hard enough for us to park the cars. We'll take twelve men to
the house and two can go with you to the power station.' He handed
McKendrick a small military radio. 'Only use that if you have to, and
no matter what you think, don't forget we're doing this for more than
one reason.'

'I know.'

'Good luck then.' He turned to leave. 'If Lucy's at the house, Zoe
will give you a call.'

McKendrick didn't answer, conscious of how many hours it had
taken them to get this far, and only slightly more confident than he had
been before they'd left Zurich on their long drive north.

'Hey.' Harland broke his train of thought. 'What do you reckon?'

'About what?'

'Zoe.'

'Probably like her brother – tougher than she looks. Did you bring the bolt-cutters?'

'They're in the car. Come on, wagons are moving out.' Harland went to the Peugeot and waited for McKendrick to climb in. 'I brought you something else, too. It's on the floor in the back. You can have it as a present.'

While Harland pushed the Peugeot out into the traffic and started overtaking cars to join the tail of the convoy, McKendrick inspected his present.

It was a brand new 9mm Walther automatic, still in its box and with two fresh clips of ammunition to go with it.

'What about you?' he asked. 'Didn't you bring the Uzi?'

The American patted his pocket. 'Wouldn't leave home without it. Not that I can see it doing us much good. Squirting an Uzi around in an underground cave full of TTX will be about as smart as playing catch with a hand grenade in a shit-house. If the ricochets don't get us, the TTX will.'

'It won't be a cave. It's a tunnel under the lake.'

'If it exists.'

'Yeah, if it does.' By now, in between worrying about Lucy, McKendrick had been struggling with his doubts for nearly twenty-two hours, refusing to accept he could be wrong, but unable to forget Linder's warning about how wrong they'd been about everything else.

To control his nerves, he started cleaning the Walther, removing every scrap of grease from the action, making himself believe he was doing something useful during the ten-kilometre drive to Weiskirchen – the final step of a journey that had brought him from a fire-front in Kalimantan to what might or might not be a burned-out seam beneath a sterile lake in Germany where maybe – just maybe – if he wasn't too late already, he would discover if his fears were as real as he thought they were.

Nothing had changed. Despite a lack of moonlight, the bullet scars in the stone wall had been fresh enough to see, and on the south side of the lake where the old section of fencing had been replaced, the slack bottom wire had been as easy to crawl under as it had been on the night when McKendrick had been here last.

The lake too was the same, no less sinister than he remembered it, still smelling powerfully of antiseptic, still filled with the same milk-coloured water, and still surrounded by a foreshore of sickly yellow mud.

Although from a distance the derelict power station appeared to be in darkness with its doors shut tight, he nevertheless approached it with some caution, leaving Harland and Linder's men to cover him from the shadows until he'd found what he'd hoped to find, and only then using his flashlight to signal the all clear.

Harland came to see. 'Any outside cameras?' he asked.

'Not on this wall. We shouldn't have to worry about cameras – not if Zoe's going to knock out the whole system for us.' McKendrick pointed at the doors. 'Take a look.'

'At what?'

'The hasps. Where the padlock's supposed to be.'

'So there isn't one. Big deal.' Harland put down the bolt-cutters and slipped his Uzi back into his pocket. 'That doesn't mean someone's inside. Maybe Zitelmann never got around to replacing the old one.'

'Or maybe he did, and whoever's in there has taken it with them.'

'Depends if this is the only way in and out of your tunnel.' Harland checked his watch. 'We're going to know that pretty soon now.'

Linder's men had gone to reconnoitre, keeping in the shadows of the building while they searched for another entrance and looked for hidden cameras. They too were wearing balaclavas, and both were armed, one with a Valmet assault rifle, the other with a SIG-AMT – guns with sufficient fire-power to hold off the most determined of attacks if things went wrong and it came to that.

McKendrick was beginning to believe it wouldn't. Up at the house, a solitary light was visible in one of the upstairs rooms, but so far no others had come on, and there had been no shouting, nor the barking of any dogs.

So why was he apprehensive, he wondered? And why was he so damn cold?

Over the last ten or fifteen minutes there had been a marked drop in temperature, and now he'd stopped moving he was shivering, conscious of the chill of his sweat against his skin, and no longer able to keep a proper grip on his gun.

Harland appeared to be neither cold nor apprehensive. He stopped talking to the two men who'd returned from their reconnaissance and came over to ask if McKendrick had heard anything over the radio.

'Not yet. Maybe Zoe couldn't find the phone lines.'

But she obviously had. No sooner had he finished speaking, than from the ground floor of the house came the sound of exploding stun grenades. At the same time, there was barking, and suddenly there were lights on everywhere. A second later he heard the stuttering of automatic weapons.

Although the gunfire was short-lived, from this far away it was impossible to tell whether the element of surprise had worked in Linder's favour or how successful the raid was going to be.

The odd muffled burst was still coming from the outbuildings and from some of the upstairs rooms, but most of the disturbance was now being created by the dogs.

'How long do you want to wait?' Harland pulled back the slide on his Uzi.

McKendrick wasn't sure. 'A couple more minutes aren't going to make any difference,' he said. 'You're the one who's worried about us getting trapped underground.'

'Not much chance of that while we're standing out here, is there?'

'Keep your voice down.' He pointed.

A moment ago the implement shed had been in darkness, but it wasn't any more. Light was filtering through the crack between the doors and shining through some of the fractured joints in the concrete panels.

Quickly, he took the risk of putting his eye to the crack.

Like the stone wall, the fence and the lake, the inside of the build-ing was as it had been. Just as the orchard tractor and the lawn mower were parked where they'd been parked before, so were the same gardening tools hanging from the hooks on the wall, and the wheel-barrow and the cans of phenol were still standing beside the unopened bags of grass seed on the wooden pallets.

The only thing that had changed was his luck.

If the light hadn't come on, he wouldn't have been looking through the crack. And if he hadn't been looking through the crack, he would-n't have seen that one of the pallets was moving.

It was sliding sideways to expose a rectangular opening in the floor, being driven by an electric motor or what he thought could be a hydraulic ram concealed inside the pallet itself.

Uncertain of what to do, he checked the safety on the Walther and moved back, bumping into Harland who'd come to stand behind him.

'Easy there.' The American deflected McKendrick's gun arm. 'What is it?'

'Some kind of hatch or trapdoor opening up in the floor.'

'OK. Leave this to me. If someone's heard what's going on at the house, they'll be using this as a bolthole or wanting to find out if they're better off staying where they are. Which way do the doors open?'

McKendrick checked. 'Outwards.'

'Right. Make sure your radio's off, no fucking heroics and don't shoot me or anyone else.' Harland hurried over to brief Linder's men, waiting until they'd taken up positions out of sight at the corners of the building before he made his own preparations, taking off his jerkin and giving the Uzi to McKendrick. 'If this turns to shit, the minute I yell at you, throw me my gun.'

From inside the building, the clang of engaging catches was accompanied by the soft hiss of escaping air or of hydraulics losing pressure.

Holding the Walther in one hand and the Uzi in the other, McKendrick stationed himself by the left-hand door, as ready as he was ever going to be.

Whether Harland was ready, he couldn't tell. The American was lost in the shadows, a shapeless figure crouched among the pieces of rusted steel and slabs of broken concrete.

Whoever was inside was being slow to reveal themselves – alerted perhaps by a sudden loss of communications with the house or by the distant gunfire coming from it. But they weren't going to wait much longer.

A creak from an unoiled hinge was a warning that the right-hand door was about to open.

It was Meyer, stepping forwards until he was silhouetted against the light, entirely unaware of how foolish he was being.

Harland had him before he could move, locking a forearm round his throat and lifting his feet off the ground, easily evading his flailing

222

arms and his ineffectual kicks.

Although the German was wiry and stronger than he looked, he was no match for Harland who, without apparent effort, was choking off his windpipe and exerting more and more pressure on his neck and spine.

It was hard to watch, a slow-motion lesson in submission that only ended when the American rammed his victim face-first into the door and allowed him to gulp a single breath of air.

'You get one chance at this,' Harland said. 'Give me the wrong answer, and I'll break your fucking neck. How many men?'

'At the house, I think no more than seven.' Meyer tried to cough. 'Underground, Herr Zitelmann, Fraulein Kessel and myself only.'

'OK.' Harland glanced at McKendrick. 'Get his arms behind his back and wrap two cable-ties round his wrists. They're in my jerkin. Pull them so tight they cut off his circulation.'

'How about his ankles?'

'Not unless you want to carry him while he takes us down to meet his friends.'

Meyer made no effort to resist while his wrists were tied, still coughing and still desperately trying to breathe until Harland let him go.

'We'd better contact Zoe,' McKendrick said.

Harland nodded. 'Tell her we've got Meyer and find out what's happening at her end.'

Zoe answered at once, sounding more relieved to hear McKendrick's voice than she was to hear about Meyer. 'You've had your radio off,' she said. 'We've been worried.'

'We're fine. How have you got on?'

'Easier than we thought. Everything's secure here, but we have two men down. They'll be all right though – nothing serious.'

'Have you found Lucy?' He made himself ask the question.

'We're still looking. The rooms in the west wing are all locked and we've only just got the keys for them. And there's a cellar we're still trying to get into – well, we think that's what it is – unless it's the way into the tunnel.'

'It isn't. It's here. We're about to head down to have a look. Let me know when you've been through the house, will you?'

'If Lucy's here, I promise we'll find her. We'll smash open the cellar door if we have to.'

'OK.' McKendrick was anxious to get on. 'I'll call you in about five minutes.' He pocketed the radio and turned to level his gun at Meyer. 'Where is she?' he said.

The German was nervous. 'The girl you call Lucy I have seen only once – when you bring her to the San Michel restaurant in São Paulo. Why would she come here?'

Harland retrieved his Uzi and put his jerkin back on. 'You're wasting your time with a piece of shit like him,' he said. 'He figures if he can keep you talking long enough, Kessel and Zitelmann will guess he's run into trouble. You close the doors while I work out how to use the lift.'

There wasn't much to work out. The lift was simplicity itself, a hydraulically actuated platform surrounded by a waist-high guardrail with a gate in it on which was mounted a small control unit.

Prodding Meyer on to the platform ahead of him, Harland waited for McKendrick to step on board then thrust the muzzle of his gun between the German's buttocks. 'You speak when I say you can,' he said. 'And you go where and when I tell you to go. Open your mouth at the wrong time or move too fast, and you'll be a nasty little skinhead who hasn't got any balls.'

McKendrick positioned his thumb over the button on the control unit. 'You all set?' he said.

'Sure.' Harland nodded. 'Go.'

For the first few metres of their descent, there was sufficient light coming down from the implement shed for McKendrick to see that the lift shaft had been part of the seam, a tall chimney of unknown height that had once been full of red-hot burning coal.

Since then, to prevent it from collapsing inwards and to stop the lake water from seeping into it, at some point in the more recent past, the walls had been coated with a layer of sprayed-on concrete.

But there was no mistaking its origins, and no mistaking the warmth and the peculiar odour that was drifting up from below – the same, not unpleasant smell of seaweed and salt water that McKendrick had last encountered in Maria Kessel's warehouse.

After continuing on down to a depth of what he thought was nearly twenty metres, the lift shuddered to a standstill and the light went out.

For a second or two the platform was in darkness. Then, after the hissing sound had died away, a section of the shaft began to open up as a large steel door swung open.

And there, illuminated in the cold blue glare of countless rows of fluorescent tubes, was McKendrick's tunnel – except that it wasn't one. It was a vaulted chamber, a huge, white-painted underground cavern that had been reinforced with man-made buttresses and columns, its roof soaring in places to a height of eight or ten metres, while in others the seam had fanned out sideways like veins or strata in a rock-face to create a labyrinth of dead-end passageways and alleys so shallow that only a child could have hoped to enter them.

In different circumstances, the formation would have held some interest for McKendrick. As it was, he barely noticed, his attention concentrated entirely on the figures of two people who, now they'd realized what was happening, had already started to retreat.

Harland didn't hesitate, firing two successive rounds into one of the blind passageways beside them.

In the confines of the cavern, and at such short range, the muzzle blast alone was enough of a shock to stop Zitelmann in his tracks. Kessel, though, was not intimidated. She'd ducked behind a large fish tank to use it as a shield and was continuing to feel her way along a workbench with one of her hands behind her back.

Harland moved the barrel of the Uzi. 'Wherever you're off to, I wouldn't go there if I were you,' he said.

She stopped, but in contrast to Zitelmann who was cowering up against one of the concrete columns she wasn't frightened, staring back at Harland as if deciding whether he'd fire again.

Hoping he wouldn't, McKendrick tried to get a better fix on his surroundings.

The size of the cavern was an illusion created largely by its height. Most of the useable space was taken up by fish tanks and aquariums, leaving little room for the laboratory section, which in itself was quite small, a self-contained biohazard area consisting of three freestanding glass-panelled cubicles interconnected via a series of air locks, seals and filters, and all of it standing on a floor of highly polished stainless steel.

The cubicle nearest to him was the only one with an outside door, but was otherwise uninteresting, housing a computer work-station, a biological wash-down shower, and sandwiched between a pair of storage cabinets and a rack of protective clothing what looked like an ultra-violet sterilization booth.

Inside the other two, illuminated by more fluorescent lights and standing on polished metal benches, was the expensive, high-tech apparatus Zitelmann had used to pioneer the development and manufacture of a toxin that no one had ever made before, equipment that was as surgically clean and gleaming as the glass panels and the floor.

Had McKendrick been paying less attention to the equipment and more to Maria Kessel he might have had time to shout a warning. But he was too late, and Harland was too slow.

In one quick movement, she'd brought out her hand from behind her back and was holding up a small glass vial. 'You will not succeed,' she said. 'We are already too strong, and soon the seeds we have sown will make us stronger.'

'Who gives a fuck.' Harland motioned with his gun. 'Get over there with Zitelmann.'

'Do you not understand what this is?' She held the vial up higher. 'In such a closed environment, if I crush this with my fingers or drop it on the floor, the air-conditioning system will disperse the TTX before we are able to reach the surface. So, unless you are very brave or very stupid, you must allow us to leave now. If you do not, together we will breathe in the powder which will dissolve on the membranes of our throats and noses, and, one by one, together we will die.'

The threat was real enough. But apparently of no concern to Harland.

He looked at her in disdain. Then, without compunction shot her.

The bullet caught her high in the shoulder, splintering the bone and slamming her backwards so hard against the bench that the vial dropped from her nerveless fingers, not on to the floor, but into the water of the fish tank.

How lucky or how calculated the shot had been, McKendrick wasn't sure. But now that Kessel had collapsed moaning beneath the bench, and with the vial floating harmlessly in the tank, he was willing to give the American the benefit of the doubt.

As though nothing much had happened, Harland produced more of his cable-ties. 'Do you want to waste your time tying up a two-bit Nazi whore?' he asked. 'Or shall I try again?'

In case he wasn't bluffing, and because Kessel could have vital information about Lucy, McKendrick made the mistake of kneeling down while he secured her wrists and ankles.

She spat at him, then despite her pain, split his cheek open by kicking him savagely in the face.

He didn't mind, cinching up the ties as hard as he possibly could, feeling no more pity for her than she had shown the children at the schools and finding it as easy to ignore the pieces of bone that were protruding from her shoulder as it was to side-step the pool of blood beneath her.

Harland had been right, he thought, except that this place wasn't just a rat's nest: it was worse – a place so evil that you could almost taste it.

'Hey.' The American was growing impatient. 'Have you forgotten why you've come?' he said. 'Ask her about Lucy.'

'You will not find her.' Kessel tried to sit up. 'But before your son's next birthday, I guarantee he will be dead.'

'Let her bleed.' Harland retrieved the floating vial of TTX and picked up a roll of tape from the bench. 'We'll do this another way.' He marched Meyer over to the column where Zitelmann was standing and held up the vial in front of them. 'OK,' he said. 'This is the deal. Unless you tell me what I want to know, just like those schools you chose, I'm going to choose one of you. First I'm going to ram my gun down your throat, then, before I tape your mouth shut, I'm going to stick this nice little glass vial between your teeth. If you're quick, you can swallow it before I whack you under the chin, but then you'll have to worry about how hard I'm going to kick you in the guts.' He tore off a length of tape. 'What do you say we start right away?'

Meyer was frightened, but nothing like as frightened as Zitelmann. The German was a distinguished-looking man in his sixties, taller than he'd appeared to be in the photos, with bushy eyebrows, a full head of steel-grey hair and a face that had gone as white as the lab coat he was wearing.

'No, no,' he stammered. 'It is not necessary. If you will let me go to my car at the house, in return I give you the antidote for the girl.'

McKendrick's stomach lurched. He'd been fearing the worst, but never had he imagined this.

Even Harland was shaken. 'TTX,' he said slowly. 'You gave her TTX?'

Realizing how badly he'd miscalculated, Zitelmann had lost his nerve and seemed incapable of answering.

Meyer, though, had sensed an opportunity. 'For Herr Zitelmann, the girl is like the little Goddard bitch,' he said. 'Once she tells him what he wishes to hear, I think he uses her for a good experiment.'

McKendrick was close to throwing up. Not trusting himself to keep his finger away from the trigger, he shoved the Walther into Zitelmann's chest. 'You have one second,' he said. 'Either you give me the antidote right now, or I swear I'll kill you.'

'Do it anyway.' Harland interrupted. 'He's lying to save his skin. There isn't any antidote. You know there isn't and he knows there isn't. Come on, we'll shoot both the bastards and go and see if Lucy's up at the house somewhere.'

'Please.' Meyer stepped forwards. 'You make a mistake. I will take you to her.' He looked nervously at McKendrick. 'If you kill me, how then can I help you?'

'Show me. Now.' Feeling sicker by the minute and not caring whether he was walking into some kind of biological trap, McKendrick ignored Harland's warning and accompanied Meyer over to the laboratory door.

'You must open it,' Meyer said.

There were four seals on the door, each releasing a puff of pressurized air as McKendrick swung it open and escorted Meyer into the first of the cubicles.

The atmosphere inside was even warmer and more humid than it had been in the cavern, an environment as foreign to McKendrick as anywhere he'd ever been. The equipment in the other cubicles was equally foreign to him – incubators, centrifuges and what he thought were evaporators for turning substances like anthrax and fungi into an easily deployable powdered form – the expensive, state-of-the-art apparatus that Zitelmann had employed to produce his TTX.

Instead of continuing on through an air lock into another part of the facility, Meyer stopped in front of one of the storage cabinets, a large metal box that was being fed with clean air through its own dedicated filtering system.

'There is no danger.' Meyer stood aside. 'It is safe for you to look.'

Half-expecting to be enveloped in a cloud of TTX, McKendrick released the catches and wrenched open the door.

Lucy was still breathing but unconscious, lying crumpled on the floor.

She had a cut lip, both her arms were badly bruised from being held still, and her blouse had been ripped open by someone who'd played a game of join-the-dots with her freckles to scrawl a series of swastikas across her breasts with a felt-tipped pen.

Unwilling to put down his gun, he used his free hand to drag her out by her ankles, making sure she was clear of the door before he told Meyer to take her place.

'But I have helped you.' The German was hesitant.

McKendrick hit him in the stomach, kicked him inside and slammed the door.

Lucy's pulse was regular, but because he couldn't tell how far her paralysis had progressed, he knew he'd have to move fast if she was to stand any chance at all.

After discovering that he was too far underground for his radio to operate, he did up the one remaining button on her blouse and started carrying her back through the laboratory in his arms.

Harland met him at the door. 'Is she alive?'

'Just, but I don't know how long she's got. I have to get her to a hospital. The Italians had a drug that someone needs to get hold of. Did Zitelmann say any more about an antidote?'

Harland shook his head. 'Leave that to me. You get Zoe on the radio and tell her to meet you up top in Linder's car. Soon as you've got Lucy away, we can have a proper look around down here.'

'You don't need me. Meyer's locked up and Kessel isn't going anywhere. You can handle things by yourself, can't you?'

'It's not that.' Harland searched for the right words. 'Look, there's nothing you can do for Lucy that Zoe can't do better. She'll know where the nearest hospital is and she'll know the quickest way to get there. If you go with her, you'll only slow her down, and you'll be hanging around all night getting yourself in a real state. Leave it to her.'

'I'll see.' McKendrick headed for the lift shaft, holding down the transmit button on his radio in the hope of saving precious seconds.

The platform was nearly at the surface before he heard Zoe answer him. He didn't let her speak, relaying his instructions, telling her not to stop for anything or anyone and cutting her off short when the platform juddered to a halt.

He'd forgotten how cold it was. After the moist warmth of the cavern, the temperature in the implement shed was almost as much of a shock as the temperature outside in the open.

Wrapping his arms around Lucy to hold her more closely he stumbled his way over to the gate, hurrying now he could see headlights travelling towards him.

Zoe was driving fast, showering McKendrick with gravel when she braked at the last minute and put the Mercedes into a slide in her haste to turn it round.

She jumped out and opened one of the rear doors. 'How long do I have?'

'I don't know.' He laid Lucy on the back seat and covered her with his jacket. 'You have to remember the name Neostigmine,' he said. 'It's a drug that might just help her. Tell the doctors, and don't let them waste time trying to do tests for tetrodotoxin because there aren't any.'

'Does that mean you're not coming?' Zoe got back behind the wheel.

'Do you want me to?'

'No. I wasn't going to let you.' Giving him a tight smile, she closed her door and put her foot down, spinning her wheels on the wet grass before the Mercedes slithered on to the gravel and began to gather speed.

McKendrick watched it go, standing in the cold by the gate until the tail lights disappeared as Zoe swung the car out on to the road and took off on a drive that, if he was truthful to himself, he knew could only have one ending.

Now Lucy had gone – now he'd done all that he could for her – he was conscious of an overwhelming need for retribution, choking on his vindictiveness towards those who, for their own terrible purposes had chosen to take her from him.

For a few minutes more he remained standing in the dark, breathing in the smell of the lake until some of his anger had dissipated, and only then walking back slowly to the power station.

Harland had given up waiting for him. The American had returned from below and was in the process of disabling the lift by jamming the wheelbarrow between the guardrails and the floor.

'Lot of help you are.' Harland gave him a cardboard box to hold. 'I had to figure out how to get up here by myself. I thought you were coming back.'

'I was. What's in the box?'

'Documents, computer disks, print-outs, Quaid's political agenda, TTX targets, Kessel's distribution channels, money-laundering routes and the names and addresses of every Christian Freedom Party member in eleven different countries.'

'Zitelmann just gave them to you, did he?'

'Sort of. You know how it is.'

'But he didn't give you an antidote.'

'What do you think?' Harland squinted in the light. 'Are you OK?'

'No.'

'Did Zoe say where she was taking Lucy?'

'No.' McKendrick gave the box back.

'Linder might have an idea.' Harland took a last look around. 'Come on. Let's ask him. We ought to see how he's been getting on.'

McKendrick wasn't going anywhere just yet. Instead he went over to the wall and ripped the piece of burlap sacking from the nail to expose the plastic warning sign and the switch below it.

'What are you doing?' Harland came to see.

'I don't know.' In his mind now, the images were coming back: the smoke from Goddard's burning Porsche, Linder's Mercedes engulfed in fire on the bridge, the bloodstained eye socket in Vicente's skull, the little golden-haired Virgin Mary spreadeagled on the floor of her school, and finally, the freshest of them all – Lucy lying paralysed in the cabinet with her breasts defiled by swastikas.

There were two interlocks on the switch, and the toggle was stiff to move, forcing him to use both thumbs until it suddenly snicked into place.

The wail of a siren was the first sign that he'd guessed correctly. The noise was faint, drifting up the lift shaft, but unmistakably the sound of an evacuation alarm and an indication of what he hoped would happen next.

To find out whether it would or not, he went outside and stared back at the lake, counting out loud for the benefit of Harland who was looking mystified.

He didn't have long to wait. He'd counted off forty-six seconds when the siren stopped abruptly and the ground was shaken by a number of thuds from somewhere deep beneath the lake. At the same time, a five metre-high fountain of water erupted from the surface.

'Shit.' Suddenly, Harland had understood what he was witnessing. 'Rupture discs,' he said quietly. 'Or maybe a hatch with explosive bolts.'

McKendrick didn't care what it was or what it had been. That millions of litres of contaminated water were pouring in to flood the cavern was all that mattered now, and all he'd wanted to achieve – an end not just of a coal seam that had been burned out long ago by the fires of Hitler's Reich, but an end of a woman and two men who, in this very same place, had sought to keep the Nazi flame alive.

Now the lake level had begun to drop, Harland had gone back to the power station where he was listening to something. 'Can you hear that?' he asked.

The sound was just audible, but getting louder, a continuous roar that was being accompanied by a powerful smell of phenol.

'It's air being driven up the lift shaft by the water.' McKendrick stopped himself from breathing it. 'We ought to get away from here. It might not be too safe.'

'So what's new? Nowhere is when you're around. If you don't smarten up and stop trying to get even with all the bad guys, you're going to wind up being one of them. Payback doesn't do you any good. It never does. How much better do you feel for flipping that switch?'

'Not a lot.' He didn't want to talk. What he wanted was to be alone. 'Look, if you can grab a ride with someone, will you lend me your car? I'll let you have it back in the morning.'

'Help yourself.' Harland handed over his keys. 'Why not wait until you get some news from Zoe?'

'Why the hell would I want to hear that? It's a stupid question.'

'OK. So it's a stupid question. I'm only trying to help.'

'Yeah, I know.' McKendrick stuck out his hand. 'Thanks for doing what you did tonight.' He left the American leaning against the wall of the building and walked quickly to the gate, heading not for the pathway or the house where there was the chance of him running into other people, but for the stone wall and the lane, returning the way he'd come until he reached the field where they'd parked the cars and where, in the vain hope that it would somehow ease his bitterness, he set off in no particular direction on a long and very lonely drive into the night.

# Chapter 18

He had no idea how long he'd been here. He knew only that he'd been asleep and that he was cold – so cold he'd lost all feeling in his legs and was unable to clench his hands properly.

With some difficulty he twisted the ignition key to start the Peugeot's engine, then used his fingernails to scrape some ice off the inside of the windscreen, peering out into a thick morning fog that made it impossible to see where he was parked.

Having driven for what had seemed like half the night, he could remember pulling off the road and he could remember every minute of what had taken place at Weiskirchen. But that was all he could remember.

Now the heater was beginning to work, and his legs were no longer quite so numb, the need to empty his bladder was becoming urgent.

Wishing he still had his jacket, he stepped out on to the frost-covered lay-by and went to relieve himself against a tree, trying to identify a landmark through the fog and mist while he tried to summon the courage to return to the car and search for his phone.

He found it lodged beneath one of the seats, but even after he had it in his hands he put off using it, waiting for several seconds before fumbling to press buttons with fingers that were still refusing to do what he wanted them to do.

There was no dial tone coming from Linder's phone, but Harland answered his at once.

'It's me,' McKendrick said.

'Where the hell are you?'

'I don't know.'

'What do you mean, you don't know?'

'What I said. Did you hear anything?'

'Not yet.' The American sounded cautious. 'Linder figures Zoe would have gone to Saarbrücken. He said there's a big general hospital there, but I haven't heard anything from him since he dropped me off back here last night.'

'Where's here?'

'I'm at Emily's. I brought her home yesterday on my way down from Bonn. Have you tried calling Zoe?'

'I don't know her number. I'll try Linder again and then phone the hospital.'

'I'll do it,' Harland said. 'You just find out where you are and get my car back to me. I need it. By the time you arrive I'll have a better fix on things. I wouldn't bother trying to get hold of Linder. The minute he saw that stuff from Zitelmann he was on the phone to God knows how many people. Last I heard he was off to see the police in Trier.'

'In the middle of the night?'

'Sure. He'll still be there. No one's going to stop him now. He knows that anything with a neo-Nazi label on it scares the shit out of the Germans, so he's got exactly what he needs to make them sit up and listen real hard.'

'They'll still try to bury it,' McKendrick said.

'This is too big for anyone to bury. In a couple of hours the story's going to explode in every country that's been stupid enough to let a Christian Freedom Party tell the public what they ought to be thinking.' Harland paused. 'I've got a couple of things here for you.'

'What?'

'A bunch of photos and a letter from Andrew that the DEA have sent on. How long will you be?'

'No idea. I'll see you when I get there.' Feeling warmer, but otherwise not much better than he had done five minutes ago, McKendrick ended the call, stuck the Peugeot in gear and let it roll down out of the lay-by on to the road where, for no good reason he could think of, he turned right and headed off into the fog, continuing to drive until he came across a sign-post that told him he was travelling in the wrong direction.

He was more than 100 kilometres from Trier on a minor side-road somewhere south of Koblenz near a place called Nastätten, but not too far away from highway 407 which was the only route he knew that would take him back to where he was supposed to be going.

Why he should be going anywhere, he wasn't sure, doubting that Andrew's letter would be a good enough reminder of how things had been before, and knowing that no reminder of the past was going to help him forget how futile and short-lived his hopes for the future had been.

He drove without thinking, keeping his speed down until he'd passed through the village of Reinfeld and turned south on to the 268 where most of the fog had gone, and by which time what little sense of purpose he'd set out with had gone as well.

Emily's gate was open, a plume of white woodsmoke was curling from the chimney of the house, and the puddles in the driveway were either frozen solid or covered with a thick film of ice.

Harland met him at the door, pre-empting questions by explaining at once that there was no fresh information.

'Did you try Zoe?' McKendrick followed him into the lounge.

'She's not answering, nor is Linder, and the hospital in Saarbrücken won't give out patients' names over the phone unless you can prove you're a relation or a next of kin. Some crap about German privacy laws.'

'You should've said you were her father or a brother or something.'

'I did, but it didn't wash. Have a go yourself if you want – or ask Emily to. She might be our best bet.' Harland glanced at the cut on McKendrick's cheek. 'You look like hell. How about some coffee?'

'I will make it.' Emily had come to say hello. 'Now I am again back in my own kitchen, if you have not already eaten I shall also cook you breakfast.'

'Coffee's fine thanks.'

'Then while you wait, you must warm yourself.' She smiled. 'Outside it is very cold today, I think.'

Harland tossed another log on the fire. 'You probably don't give a shit,' he said, 'but Quaid's been arrested. The US Department of Homeland Security got him last night in Alabama. He's crying religious persecution, but even without the way things are in the States

236

right now, there's enough evidence to lock the bastard away forever.'

'What about his Christian Freedom Party?'

'A week from now there won't be one in the States and a week after that, there won't be any in Europe or South America either. I know you think Washington is wet behind the ears when it comes to foreign policy, but there are a few things that the US Government is pretty damn good at.'

'Like guaranteeing oil supplies.'

'And getting themselves re-elected. Once the public realizes not all Muslims are terrorists, the Arabs are going to be real grateful, and that'll take some of the pressure off the US in the Middle East. Right now, Washington will be putting the Rosenberg Principle into reverse so fast that by Sunday you won't know whether to go to a mosque or a church.'

'That'll be the weekend the oil companies throw themselves a big party, will it?' McKendrick said.

'Why not? You've got your agenda – they've got theirs.' Harland looked at him. 'Are you going to tell me how you knew what that switch was for?'

'Lucy thought it was something to do with flushing the phenol out of the lake.'

'But you didn't. You decided it was how Zitelmann planned to wipe out all evidence of his TTX lab if anyone ever found out about it, right?'

'Lucky guess. With that much phenol you could sterilize anything you want.' McKendrick changed the subject. 'Any TTX show up at the schools?'

'Yeah it did. I heard first thing this morning. The Italians nailed it. They worked out why some children died and why some didn't. The kids at both schools had all been given soft drinks, but not all of them used straws. There were two boxes at St Catherine's and one at St Gabriel's – all three loaded with tetrodotoxin powder.'

'Drinking straws?' McKendrick tried to remember if he'd seen any in the warehouse. 'Not plastic cups? Not sachets of sugar or . . . .'

Harland had recognized the signs. 'Don't go beating yourself up,' he said. 'The Coalition's fucked, so nothing like that's going to happen again. Forget the TTX programme. It's gone. There isn't one any more.'

'Did you find out what the new targets were going to be?'

'Linder did. There was an updated manifesto on one of the disks. Looks as though they were still making up their minds, but there was a list of possibles – mostly political – things like a Republican conference in the States and a meeting of young Conservatives in the UK. They're both on this coming weekend.'

'What about the Christmas Day hit?'

'Just something pencilled in. The programme was designed to rack up. Fallièrs, Bowden and Pattullo first, then the kids, then a couple of political rallies followed by a bang at the end.'

'How big a bang?'

'Big as you can get. How does the Vatican grab you?' Harland went to his brief case and took out some photographs. 'I wouldn't get excited. Saving the Pope isn't going to buy someone like you a ticket to Heaven. Have a look at those.'

There were eight photographs, all pictures of the Kalimantan clearing, four taken from a distance, two shot at reasonably short range and two close-up, all in colour, and all of them illuminated by the reflected rays of a setting sun that had turned everything to an unearthly red.

Even the ghost trees were red, but not as red as the blood that was streaming down the legs of the six naked men who were tied to them.

Each man had been castrated and left to die, photographed by the *Kopassus* in unnecessary detail to show exactly how uncompromising they were prepared to be in their fight against the trafficking of drugs and guns, and to demonstrate how willing they were to avenge the rape and deaths of innocent civilians.

The photos were gruesome in the extreme, evidence of the retribution McKendrick had thought he'd wanted, but too sickening to examine for any length of time.

He checked a close-up print showing a tattooed hand, then threw the whole lot into the fire.

'Did the *Kopassus* get it right?' Harland asked.

'Yeah, they got it right.'

'You and I are all square then, are we?'

'I didn't do a deal with you just for that.'

'I know you didn't.'

'So don't start asking if I feel any better.'

Emily came to interrupt. She'd been waiting for McKendrick to stop talking, standing in the doorway holding the cup of coffee she'd made him.

'Thank you.' He took it from her.

She studied his cut cheek. 'It is not good to leave such things too long,' she said. 'I shall attend to it for you.'

'It's OK.'

'Finish your drink, then we shall see.'

Harland had gone to fetch an envelope from his case. 'This is what came from Andrew,' he said. 'It was sitting on my desk.'

The letter was dated Nov 29 and carefully handwritten in ballpoint pen:

*Dear Dad,*

*I'm not allowed to send letters from here, but Sam says it's OK as long as he does it for me.*

*Sam is the agent who's looking after us in San Elijo. He drives a four-by-four Nissan and wears a gun that no one is supposed to see, although Mom says she knows about it.*

*She's still real mad about us having to move. I think we had to because of what happened to Lieutenant Goddard in Hawaii, but you said not to tell her about that, so I haven't.*

*San Elijo is a neat place and I like going out in the Nissan with Sam. He says you can get a letter to me by giving it to a Mr Harland, but I don't know who he is or where he lives, so maybe you won't be able to do that.*

*Love Andrew*

'Everything OK?' Harland asked.

'Sort of.' Although he was pleased to get the letter, it was cold comfort, and as well as doing nothing to offset the repulsiveness of the *Kopassus* photos, it had left him feeling flat and dispirited.

'Right. I'm off.' Harland waved his goodbye to Emily through the kitchen door. 'Do you have my keys?'

'They're in the car. What's the rush?'

'Meeting with the US Ambassador scheduled for four o'clock. If there are any pats on the head going around, I don't want to miss out on mine. If you want me to drop you off somewhere, I'll be happy to, or I can call Linder's office and tell them they need to get a message to him about picking you up from here. What do you want to do?'

'I'll wait here.' McKendrick accompanied him to the car. 'Find a new home for the Walther,' he said. 'It's in the glove box.'

'I might just hang on to it.' Harland zipped up his jerkin. 'Don't freeze your balls off. Go and get some more coffee, and get that cut of yours fixed up.'

'If you hear from Zoe, I want to hear from you. I don't care where you are or who you're talking to.'

'Sure. I'll be in touch anyway.'

Shivering for the second time today, McKendrick waited until the Peugeot had gone, then crunched his way back through the frost and went to find Emily.

She was standing on a chair in the lounge, busy dusting her collection of porcelain figurines. 'Ah. So you are ready.' She let him help her step down. 'I shall wash my hands while you go upstairs to clean your face, then we can begin to make you look better.'

'It's not that bad. All I need are a couple of plasters.'

'You will find some in the dressing-table in the room where you stayed before.' She put the chair back by the wall. You will also see there scissors and gauze which you must bring to me.'

When he'd been here last, it had been Lucy who'd been in need of attention for her injured foot – another persistent recollection of her that didn't go away until he saw himself in the bathroom mirror.

His face was a mess, and even after he'd washed off the dried blood it remained a mess – a reflection more of how he felt than of his appearance, he decided, made worse by a large bruise and because he hadn't shaved since leaving his hotel in Guilianova on Sunday morning.

After drying himself with a paper towel, he ran his fingers through his hair to try and make himself more presentable and went to fetch the plasters.

There weren't any in the top drawer of the dressing-table, and the drawer below it was empty except for a neatly folded jacket.

But it wasn't just a jacket, and it wasn't just neatly folded. It was his jacket – the jacket he'd put over Lucy to keep her warm in the car last night.

He couldn't bring himself to turn round, refusing to believe the impossible even when he heard her whisper his name.

She was sitting up in bed, clasping a sheet to her as though she was no more certain this could be happening than he was.

'Don't I get a hello?' She endeavoured to smile.

He was overwhelmed, incapable of doing anything until he saw the tears rolling down her cheeks.

He went to her then, kneeling beside her on the bed, holding her to him, burying his face in her hair, too bewildered to make sense of the miracle that had brought her back.

When she'd recovered sufficiently to speak, she pushed him away so she could see his face. 'I promised myself I wouldn't do this,' she said. 'I was all right until I heard you come upstairs.'

'Harland knew all along? And Linder?'

'I think they wanted me to be a surprise.'

How much of a surprise she would never know, McKendrick thought. 'Why in God's name didn't you tell me?' he said, 'Why?'

'I couldn't. No one could. Your mobile was switched off all night, and I was still asleep when you phoned this morning. I've been waiting for you ever since. Where have you been?'

'Nowhere.' To stop her asking questions, he kissed her gently on the mouth, taking care to avoid the cut on her lip, tasting her tears and breathing in the fresh smell of her skin. 'No TTX,' he said quietly.

'No. It was sodium pentothal. Two hundred milligrams.' She showed him a needle mark on her arm. 'Zitelmann injected me with it. He called it a truth serum.'

'To make you tell him how much we knew?'

'I'd already told Meyer everything, but he wouldn't believe me. He was an animal. Before I was taken to see Kessel and Zitelmann he spent hours questioning me in a room at the house.' She shuddered. 'He brought in men to hold me down on a table and kept telling them about all the awful things he was going to do before he'd allow them to rape me.'

'Jesus.' McKendrick didn't know what else to say.

'It's all right. Nothing bad happened. I think Meyer had been told not to hurt me until Kessel and Zitelmann had used the sodium pentothal.'

'But you didn't know that?'

'No, not until I was taken down into the laboratory. That's when I really got terrified. I couldn't stop thinking about those holes in Bridget Goddard's teeth. The only thing that helped was telling myself you'd be able to guess where I was.'

'I shouldn't have had to,' McKendrick said. 'If I hadn't let you go to Germany no one would have had to guess. I must have been out of my mind.'

'It wasn't your fault. It was my idea to see if it was Meyer who was staying at that boarding-house in Cologne. I didn't go in, but I might as well have done. The first thing I remember is him standing outside the car pointing a gun at me through the window.'

'How did he get you to Weiskirchen?'

'In the boot of a car. He locked me in.' She touched her lip. 'That's how I got this. Whenever he was anywhere near me he either had his hands inside my bra or between my legs.'

'Was it him who drew the swastikas?'

She nodded. 'Emily had to scrub them off with olive oil and wood ash from the fire. She used up a whole packet of cotton buds on me.'

'Let me see.'

'No.' She prevented him from pulling down the sheet. 'You can look when I want you to look.'

'How sure are you about the sodium pentothal?' He was unwilling to take any risks at all.

'That's what Zitelmann said it was. Stop worrying. It's not that dangerous, and it's not supposed to have any serious side effects.'

'You don't know that.'

'Yes I do. The minute I woke up in the car, Zoe phoned ahead to the hospital. They told her sodium pentothal just makes people suscep- tible to suggestion by depressing their central nervous system, slowing their heart rate and lowering their blood pressure.'

McKendrick wasn't reassured. 'If it does all those things, you shouldn't be here,' he said. 'You ought to still be in hospital.'

'I didn't go. I didn't feel too awful once I'd come round, and at that point we weren't even halfway to Saarbrücken, so Zoe checked with

Harland who said, if she really believed I was all right, he thought Emily would be happy to look after me. You don't have to fuss. I'm just sleepy.'

'You're in shock.'

'Because you're here. I wasn't before. Do you know what the worst part was?'

'Wondering if you were going to wake up from the injection.'

She shook her head. 'The feeling that after I'd spent all this time finding you, I wouldn't ever see you again.'

'You're out of luck,' McKendrick said. 'From here on, you're pretty much stuck with me.'

'No I'm not. I haven't told you about my Christmas present from Mr Linder. He's paying for me to spend Christmas anywhere I like for as long as I like.'

'That's not a present, it's an excuse. He's feeling guilty and he wants you out of the way until things settle down. It's what he did before when he let you go to Brazil.'

'So if I've decided to spend a month in Florida, you don't care?'

'I don't care because you're not going.' He pushed her back against the pillow. 'I've told you. You're not going anywhere by yourself again.'

'Oh. Do you suppose that's why Mr Linder said I have to take you with me?'

'To Florida?'

'He thought it was the least he could do.' She waited for his reaction. 'If you don't want to go, I can make you.' Placing a finger over the split in his cheek, she kissed him open-mouthed, refusing to release him until she'd run out of breath and realized that her sheet had slipped. 'I know Emily's waiting for you,' she whispered. 'But I want you to stay with me.'

He stayed with her for a long time, cradling her in his arms as the rays of a cold December sun began to bathe the room with light, not yet certain whether the past had been finally put to rest, but no longer seeking a reason for his change in fortune, and thinking now only of a future that no one but the girl he'd so nearly lost could have ever promised him.

# Chapter 19

Yesterday it had been the boat trip to see loggerhead turtles in the Dry Tortugas National Park, and the day before that it had been snorkelling at Marquesas Keys and the obligatory visit to Hemingway House.

Today, though, was going to be different.

How different, McKendrick was still waiting to find out, although he suspected it had something to do with the fax Lucy had gone to get.

They'd still been asleep when she'd received the phone call to say it had come, and since then she'd been rather quiet and subdued, ordering breakfast in their room for the first time in the three days they'd been here and putting off going downstairs to collect it from reception as though she was as reluctant as he was to learn who it was from and what it was about.

It was an interruption they could have done without, he thought, although it was going to take more than a fax to upset her now.

Three days in the Florida sunshine had worked wonders with her. She'd not only recovered from her ordeal more quickly than he'd expected her to, but she was as happy and bubbly as he'd ever seen her, holding his hand wherever they went, and on the odd occasion when they'd been in the company of other people, being as confident as she was possessive.

For McKendrick, having her to himself would have been reward enough. That she was here with him in the sultry warmth of the Florida Keys, where sun and colour were as much a part of life as beaches and the ocean, had just made things that much better – or so he'd thought until the fax had arrived.

He was standing on the balcony watching a fishing trawler that was heading out into the Gulf when he heard her come back into the room.

This morning, because she seemed at last to have stopped worrying about her freckles, she'd put on a halter-top and was wearing the yellow skirt and the Kino sandals they'd bought at the market yesterday.

'What's the matter?' She closed the door behind her. 'Why are you looking at me like that?'

'Like what?'

'Don't pretend you don't know.' She held up some sheets of paper. 'Guess who it's from.'

'Give me a clue.'

She smiled at him. 'It's not from Harland.'

'Has Linder decided he can't run his office by himself?'

'I don't know yet. Do you want me to read it now, or shall we wait until we get back from the beach?'

'What beach?' This was the first he'd heard about her plans for the day.

'That one at Fort Zachary Taylor. It's supposed to be really nice. We can take lunch with us.'

'See what Linder has to say first, then if it's bad news, we can talk about it while we're lying in the sun.'

'All right.' She sat down on the bed and began to read out loud. *'Dear Lucy, I'm sure work is the furthest thing from your mind, but I thought you'd be pleased to hear that the St-Gilles-Croix-de-St-Vie contract was signed yesterday.'* She looked up. 'That's not bad news. That's good news – really good news.'

'Lots of money for lots of wind turbines,' McKendrick said.

'How do you know it's for wind turbines?'

He grinned. 'You'd be surprised what I know. What else does he say?'

'There's something about the project timing, then he goes on: *The German police are continuing their mock search for Zitelmann, but there has been no mention of Jürgen Meyer or Maria Kessel during any Press conferences or in the media, so I think we can assume government pressure has been brought to bear, and that political expediency has carried the day. For the same reason, the Germans will not be pumping out the tunnel. Officially this is because environmentalists believe*

245

*the contaminated water should remain underground where it is, the hope being that, once the lake has been resealed, it should eventually recover over a period of time.'*

'Smart move,' McKendrick said. 'Best no one ever knows what went on down there.'

'The same way it's best if no one ever knows what happened to those guerrillas?'

So this was the problem, he thought. It hadn't been the fax. It was Indonesia. She'd made him tell her about it before they'd left, but she'd been wanting to raise the subject again ever since and had evidently decided to use the fax as an excuse. 'You still don't understand, do you?' he said.

She confused him completely by giving him another smile. 'If I didn't understand, I wouldn't feel like this, would I?'

'Like what?'

'Safe. I've never had anyone to look after me before – well, not properly and not anyone like you.' She looked awkward. 'I haven't explained that very well.'

'No, you haven't.' He didn't know whether to be relieved or not. 'Read the rest of the fax.'

'The next bit's only about how many Christian Freedom Party activists have been arrested in Europe and America, and how the US government and the European Union are getting themselves into trouble.'

'For not stamping out the Coalition earlier?'

'No.' She shook her head. 'For helping them. Listen to what Mr Linder says. *If the pair of you have been too busy to watch TV or read the papers, you may not know that western governments are being accused of secretly funding the Coalition's aims. Numerous websites are claiming · that some months ago a number of US and British politicians decided that the more appalling Islamic violence was seen to be, the more likely the public would be to support the invasion of Iraq. How true this is remains to be seen, however, the irony of it will not have been lost on Quaid and his supporters who will doubtless be exploiting these rumours while they can.'*

Another damn twist, McKendrick thought, and another conspiracy theory no one would ever be able to prove or disprove. 'Is that it?' he said.

'Except for something I'm supposed to tell you, and a message from Zoe.'

'What is it you're supposed to tell me?'

'*Please inform Mr McKendrick I have been in touch with his Brussels office and provided them with what I trust is a plausible explanation for his recent absence. He will also be pleased to hear that an account in his name has been opened in a Zurich bank into which I have today deposited the sum of US$73,000, this being a consultancy fee of $3000 per day for 21 days, plus an additional payment of $10,000 as some compensation for his contribution to a project that has had rather wider ramifications than any of us thought. Zoe sends her regards and says she expects a card from you. Enjoy your break from the office and, of course, my best wishes to you both for a very happy Christmas.*'

McKendrick was surprised. He'd guessed Linder would be generous, but not this generous.

Lucy was equally surprised. 'I never knew how well people like you got paid,' she said. 'I'd better start learning how to put out underground fires.'

'Nothing to it.' He grinned at her. 'I'll give you a quick course at the beach. Are you ready?'

'I will be. I'll do my hair while you put a fresh plaster on your cheek and get my sunscreen lotion. It's on the vanity in the bathroom.'

Still inclined to believe he was misreading the situation, he went to fetch the bottle, only understanding what had been going on when he returned to the bedroom.

She wasn't brushing her hair. Instead, she'd kicked off her sandals and was standing barefoot by the bed with a peculiar expression on her face.

It hadn't been Indonesia or the fax, he realized. She'd been quiet and subdued for an entirely different reason – because of something that had been on her mind for a long time.

'You'll have to help me with the sunscreen,' she said. 'Unless I put it on all over, my freckles just get worse.'

'Wait until we're at the beach.'

'I want you to do it now.'

'Why?'

'Because it's not night-time.' She removed her top and her bra. 'You've only seen me undressed when it's dark, so I want you to see me while the room's all full of light like it is now – so I can tell what you really think of the way I look.'

247

'You already know what I think.'

'No I don't.' Unbuckling her belt she let her skirt drop to the floor and very carefully and very slowly stepped out of her bikini briefs.

So bright was the light, and so achingly beautiful was she that McKendrick couldn't take his eyes off her, marvelling at the provocative tautness of her skin, aroused as much by her flawless figure as he was by the already-erect pink buds of her nipples and the tantalizing swell between her thighs.

'Don't you want to?' She went to the bed and stretched out on her back.

Without saying anything, he gave her the only answer he could give her, going to sit beside her and kissing her to make her relax before he started applying the lotion to her skin.

To begin with she seemed to be content with kisses, but it was a pretence she could not maintain.

The minute his hands began to stray, she sat up straight and brushed her nipples across his lips, murmuring to him to make it plain that she wanted his mouth on her breasts as well.

She was restrained while she helped him strip off his shorts and T-shirt, but soon reached out to grasp him, unable to deny herself the pleasure of stroking him with her fingers.

Although she was trying to linger, she was already breathing quickly, lying back on to her pillow when he became more enterprising and gradually parting her thighs to prepare herself for the moment when his hands would slip down over her stomach to touch her where she was eager to be touched.

On the two previous occasions when they'd made love, she'd been willing to let him take the initiative. But today her demands were greater, and she was being more ambitious.

She offered herself to him as freely as she had done before, gasping when he opened her gently with the edge of his hand, but this time responded with her own hands, watching wide-eyed to see if she could excite him and stimulate him further.

Now that she was closer to receiving what she sought, instead of prolonging her enjoyment of him, she raised her knees, inviting him to discover how wet and swollen she was, encouraging him to explore her more thoroughly by welcoming each of his caresses with a flurry of kisses until she was suddenly overtaken by a wave of anticipation.

Trembling slightly, she pushed away his wrists, spread her legs and urgently guided him inside her.

Once she'd started to accept him she tightened her muscles and lay still, showing him that, until she'd taught him what to do, she would not allow herself to be penetrated fully, teasing him with her tongue when she wanted him to push, or biting his lip to stop him if she grew over-eager or felt her contractions beginning early.

Even then, as though still anxious for reassurance, she refused to submit completely, twice making him withdraw and forcing him to look at her, and only surrendering after the last of her reservations had been dispelled.

McKendrick hadn't needed to look at her to remind himself of how truly irresistible she was and how irresistible she'd always been, but he'd never seen her like this before.

Her whole body was glowing in the sunshine, while across her shoulders and the curve of her breasts where the patterning of her freckles was being enhanced by a sheen of lotion and perspiration, the wonderful smoothness and colour of her skin had been highlighted to such an extent that he was no longer capable of waiting, determined to possess her whether or not she was ready to be taken.

But she was ready, immediately moving with him, whispering his name and using a newfound confidence to draw him into a world she knew no one else would ever or could ever give him.

He endeavoured to slow things down, sensing from her shudders that she would be quick to climax, but in so doing fell victim to his own desire.

Lucy was already lost, clinging to him as she let him bring her to her peak and crying out when at last they were able to share a burst of such exquisite pleasure that it drove the breath from her body and left McKendrick's heart pounding so hard against her she could feel it.

For nearly quarter of an hour he stayed beside her, unwilling to break the spell, and only leaving the room to go out on to the balcony after she'd become drowsy and he'd seen her eyes begin to close.

The fishing trawler had disappeared from sight. In its place, floating beneath a cloudless sky on an ocean of turquoise blue, a number of smaller boats were leaving frothy white wakes behind them, while further out to sea, a freighter was crawling south through the heat-haze.

He tried to guess where it had come from and where it might be going, wondering whether it was on a coastal route or bound for more distant shores – somewhere as remote as Indonesia perhaps, a long journey that would carry it halfway round the world, he thought, but nothing like as long a journey as the one that had brought him here from the burning forests of Kalimantan, and not as long as the one that had finally brought him peace and contentment in the arms of the young woman who lay curled up asleep in the warmth and safety of the sunlit room behind him.

# AUTHOR'S NOTE

Although this book is a work of fiction, the existence of laboratory-produced tetrodotoxin is an established fact.

As well as being one of the deadliest poisons on Earth for which there is no known antidote, and which once ingested is undetectable by any known means, TTX is regarded as being a toxin of such extreme lethality that it has the potential to become the ultimate bioweapon for international terrorists.

For this reason, scientists hoping to prove that in vanishingly small doses TTX may have some therapeutic value are expressing alarm at the prospect of it ever falling into the wrong hands.

The recent interception of a quantity being shipped illegally from Japan to the US shows that it already has done.

CDP